Murder
in the Mist

by

Loretta C. Rogers

Murder in the Mist

Cover Art by *Rae Monet, Inc. Design*

The Wild Rose Press, Inc.
PO Box 708
Adams Basin, NY 14410-0708
Visit us at www.thewildrosepress.com

Publishing History
First Mainstream Mystery Rose Edition, 2015
Print ISBN 978-1-62830-832-7
Digital ISBN 978-1-62830-833-4

"Mitch, line one. It's Bryan Cole. Sounds urgent."

He pushed the button. "Ranger Cole?"

"Got an emergency at Thunder Hole, and it's a hellish nightmare."

Mitch stopped smiling and listened. "Close off the area to spectators. We don't need a panic. Don't touch anything. Try to preserve the scene as much as possible. As for witnesses, isolate them from each other. It will keep them from feeding off each other's recollections. Get them coffee, and pencil and paper to write down everything they can remember. I'll get there asap!"

"Will do."

As Mitch hung up the phone, he issued instructions to Louise. "Call Dr. Musuyo, tell him he'll need his forensics kit, an EMT, and the ambulance, and to meet me at the main entrance of the national park. Musuyo is to ask for Ranger Jane Dorsey. She'll direct him to the scene."

Louise adjusted the eyeglasses that had slipped down on her nose. "What is it, Mitch? What's happened?"

His voice brooked no nonsense. "In a minute, Louise. Right now, do as I've asked."

He punched auto-dial for Laura's number and was relieved when she answered on the first ring.

"Hey, Mitch, I've been meaning to call and thank you for telling me about Elio—"

He didn't have time for platitudes. He glanced at his watch. Eleven fifteen. "Friday, I'll pick you up in fifteen minutes. Bring your camera."

Other Books by Loretta C. Rogers

Acknowledgements

A little bit of research went into the making of this novel. I needed some experts, and boy, did I hit the mother lode with friends Carol Brennan and Greg Bannon, native Mainers. With their information, I have done my best to create the facilities, culture, and the ambiance of this fictional town located on coastal Maine.

A special thanks goes to Phyllis Webber and The Friday Sisters Book Club. When these lovely ladies in Palmetto Bay, FL hosted me as their guest author, I promised that if I ever wrote a mystery novel, I would somehow feature them in the story. Happy Reading, ladies!

Thanks to my favorite physician, Dr. Timothy Peterson, for his invaluable information about forensics and how a forensics team might process a crime scene.

Any discrepancies in the information these special people gave me is entirely my fault.

My deepest thanks to Greg Bannon and Carol Brennan, who made cameo appearances in this novel.

To all my faithful readers, I hope you enjoy *Murder in the Mist*, and forgive me for writing out of my usual historical western romance genre.

Finally, to my wonderful editor, Nan Swanson. You are the best.

Happy Reading!

Loretta C. Rogers

Prologue

We are so accustomed to disguising ourselves to others, that in the end, we become disguised to ourselves.

~Francois La Rouchefoucauld

It wasn't the dense sea fog or the cool air that prickled the hairs on Lynnette Braswell's neck, but the sound of footsteps that accompanied it. She stood still and listened. "Who's there?"

Goosebumps rippled up and down her arms beneath her sweater. She squinted to see through the thick white mist. Her heart kept pace with the adrenalin shooting through her veins. Glancing over her shoulder to discern the source of the sound, she noted the bank's parking lot stood empty. She chided herself. Of course the bank was closed. It was Thursday and nearly midnight. Her shift at the hospital had ended, and before walking home she'd decided to stop at the ATM to get enough cash for her long weekend trip into the city. She loved Cole Harbor, but spending party time in Bangor with her best friend was to die for. Lynnette focused her thoughts on how many Long Island Iced Teas she planned to drink, the laughter she and her friend would share, and sleeping late for the next three days.

A movement shrouded in deep shadows caused her

to glance left and then right. The dim halo from a street lamp provided minimal comfort. In spite of the night's chill, her palms sweated as she reached inside the zippered section of her purse where she kept the debit card.

Shrugging off the clop of imaginary footsteps as the aftereffects of pulling an exhaustive double shift, Lynnette relaxed her death grip on the plastic card and inserted it into the ATM's slot. She leaned closer to punch in her pin number. The seconds it took for the money to roll through the dispenser seemed like a lifetime.

She thought about her own stupidity in turning down a ride home, opting instead to walk the four blocks to her apartment. This was Cole Harbor—crime free, mundane, where nothing out of the ordinary ever happened, not even during the annual Lobster Fest that drew several thousand sailing enthusiasts and a few weirdoes from the mainland.

Weirdo. The word plucked at her brain. Stuffing the money inside her purse, Lynnette searched until her fingers wrapped around the keychain. Chill bumps prickled her skin as she moved away from the building, and she picked up her pace as she crossed the parking lot to the sidewalk. The ghostly shapes of closed businesses and the lights inside them calmed her. Never had she feared walking home after her shift. This feeling of trepidation was a puzzle.

"Lynnette?"

For a split second, her heart stopped. She blinked to clear the moisture from her eyelashes, to bring the dark figure into focus. Murky lamplight revealed his hair was pulled back from his face. She imagined he wore it in a ponytail.

She ran his voice through her mind and drew a blank. Swallowing hard, she looked up at him. Way up at him. Over six foot, he towered above her diminutive five-foot frame. "Do I know you?"

A lurid grin curled over his lips. Something about that smile, the dark anticipation that filled his weasel-eyed features, produced icy fingers of terror in the pit of her stomach.

One thought registered—*shit!*

****

Night after night, he'd watched Lynnette leave the hospital, hoping to gain enough courage to approach her. Each time, his nerve let him down. Not tonight. He'd fortified himself with two joints and a couple of boilermakers. Yeah, he was on top of his game. Mr Irresistible. Conqueror of women.

She was pretty. And small. And seemed to radiate innocence. He hesitated.

"Pretty lady like you shouldn't be out alone. 'Specially on a night like this."

Lynnette moved a step backward. "Yes, of course, you're right. It's late and I'm meeting some friends, so I should go."

"Sure, no sweat. I'll walk with you…to make sure you're safe."

Lengthening her stride, she said, "Were you a patient at the hospital? Is that how you know my name?"

He snorted. "I really didn't expect you to remember me. A girl raised with everything—money and beauty, and never knowing what it's like to have highfalutin' people look down their snobby noses at you."

Her tone turned arctic at the insult. "I am none of those things. How dare you judge me, whoever you are!"

"Ben Wiener. Now do you remember?"

"Beenie…" She stopped abruptly.

"Yeah, go ahead and say what you're thinking—Beenie with the little weenie. I've been away ten years, and nothing's changed. Except I've taken my mother's maiden name. No one here knew her because I lived with my grandpa. I'm Benjamin…" He hesitated, deciding not to reveal his new last name. "Anyhow, Beenie Weenie died in the hospital when they treated him for paranoid schizophrenia. Stuck him with all kind of needles and electrodes. Ice water baths."

He snapped his fingers. "Poof, Beenie Weenie disappeared like a puff of smoke." The expression she wore caused him to hasten on. "I'm better now. The doctors said I'm no longer a menace to society. So, see, you don't have to be afraid."

"I'm sorry. That was unfair of me. It just slipped out. You were sixteen when you…when you were sent away."

"I didn't mean to hurt that girl. Sh-she shouldn't have taunted me, but I'm okay as long as I don't forget to take my medication." He reached out and grabbed her arm. "You were nice to me when nobody else in this stinking town was."

Lynnette struggled to break the viselike grip. "Then why did you come back?"

He stared at her with those empty eyes. "For you. I thought about you every day while I was locked up. The doctors said I was mentally unstable, but, like I said, I'm better now. All because of you."

Dizzy with fear, she shuddered. "You're hurting me. Please, my friends will worry if I'm late."

He stood, towering over her, imposing. "I've watched you every day since my return. You live alone. Your parents are dead. You like one cream and one sugar in your coffee. You're a workaholic, and when you're not working, you spend most of your time alone."

Lynnette made a one-punch move. Surprised, he released her. Arms now free, she kicked upward, her knee connecting with his groin.

Air swooshed from his mouth as his knees sagged. He cursed, trying to regain his balance, and his hold on her. "Don't run away. I only want to love you."

****

Options ran through Lynnette's mind. Blood pumped furiously through her brain. She had to stay calm. Calm enough to think. Her brain agreed with her feet. Run like hell until she reached her apartment. Two blocks. Two blocks to safety.

Her purse, still unzipped, draped against her hip. She reached for her cell phone. Unable to see the numbers through the grey fog, she prayed her fingers were punching 911. She forgot about the uneven section of sidewalk until she was thrown off balance. The phone flew from her hand, and the stumble cost her what little edge she had gained.

Quick as a whip, he caught her by both arms. Like a giant octopus, he imprisoned her against his chest.

She struggled and sensed the futility of it. She tried to slow her breathing, to calm herself. Panic might get her killed. Maybe she could reason with him.

5

"Hey, Ben. No one has to get hurt here. Let me go, and we'll forget this ever happened. It's a big mistake, a misunderstanding. Right?"

"Right." The way he said that one word was as chilling as a block of ice.

Her throat tightened. Her mind sped back sixteen years to the gruesome images of Brenda Alligood's tortured body, and Bennie Wiener sobbing and apologizing for hurting Brenda.

Lynnette tried a different tactic. "If you *don't* let me go, I'll scream."

"Shh…shh. Don't scream. Please. I *won't* hurt you."

His reassurance meant nothing to her. She had lived in Cole Harbor most of her life, and the only real crime the community had ever suffered was from Bennie's hands. And now he had returned.

The pounding in her ears was more deafening than the constant waves lapping against pier pylons. Her chest rose and fell faster with each breath.

She tensed when he leaned down and sniffed her hair. "I like the way you smell." He inhaled again, as if he were savoring each sniff. "You smell the way a real woman should. Clean and fresh, like a spring day. Nice. Not like a cheap whore doused in even cheaper perfume. That's what Brenda was—cheap. Every guy in school knew about her."

He nuzzled Lynnette's hair. Her nerves tangled in a frenzy. Rage punched its way past her fear. She screamed, and screamed again. Twisted and squirmed until she broke from his arms. She clawed his face, the backs of his hands. At the hospital, she had seen death. She wasn't ready to die.

Out of the gray mist, one large hand wrapped around her forehead, the other around her chin. The crack echoed through her brain, and for one intense moment she had the feeling she could escape.

"You should've listened to me. I warned you. I don't like screaming."

****

Ben staggered through the back door of the cabin he'd inherited from his grandfather, closed it, and leaned back, touching the wooden slats.

Weary, he let his head rest against the door. A dog howled, way off in the distance. The sound rallied his senses. His eyes adjusting to the dark, he walked to the bathroom and switched on the light. With a groan, he turned on the faucet and placed his hands under the warm running water. Looking down, he saw the source of the stinging pain. Streams of crimson ran stark against the white sink.

He stared into the mirror. Bloody lacerations covered both cheeks where Lynnette's nails had punished him. Blood had already begun to clot in the deep scratches on the tops of both hands. He lathered his hands with soap and scrubbed his face. He peeled off his bloodstained jacket and let it fall in a heap on the old-fashioned braided rug. Dirt, grass, and leaves clung to the dark T-shirt and jeans he wore. Mud laced the rims of his brogans. He undressed, tossing the clothing and shoes aside. All the time, he mumbled, "She shouldn't have screamed. I told her, didn't I?"

He beat his fist against his forehead. "No…no…no. I promised not to hurt her. She shouldn't have screamed."

He strode to the bed, knelt on the floor, then

reached between the mattress and box spring until his fingers found the pouch. In a matter of seconds, he had lit the joint and inhaled until he felt certain his lungs could hold no more of the calming drags. He sat naked, legs stretched in front of him, back against the box spring, until he'd siphoned the stick and nothing remained to hold between his fingers.

Climbing into bed, he pulled the quilt over his trembling body. Tears sprang to his eyes. "It wasn't my fault."

Vrrrr vrrrr vrrrr. Ben crawled from the bed. He shivered as the cold prickled across his body. V*rrrr vrrrr vrrrr.* He reached down and plucked his pants from the bathroom floor to extract the cell phone from the pocket. The whirring vibrated his hand. He walked into the kitchen, then lifted the latch on the back door. With quiet reverence, he set the phone on the step. A shovel leaned against the cabin. Gripping the long wooden handle, he smashed the metal end against the piece of plastic. In a frenzy, he hit the cell phone again and again, until broken pieces scattered and rolled to the ground. He'd bury them in the morning.

He was exhausted. Depleted of energy.

Sleep.

All he wanted now was to sleep and to forget about Lynnette Braswell.

****

In the center of the town's park, Ben knelt in the raw dirt that surrounded the gazebo. He lifted a large plastic pot, turned it upside down, and carefully removed the white rosebush. He used the small spade to dig a hole deep enough to accommodate the plant. Then with his hands he filled in the gap around the roots. He carefully measured the distance and marked the space for another rosebush. A red one, this time.

Buoys clanged in the bay, the sea fog had lifted, and the sun shone. He stopped long enough to draw in a breath of salt air. He watched the town come alive as shop owners opened their doors, rolled out displays, and called greetings to each other. It was like watching a grand Victorian lady put on her jewelry.

He blinked back the fleeting image of Lynnette. He had hoped, when he awakened this morning, that it was all a bad dream. No, it had not been a nightmare; it had really happened. The full reality of what he'd done settled firmly in his mind.

A cheery voice startled him back to reality. "Good morning, Mr. Noone."

He squinted up at the mayor's wife. "Ayuh, 'tis a fine morning, Mrs. Shipley."

At that moment, Mrs. Perry, who owned the pastry shop, walked up. "Lovely, Mr. Noone. Just lovely. Don't you think so, Martha?"

Martha Shipley gathered her plump body like a hen fluffing its feathers. "Ayuh. I believe you are a better gardener than old Mr. Wilton. The flowers will look beautiful for the annual Lobstah Fest and Fourth of July fireworks. Well, ta-ta. As president of the women's society, I have much to do before next week's opening ceremonies."

Mrs. Perry offered a large disposable cup filled with steaming coffee, along with a sack containing a bagel spread with cream cheese and thin-sliced lox. "A young man needs to keep up his strength."

He accepted the refreshments. "Thank you kindly. I'll stop by and pay you after I finish up he-ah."

"Oh, pshaw. It's the least I can do while you work to beautify the town square."

A shard of panic raced through him when the middle-aged woman grabbed his hand. "You orta wear gloves. Scratches like that can turn septic from working in the dirt. What happened? Oh, my, and look at your poor face."

A streak of dirt stained his cheek where he reached up and touched it. "I'll heed your advice, Mrs. Perry, and buy a pair of leather gloves. Rose thorns can make a mess of your hands. B-but I found a kitten in the woods. It's kinda wild and didn't take kindly to me. Between the kitten and the scratches from the rose thorns, I probably look like I've been in a fight."

Maudine Perry patted Ben on the shoulder. "You are a kind soul. Now, sit and enjoy your breakfast before the coffee gets cold."

He opened his mouth but closed it without speaking, merely acknowledging her with a nod. Seated inside the summer house, he looked across the bay toward Pine Island. He watched the world go by until he was finished with his snack. Disposing of the sack and cup in a public garbage bin, he knelt down, enjoying the feel of the soft earth that sent its cool dampness through his old blue jeans to his skin.

As he began his careful effort to plant rows of petunias, then variegated border grass, a feeling of unease settled in his mind. He found himself thinking of the young woman who lay in a lonely grave. And then he smiled. How incredibly smart of him to bury the body right under the town's regal noses. He sucked in gulps of fresh air, clearing the residue of death from his lungs.

Chapter One

Ten years later

The weeks had passed in a blur of pain and sorrow. Although the windshield wipers worked at full speed, Laura Friday leaned forward to peer through the heavy mist that blanketed the two-lane highway to Cole Harbor.

Justice. The word left a bitter taste in her mouth as she thought back to the night she'd cradled Jolly's head in her lap. Jaali Zuri, her cameraman and friend of many years. In Swahili his name meant "fearless and beautiful." Always smiling, he lived up to that and to his nickname.

Overly zealous, and not heeding her editor's warning about checking the reliability of an informant's sources, the only thing that had mattered to Laura was to out-scoop her competitor. She'd beat him, all right. And at what cost? Jolly was dead, and she was left with scars deeper than the permanent limp from bullets that had nearly taken her life.

Other reporters had jockeyed for positions, flashed cameras, yelled questions. In spite of wavering in and out of consciousness, she'd heard every profane word shouted by the two drug mules being shoved into the patrol car. She'd swung her gaze to the two lumps covered by white sheets. She wanted to scream that she hoped they rotted in hell. And then she had shifted to look at the kid, handcuffed, his eyes glittering with pure hatred. The informant. He'd set her up, and she had trusted those childlike brown eyes, the innocent baby face. He shouted something. She didn't understand the language, but even amid the noise and confusion the gist of his words was not lost on her: *I'll get you.*

She had dropped her gaze to Jolly's dark curly hair and with one hand stroked his cheek, her fingers laced with blood that glistened in the street light. From somewhere far away she heard someone say her name.

Pain, sharp and intense, had slammed into her with blinding force. She recalled nothing else until she opened her eyes to see a nurse adjusting the IV and asking if she needed anything.

She'd been a crime reporter for ten years. Her job had always meant everything—her career, her obsession. With her nearest relative living in another state, the newspaper had become her family. Nothing had mattered except getting the story, exposing the bad guys.

None of that mattered now. Nothing would erase the guilt from her soul.

Shaking off the memories, she squinted through the windshield to see the road ahead. The endless sweep of trees on one side reminded her of ominous giants, balanced against the cold waters of the bay on the other side. An unexpected sense of loneliness twisted her heart.

A blast of wind slammed against the side of her car, sending it with a lurch into the opposite lane. Wrestling the steering wheel for control, Laura scanned the darkness on either side of the road. She hadn't seen another vehicle for more than an hour. If she careened down the steep embankment, she likely wouldn't be found for months. But then, who was there to miss her? She hadn't bothered telephoning her Aunt Phyllis. Foolish! Her nearest living relative, and she hadn't considered the possibility of not being welcomed. Their last contact was a brief encounter at her mother's funeral. Aunt Phyllis had invited Laura then to stay a few days in Cole Harbor. She had used the excuse of needing to return to New York City for a news story she was following. Yeah, foolish.

Laura checked the odometer. The highway seemed to stretch on forever. The sheer desolation made her shiver. Already she missed the bustle of crowds, the honking horns of irate taxi drivers during rush hour traffic, and the comingling of savory aromas from food vendor trucks.

She lifted the container from the cup holder and shook it. Empty. What she needed now was an extra dose of caffeine.

The large stop sign loomed in front of her like an unexpected red eye. She touched the brakes. Hitting the electric button to lower the window, she listened for the sound of another vehicle. Poor visibility, the throbbing pain in her hip, and the overwhelming need for a strong cup of coffee made her wonder if she'd made the biggest mistake of her life.

A familiar wash of grief and anger flowed through her. No, she'd made a worse mistake. The one that had cost her friend's life. The whoop-whoop of a siren invaded her thoughts. She glanced into the rearview mirror and spotted the flashing amber bubble.

Every sense she owned went on red alert. An

isolated location. She pressed the button to close the window, then opened it again, a few inches. A light flashed, momentarily blinded her.

"Car trouble?"

She met his gaze squarely. "No. Because of the fog, I was being extra careful."

The badge on his jacket meant nothing to her, although his body language didn't seem threatening. But looks were deceiving. Out here, totally alone. Fingers of fear chilled her. What if Elio Casper had escaped prison and somehow found her?

She gave the man with the badge a bland smile. "My aunt is expecting me. She's probably worried because I'm running late; and I have no bars on my cell phone to call her."

"I assume you're on your way to Cole Harbor?"

Swallowing hard, she said, "Why would you think that?"

He pointed to the right. "Unless you plan to spend the night outside the national park, except for a few cabins, not many people live in that direction. If your aunt lives close to the park, you can follow me."

"Mmph, no. She lives in town, above her store. Again, thanks for the directions."

"I'd escort you in, but I need to check on a complaint." He pointed. "Hang a left. The town is less than a half mile."

She caught herself captivated by his slight southern drawl. Maybe he wasn't what she'd thought after all. Consorting with narcs and stoolies had made her edgy, had honed her sense of caution. Not that it had helped in Jolly's case. Still, a crime reporter who didn't develop a sense of awareness didn't last long in a tough business. She drew in a deep, steadying breath and slowly exhaled. "Thank you."

He offered a nod before returning to his vehicle.

As a matter of caution, she waited for the deputy's car to pull around hers. She gripped the steering wheel with both hands until the flashing blinker light showed the car turning to the right. After she'd turned in the opposite direction, and again as a matter of caution, she checked the rearview mirror to make certain no one followed her.

As he'd predicted, in less than a minute the town opened up. Even with the buildings shrouded in gray mist it was a welcome sight. Laura drove down the main boulevard until she spotted the gazebo. She swung the car into an empty parking space in front of Friday's Bookstore and Tea Room.

Chapter Two

The last dregs of winter air hung mild and misty as dense sea fog blanketed Cole Harbor. Inside the conference area of Friday's Bookstore and Tea Room, Phyllis Friday glanced around the table at the other five participants. "Perfect weather for our little experiment. I believe we've followed all the instructions to conduct a proper séance. Let us join hands, and no matter what happens, don't break the circle."

In the center of the round table, lighted candles emitted eerie shadows over the tureen of steaming lobster chowder and a platter of crusty bread. Phyllis adjusted the glasses on the bridge of her nose as she peered at the open book. "It says to call forth spirits we must provide them with physical nourishment and lighted candles—enough divisible by three." She sniffed and sighed her appreciation for the food's savory aromas.

Maudine Perry lamented, "I'm not so sure we should dabble in the arts of dark magic, Phyllis. What if we accidently call forth an evil spirit?"

Phyllis studied the pale, pinched features of her friend. "Maudie, are you a mouse or a woman? We're merely trying to contact Sally Wentworth's spirit, and none other." Once again, she glanced around the table at the faces of women past their prime, some widows of lobstermen and crabbers. She herself was a spinster.

Maudie baked the pastries and ran the tea and pastry shop inside the bookstore, and the others were a teacher, a minister's wife, a librarian, and a travel agent, all long retired and often feeling cast aside because of their age and various stages of mobility.

During their last monthly Friday Sisters Book Club meeting, which had included a discussion of Sherlock Holmes and *The Disappearance of Lady Carfax*, the group compared the case to that of a teenage girl whose family had moved to Cole Harbor over fifty years ago.

"Stay or go, we thank you for preparing the chowdah. If you decide to go, that will leave us with a numbah not divisible by three." Phyllis sighed. "In that case I'm afraid, ladies, we'll have to cancel the séance and find anothah way to figure out who murdered poor Sally."

She didn't know if the sighs filtering around the table were those of relief or disappointment. Her chin went up. "Are we mice or women? Where is your courage? While our new deputy is too handsome for his own good, and has proven his prestigious credentials, he is young and inexperienced. Plus, he himself said he wasn't interested in solving cold cases."

Maudie Perry broke the circle. She clasped her hands together. "I think we've read too many mystery novels. Look at us. Nadia is almost eighty, and deaf as stone. We're old. Not sleuths or psychic mediums. Besides, Sally Wentworth disappeared forty years ago. I agree with the majority of the town folks. She ran off with that no-good Corbin Drake. Sheriff Pitmeyer, God rest his soul, never found any evidence of foul play. Besides, Sally's parents died a long time ago, and there is no family who would care one way or the other. I don't understand your obsession with solving a mystery where there is no mystery." Maudie reached across the table and grabbed a crusty roll. "I'm hungry. Let's eat."

"Ayuh, I agree with Maudie. Ladle me a bowl of chowdah, will yah? And for your information, I'm not all that deaf. I have selective hearing." The wrinkles smoothed from Nadia Cruex's cherubic face when she smiled.

Bing bong...bing bong!

Phyllis Friday huffed, "For Pete's sake. It's aftah seven." She yelled, "The store is closed."

Bing bong...bing bong!

The incessant ringing of the doorbell was followed by, "Aunt Philly, open the door. It's me, Laura."

"By Godfrey! This is certainly unexpected. It's my niece from New York. I told you about her...the reporter." Phyllis pushed away from the table. "Coming... Hold on, I'm coming."

Phyllis unlatched the door and swung it wide. After the hugs were done, she prattled, "I wasn't expecting you until next month. Is something wrong? Oh, dear, this is a lovely surprise. Put your suitcases there." She clasped her niece by the arm. "I'm rambling like a doddering idiot. Come, you're just in time for a bowl of the best clam chowdah you've ever tasted."

Laura leaned in close and whispered, "Introduce me as Laura Friday. I'll explain later."

Her aunt gave a faint nod, although curiosity gleamed in her eyes.

After the introductions were made, questions came at her from around the table, everything from "How long do you plan to stay?" to "What's it like being a big time New York investigative reporter?"

Laura cast a haggard glance at the curious faces staring back at her. "If Aunt Philly is up to my bunking in with her until I get my own place, I'm here permanently."

Phyllis' gasp echoed those of the other ladies. "What about your job? What I mean is, of course, dear. Stay as long as you like. I have plenty of room."

Laura dipped a piece of bread into the rich, creamy soup and plopped it into her mouth. She chewed, stretching out the answer to her aunt's question. "I'm burnt out, Aunt Philly. I don't have the physical or mental energy to cover another story about murder or kidnappings or anything concerning drug pushers and gangs. My editor is friends with Dan Fremont, and—"

Phyllis interrupted, "Dan Fremont who owns the *Harbor Gazette*? You're going to work for that crotchety ole grouser?"

Laura lifted the linen napkin and dabbed her lips. "Yes and no. Yes, Dan Fremont who owns the *Harbor Gazette*, and no, I'm not going to work for him. I'm sure you've heard about his health, and that he's retiring." She spread her hands wide, "Sooo, the corporation that bought the *Harbor Gazette* has employed me. You are looking at the new editor-in-chief and reporter extraordinaire, all in one."

Maudie Perry offered, "But, dear, nothing exciting ever happens here. Life is dull, routine. In a word— boring. In time you'll tire of writing mundane articles about the women's society planting new flowers around the gazebo, or who died, or who won the annual pie-baking contest. You're young, talented, beautiful. Couldn't you find something more exciting?"

Phyllis scolded. "Maudine Perry, what my niece

does with her life is her business." She flashed a thoughtful smile toward Laura. "Part of me agrees with Maudie, but the other part is totally delighted you're here."

Phyllis noted the desperation that crept into Laura's voice. "I needed a change. A do-over, if you will. I was born in Cole Harbor and lived here until I was five. It seemed logical for me to come home."

The gaunt look and dark circles under her eyes spoke volumes. Phyllis didn't need a sixth sense or a séance to know something was amiss with her niece. She placed her hands on the table and pushed her chair backwards as she stood. "Ladies, we haven't left a drop in the pot or a crumb of bread to evoke a wisp of smoke, much less a spirit. I declare the séance officially postponed."

Laura groaned when she arose. A reaction to the pain, she gripped her hip. The wan look on her niece's face caused Phyllis to hasten her friends toward the front door. "Be careful going home. It's thick as pea soup tonight." And then to Laura, "Don't worry about your bags. I'll bring them up. Take your mother's old room. It has its own bathroom. Top of the stairs, end of the hall."

Laura let out a tired breath. "It was nice meeting all of you. Forgive me for intruding."

Maudie patted Laura's shoulder. "Now, now, none of that. We're just a bunch of dotty ole busybodies who haven't learned to mind our own business. It's my turn to host the next Friday Sisters Book Club meeting. Promise you'll join us."

"Perhaps." Laura turned toward the stairs.

Chapter Three

"Knock, knock."

"Door's open, Aunt Philly."

Phyllis used the toe of her shoe to nudge the bedroom door completely open. She set the tray containing two cups, a small teapot, and a canister of whipped cream on the end of the bed. "I thought you might like a cup of hot chocolate, with a healthy splash of amaretto. It's my specialty."

Phyllis sniffed her appreciation for the aromatic fragrance as she lifted the canister. "Whipped cream?"

Laura smiled and nodded. She accepted the cup as she sat on the bed, leaning against the headboard, knees drawn up. Her aunt relaxed in the wingbacked chair next to the window.

Neither woman spoke.

Laura closed her eyes and swallowed the knot in the back of her throat. The velvety texture of the chocolate laced with alcohol worked like a magic potion. She set the empty cup aside. A slight blush rose to her cheeks. "I'm sorry, Aunt Philly."

Phyllis tipped her own cup for the last luscious drop of liquid. "Whatever for?"

"For barging in without an invitation, for being rude to your friends, for…for—" and then like the gates of a dam had burst, her tears flowed and heart-wrenching sobs tore from Laura's throat. Damn her aunt for unleashing the vulnerability she'd chained down so she could investigate crimes without crumbling under fear.

Phyllis shifted to the bed and opened her arms. She stroked the silken strands of short blonde hair as she cradled her niece. "I knew the moment I laid eyes on you things were not right. I'm a good listener, if you're of a mind to talk."

Laura sat up. Between sobs, hiccups, and blowing her nose, she managed to relate about Jolly's death, about her own injuries, and about the implied threat to her life. "It's all my fault. I have a knack for plunging ahead without thinking. Max, my editor, warned me. If I had listened, if I had waited for DEA to arrive, Jolly would be celebrating his wedding day instead of lying in a cold grave."

Phyllis offered a sympathetic smile. "I'm sorry about your friend, but what worries me the most is the threat that young punk made about hurting you. At least he's in prison, and I assume no one knows you're here. You're safe."

Phyllis stared at Laura with genuinely kind eyes. "I'm guessing all this has something to do with you changing your name from Schofield to Friday."

"The more anonymity, the better. Max helped me make the name change legal. You don't think Dad would mind, do you?"

"It's a shame your parents aren't alive to see the fine young woman you've become. In death as well as in life, Tom and June would agree with your decision. Besides, you've always been more Friday than Schofield."

A yawn caught Laura by surprise. "You won't tell

anyone, will you?"

"The amaretto is doing the trick." She patted her niece's arm. "Don't you worry. My lips are sealed. Now, it's late, and you need to rest. I'll take the dishes to the kitchen and bring up your bags."

"I'm serious, Aunt Philly. Not even to old Sheriff Gilman."

"Amos Gilman had a fatal heart attack a few years back. His daughter, Roberta Gilman, is sheriff now. She's on temporary leave of absence—honeymoon. Mitchell Carter is the new deputy. He's arrogant, too handsome for his own good, and behind those baby-blue peepers is a man harboring a sad soul."

"I don't remember her. In fact, there isn't much I do remember about Cole Harbor. Is the new Sheriff Gilman capable?"

"Ayuh. Seemed only reasonable for her to fill Amos' shoes. She's more'n qualified."

"I wondered about the deputy's southern drawl."

Phyllis' eyebrows arched upward. "You met him?"

Laura gave a brief sketch of her encounter with Mitchell Carter, then scooted from the bed. "I'll get my travel bag, and we can leave the rest of the suitcases until morning."

The sudden motion of standing caused her to yelp when pain sliced through her thigh and her leg collapsed. She grabbed the bedpost to keep from crumpling to the floor. This time the tears that leaked from her eyes had nothing to do with emotions and everything to do with the multiple gunshot wounds that were still healing.

She swallowed back the bile. Her hands trembled as she reached for her purse and lifted out the bottle of painkillers.

Phyllis took the cue, grabbed the cup off the tray, and rushed next door to the bathroom, to return in seconds with cool water.

Laura swallowed the pills, then settled on the edge of the bed. "I should probably check in with Mr. Fremont tomorrow. How far is it to the newspaper office?"

Phyllis tsked. "Out the bookstore door…into the newspaper's door. We knew Dan had planned to sell the paper and move out west to live with his daughter. He always was a close-mouthed ole coot. I'm surprised he kept quiet about you being the new owner."

"He doesn't know it's me who bought it. I desperately need anonymity. The purchase was made through a dummy corporation, so that it appears as a subsidiary of the *New York Crier*. As far as anyone knows anywhere else, I'm merely here to run the one-person operation."

"Smart girl. You take after me." Phyllis offered a sly grin, and a wink.

Laura took a deep breath to discredit the statement. She picked at a piece of lint on the quilt. "Do you ever get tired of being alone?"

"Who says I'm alone? I have my friends, regular patrons who enjoy sipping tea and enjoying a pastry while sitting in a comfy chair with their books, and now I have you."

"You know what I mean."

"Of course, I do. I loved someone once. He died in Vietnam. I never wanted anyone else. For better or worse, we choose our own paths, Laura. If we're not happy with the choice, then we work to change it."

A smile kinked one corner of Laura's mouth. "At the office they call me the ice maiden. Behind my back, of course."

"You are no longer in New York. Plus, you said you wanted a new start. Close your eyes, sleep off the exhaustion, and when you wake up it will be a brand-new day, a brand-new job, and a perfect time to become someone other than the ice maiden."

Phyllis blew a kiss and shut the door behind her.

Laura undressed and stood naked in front of the long mirror behind the bathroom door. She had always taken pride in her early morning runs, keeping her five-seven frame lean and fit. That had been nine weeks ago. Now her eyes held dark shadows, her cheeks were two pale hollows, and her limbs had become almost too thin to bear her weight. In a word, she looked like a scarecrow in dire need of more stuffing.

She traced the line of the long scar that marred her hip and traveled the length to her knee. Bullets from an M-16 had splintered the bone, leaving little for the surgeon to repair. Yet he had saved her leg, merely leaving it shorter than the other. No more early morning runs for her. No more runs, period. She couldn't stand the sight of her own body, nor the ugly orthopedic shoes that had become a permanent part of her wardrobe.

Chapter Four

Three days later, the morning sun spilled through the glass-paned window of the newspaper office. The scent of lemon oil filled the growing warmth in the office as Laura wiped the dust cloth over the antique wooden desk. She smiled as she worked her way around the room, giving the wood a polished gleam and humming along softly to the tune on the radio.

Laura stood in the center of her new office. Hands on hips, and satisfied with her efforts, she surveyed the space. No more overflowing file cabinets, or stacks of folders piled in chairs or in every corner of the small office. Dan Fremont had said to keep what she thought was important, chuck the rest. The paper was hers to do with as she pleased.

Cleaning and organizing had a cathartic effect on her. She felt good. The floors shone with new polish, and years of dust had been removed from the venetian blinds, shelves, and the ceiling fan.

"You look like the cat who swallowed the canary. Gloating, I see."

Laura turned when the little bell over the front door dingled. "Good morning to you, too, Aunt Philly."

Phyllis handed her niece a cup of coffee, then pulled up a chair and sat down, taking a sip from her own cup. "I have an assignment for you. I'd like you to find a missing person."

Laura removed the plastic cap from the cup. "Sounds intriguing. Tell me more."

"Sally Wentworth disappeared almost fifty years ago. My theory is she was murdered and her body dumped in the bay. The night you arrived, my book club ladies and I had planned to hold a séance to see if we could call forth her spirit."

Laura chided. "Really? Don't tell me you believe in such nonsense."

Phyllis wagged her finger. "Don't poke fun. Cole Harbor isn't exactly a beehive teeming with activities. We have the Lobstah Fest, of course, and the Fourth of July Arts Festival, and in October we hold a Halloween Ghost Hunt at the Lighthouse Museum. Other than going about our daily lives, the rest of the time there isn't much to do. So if we want to hold a séance, then humor your old aunt and her cronies."

"Sorry, Aunt Philly. I didn't mean to be crass. Was Sally a close friend?"

"Yes and no. Her parents rented a cottage here for several years when we were both in grade school. She was such a pretty girl, and so much fun. She and I became inseparable during that time, and she drew boys the way honey draws flies. Shortly after her sixteenth birthday, Sally started skipping school to hang out with Corbin Drake. She was sixteen, and he was twenty. In our day, anyone who wore a black leather jacket, smoked cigarettes, and rode a motorcycle was considered a real pissah, you know, a hoodlum. Then Sally disappeared and was never heard of again. Corbin was gone too, of course.

"Her parents reported her missing. After his investigation, Amos concluded Sally had run off with

Corbin. Apparently, clothes and a suitcase were missing, and some money stolen from her mother's cookie jar"—Phyllis shrugged—"that sort of thing."

"What happened? Didn't her parents pursue it further?"

"Nothing happened. Sally was a change-of-life baby. Her parents were in their late fifties when she was born. By the time she disappeared, they were on the high side of seventy. Mr. Wentworth slipped and hit his head down at the fishing docks. Never regained consciousness. Mrs. Wentworth left Cole Harbor shortly after the funeral. We all thought the strain of losing her daughter and her husband was too much, and she went back to wherever they had come from. Case closed and, subsequently, forgotten. But Sally's disappearance stuck in my mind." Phyllis grimaced. "I always had visions of Corbin cutting poor Sally into pieces and feeding her to the sharks. My teenage imagination working overtime, I suppose."

Laura felt a quick sympathy for the sorrow she saw in her aunt's eyes, and warmed toward her. "Have you tried searching on the Internet?"

"I have not."

"Don't you use a computer for your business?"

"It takes a while for an old war horse to get into the race. I'm taking lessons at the library. Once I feel comfortable with what I'm doing, I may buy a computer. Until then, I'll depend on you to search for Sally."

Laura opened the laptop to a search engine and typed in the girl's name. When no hits came up, she tried another tactic. "Hmm, nothing comes up for Sally Wentworth. Let me try white pages?"

"Humor your ole aunt. What is—white pages?"

Laura offered a squinty smile. "It's an informational site that lists the names, addresses and phone numbers of individuals and businesses. In fact, it also shows a map for people to find you. I'll bet both you and the bookstore are listed."

"By Godfrey, is nothing sacred anymore?"

Laura ignored the question. In the search space she typed Corbin Drake. "Aha. Mystery solved. Prepare to be disappointed."

"So quick. The wonders of modern technology." A frown wrinkled Phyllis' forehead. "Why should I be disappointed?"

Laura turned the computer for her aunt to view the screen. She came around the desk, and leaned over to point at the page. "Corbin Drake. Living in the same household: spouse, Sally Wentworth Drake. Approximate age, sixty-five. Address: Washington State." She patted her aunt on the shoulder. "Sorry, it appears your mystery girl and her bad-biker boyfriend eloped and are living happily ever after."

Phyllis huffed. "By Godfrey, this frustrates me to no end. It proves Maudie's theory was right. She will *never* let me live this down."

Laura drifted to the large picture window. "Who is the man sitting in the gazebo?"

Phyllis frowned as she followed Laura's gaze. "Benjamin Noone. He's the city groundskeeper and handyman. I once called him Ben, and he let me know right quick-like that his name is *Benjamin.* Strange duck."

"How so?"

"A loner, mostly. Comes into the bookstore once in

a while. Mostly, I think he comes in for the heat in winter and air conditioning in summer. Seems to enjoy reading about flowers and fertilizers." She wrinkled her nose and gave an exaggerated shudder. "He should actually do a study on the benefits of taking a bath. Whenever people greet him, sometimes he'll respond, other times not. Lives in an old cabin close to the national park. He moved here about ten years ago. On occasion, he'll show up at one of the festivals, or the Christmas program at the church over there—for the free food, is my guess. For whatever reason, Maudie takes pity on him. Every morning she walks out to the gazebo with a cup of coffee and a bagel. And every morning, for at least an hour, he sits in the gazebo and stares out over the bay.

"I can say one thing in his favor, he is an excellent gardener and keeps the town square clean as a whistle, even though I can't say much for his own personal hygiene." Phyllis tilted her head to look at Laura. "Why the interest? Has he been out of the way with you?"

Laura rubbed her thigh as she limped to her desk chair and sat down. "I've never spoken to the man. Just curious."

Phyllis waggled her eyebrows. "Beginning to miss the excitement of investigative reporting, poking around in dark alleys and smoke-filled billiard parlors?"

Smiling, Laura ran a hand through her spiked blonde hair. "Aunt Philly, you read too many mystery novels. Even if I were getting a bit bored, my leg is a constant reminder of why I left New York. Cole Harbor is my home now. Besides, I've sunk my life savings into this newspaper. I'm not going anywhere, and I'm not looking for a story where there isn't one."

"Well, you are certainly good at what you do. It didn't take long for you to locate Sally Wentworth—which, by the way, has spoiled my chances of holding a séance."

Laura looked toward the ceiling and shook her head. "Mystery novels and mysticism. Aunt Philly, you are one in a million, and I adore you." She placed a hand on her forehead, closed her eyes, and chanted, "Ohmmah. I see a customer in your near future." The expression on her aunt's face was priceless. "Truly, a woman just walked into the bookstore."

Phyllis shook her finger toward Laura. "If you're funning with me, no more free coffee, or blueberry muffins."

Laura crossed her heart. "Hope to die." She opened the bottom desk drawer and withdrew her camera. "It's about time I start drumming up some front page news. I'll walk out with you."

The sheriff's office was first on her list. She walked the short distance to the town hall, which housed the courtroom, the city council office, the sheriff's office, and a one-person jail cell. A gray-haired woman with a cherubic smile greeted Laura. *Doesn't anyone under fifty live in Cole Harbor?* She offered the woman a business card.

Before Laura could speak, the woman said, "Pleased to meet yah, and welcome. Maybe you'll breathe new life into that ole rag Dan Fremont called a newspaper. He never printed anything worth reading." She stood and offered her hand. "I'm Louise Highland."

The sheriff's secretary had a strong grip. "Nice to meet you, Ms. Highland. Today is my meet-and-greet day. Is the sheriff in?"

"'Fraid not. Sheriff Gilman is on her honeymoon. Deputy Carter is in charge until she returns." The secretary winked, then sighed. "If I were younger, I'd give Mitchell Carter a run for his money. Anyhow, he's down at the docks. There was a smidgen of excitement a while ago." Louise's overly penciled eyebrows lifted. "Say, maybe there's a story for you."

Laura thanked the woman. What with her aunt and now the sheriff's secretary swooning, Mitchell Carter must be more than she'd noticed that night on the road. "Thanks for the tip."

Laura hurried to the bookstore. "Okay if I borrow your bicycle, Aunt Philly?"

Phyllis looked up from the circulation desk. "Ayuh. What's up?"

Laura waved. "Tell you later."

At the bike rack in front of the store she bit back a grimace as she straddled the bicycle. It took all the fortitude she could muster to set the pedal in motion with her bad leg. She told herself to push through the pain.

As she pedaled toward the docks, Laura tried to remember the last time she'd felt this invigorated. Fearing she might lose control of the bicycle and fall if she lifted her arms in the air and shouted, she opted to simply breathe in the fresh, salt air and allow the smile on her face to widen.

She braked before reaching the bottom of the hill. Her current vantage point provided a perfect view of the deputy sheriff's car, an ambulance, a gathering crowd, several expensive yachts, and two men pushing a gurney up the dock. The sheet-draped body brought back vivid memories of the night she was shot, and Elio

Casper's threat. She shook off the chill that threatened to chatter her teeth on this picturesque May morning. She lifted her camera from the bicycle's basket, set the shutter speed, and snapped pictures of the deputy lifting the sheet, random shots of the crowd, and, standing aft on the main deck, a young woman dressed in a white caftan.

Laura removed the lanyard from her pocket and placed it around her neck. The badge at the end read "Press." She pushed off and rode to the parking lot, where she parked the bike. "Good morning, Deputy, I'm Laura Friday, the new editor and sole reporter for the *Harbor Gazette*."

"We meet again, Miss Friday."

"What's happened here?"

"Wife called, said her husband collapsed. By the time we got here, he was dead. Heart attack, most likely."

"Do you mind if I look at the body?"

"You fancy yourself a medical examiner?" The sarcasm in his voice spiked Laura's own temper. She tamped it down.

"In New York, investigative reporting was my specialty."

"This isn't New York, and until proven otherwise, it appears the victim died of natural causes. Case closed."

"Just like that?"

"Yep."

"We'll see." The moment she started up the steep incline, the muscle in her leg refused to respond, causing her to stumble. "Damn."

Strong arms held her up. Laura wrested her arm

away. "I don't need your help."

"Suit yourself."

She took a moment to swallow her aggravation before she half hobbled, half limped toward the ambulance. "Hey…wait a sec…press." She held the badge forward.

The overt look from the EMT and the lawman's almost indiscernible nod in reply didn't escape Laura. "Thank you, Deputy Carter."

She lifted the sheet. No bruising, no indications of a fall, nothing to suggest foul play, until she parted the man's lips and bent forward. "Uh-huh."

"What?" Mitchell Carter said in a flat voice.

They faced each other like duelers, with that unblinking awareness. She quirked a smile, leaned in close and whispered, "I'll bet you a lobster dinner and a beer the vic didn't die of natural causes."

"First of all, he's not a victim. Secondly, I'm a steak-and-bourbon guy."

"Then you won't mind if I take pictures of the…deceased."

"That's the coroner's job."

Laura looked around. "Where is he?"

Mitch removed his hat and riffled through his hair. "This is a small community, a tourist town. He's not available at the moment."

"Wow, I didn't know Cole Harbor was a hot bed of crime."

One of the EMTs laughed, then sobered when Carter sent him a scathing scowl.

When no one offered further explanation, Laura shrugged. "Whatever." She walked to the bicycle, and quirked a smile over her shoulder. "Have a nice day,

Deputy."

She spent the rest of the morning introducing herself to business owners, soliciting ads for the paper, and taking pictures of crafters setting up their tents, along with a flurry of other activities for the annual Fourth of July festivities.

At three o' clock, Mitch Carter walked into her office. His voice betrayed his aggravation. "Not that it matters, but after the coroner examined the body, I requested he send it to the medical examiner in Bangor for an autopsy."

Laura leaned back in her chair. She smiled with harsh amusement. "You always so abrupt? No 'Good afternoon,' or 'How's it going,' just straight to the point…shoot from the hip?"

Mitch drew in a breath and let it out slowly. "Good afternoon, Miss Friday. How was your day? Mind if I sit down?"

She extended a hand toward the chair. "Let me guess. You and your drawl come from Montana? Wyoming?"

"Texas."

"Long ways from home. How did you end up here?"

His discomfort with the question piqued her curiosity. He ignored the inquiry, and she chose not to goad him further.

"My job history is none of your concern. Regardless of what you've assumed, I care about the safety of this town. Negative press for a community that depends on tourist dollars would be bad for business. Believe me, the citizens won't take kindly to it, or to you. Keep the story about Victor Forgione general until

I receive the medical examiner's report."

He stood and walked to the door. Before stepping outside, he turned. "Why did you part the deceased's lips and take a whiff? You have a fetish for smelling dead people's breath?"

Laura placed both hands on the desk to assist her in standing. "Very funny, Deputy. I was checking to see if our guy's breath smelled like garlic. An experienced cop should know garlic odor is a sign of arsenic poisoning. I'll still wager you Mr. Forgione was murdered."

Mitch's cocked eyebrows indicated his amusement. "By whom?"

"The grieving widow, of course. Unless our guy pumped himself full of Viagra, there's no way a man his age could keep her satisfied. He looked old enough to be her grandfather."

"Pure conjecture. Like I said, not a hint of foul play when you print the story. And for the record, I'm not a betting man."

"For your information, I print only facts. The *Gazette* is not a gossip rag."

She expected Mitch Carter to slam the door on his way out. Instead, he eased it closed. The click when he pulled it shut was barely audible. But he'd made his point loud and clear. He wasn't a man who liked people stepping into his territory. If she read him right, he was one tough hombre if crossed, and her instincts were rarely wrong.

Settled at the computer, she typed: Mitchell Carter, Texas.

She looked up when the door opened. Seeing her aunt, she closed the laptop. The aroma from the sack in

Phyllis' hand brought a loud rumble from Laura's stomach. Both women laughed.

"Lobstah roll, cole slaw, coffee, blueberry taht."

"You are my angel, Aunt Philly. Did you bring something for yourself?"

"Ayuh." Phyllis dipped into the bag and drew out another tart. "Saw Mitch Carter. He didn't look happy."

Laura took a large bite of her roll, her voice muffled as she spoke. "What's his story?"

"If you mean why do we have a deputy from Texas, the answer is that it's a well-kept secret. We asked Dan Fremont, but all he'd say is it was none of our business. Even gossipy ole Louise Highland's lips are cemented."

Laura uncapped the coffee to let it cool while she finished off the sandwich, then nibbled on the blueberry tart. Her aunt continued. "You have to admit Mitchell Carter is a handsome rascal. Reminds me of Robert Mitchum, the actor—tall and lanky, a little swagger to his walk, and that deep cleft in his chin." She sighed audibly. "Makes my unmentionable places twitch every time I see him."

Phyllis plopped the last of the tart into her mouth. "Don't look at me like that. I'm old…not dead."

"That's still more information than I want to hear. Let's change the topic. Who is the town's coroner?"

"Ken Musuyo."

"Is there a mystery around Dr. Musuyo, also?"

"If there is, I don't know about it."

"I can tell by the look on your face you're hedging. What, he's a third-rate doctor, a medical school failure?"

Phyllis huffed. "None of that. Ken Musuyo, his

wife, and parents are wonderful people. Ken is an excellent doctor. I'd put my life in his hands anytime. Its just that there's no veterinarian, and people don't want to drive to Bangor or Ellsworth when their pets get sick."

Laura sighed. "Why isn't there a vet?"

"Had one. Couldn't make a living. Not enough business."

"I suppose Dr. Musuyo does house calls, too?"

"Ayuh."

"That explains why he wasn't available down at the docks this morning."

"By Godfrey, we heard about that poor man having a heart attack."

"Aunt Philly, as much as I love you, I have a paper to put out. I'll be working late, so don't wait up for me."

Before her aunt left, Laura called her back. "Mitch Carter implied I should only report cutesy stuff. Are the people here closed-minded about real news?"

Phyllis touched her niece on the cheek. "This is your paper. Run it as you see fit. By Godfrey, we are hungry for news. Dan only put out a paper once a month, and he seldom reported anything from the outside world. However, just a small caution. You've made a huge investment. Keep folks happy, and that will grow. I'll bring your suppah around six."

Laura mulled over her aunt's subtle warning. She put delving into the deputy's background on hold as she bent to her computer. If it was news the citizens wanted, then it was news she planned to give them. She typed the name Vincent Forgione into the search engine. A smile lit her face.

At midnight, satisfied with her first front page headline—Wealthy Plastics Tycoon Vincent Forgione Leaves Fortune—she filled in the space beneath it with pictures of the yacht and the deputy standing next to the sheet-shrouded gurney. She followed with other news about local events, as well as UP and AP news, and a special section she was certain would win over old and new Cole Harbor citizens: Tidings, where she planned to feature folks who had historical connections to the town.

When the last copy had been printed and folded, she placed her hands to the small of her back and stretched. She understood why Dan Fremont put out a paper only monthly. With limited local news, it entailed a lot of work for one person. Nevertheless, before she turned out the light, she vowed to invest in a police scanner for the office and to turn the *Gazette* into a weekly production.

Chapter Five

Little more than a week later, during The Friday Sisters Book Club meeting, the talk was about the headlines in the morning paper.

Maudie Perry said, "I can't remember a time when there was so much excitement in Cole Habah. Two deaths, and only days apart. Land a-goshins, first a tycoon on a yacht, and now a dead body washed up on the beach."

Phyllis lifted the newspaper. "By Godfrey, I'm proud as a peacock of my niece. Dan never made Cole Harbor sound as interesting as this—" and she read, "Captain Matthias Friday, a lover of history and books, in 1893 donated his home to the town, and it is now The Matthias Friday Library. Captain Friday sailed the Asian and Middle Eastern trade routes, bringing rare spices and exotic silks to—his great-granddaughter, Phyllis Friday—"

A round of gleeful twitters and applause filled the room. Maudie Perry beamed. "I can hardly wait to see who you feature next, Laura."

One of the other ladies spoke up. "You know, I heard Harmon Taylor down at the boat yard say there might be foul play involved in that man's drowning. You're a reporter, Laura. What do you think?"

Laura closed the mystery novel selected for this evening's discussion. She weighed her words. "I only report the news. It's up to the sheriff to determine if a crime has been committed. If and when he does, you will be the first to read about it on the front page."

Like a tidal wave, the women seated around the table seemed to lean forward with Maudie as the leader. "So foul play is suspected?"

Laura bit back her amusement. "I didn't say that, Maudie. As I stated in the article, the wind was high the day Doctor McMahon dropped his sailboat off for repair. But if he didn't think his small skiff could handle the wind for his five-mile return trip across the bay to Marshwood Island, I'm sure Mr. Taylor would have gladly driven him over in a larger boat. The way it stands now, the skiff flipped and Doctor McMahon drowned."

Maudie was quick with her response. "Ah, but therein lies the mystery, Laura. The doctah was wearing a lifejacket. Perhaps his spirit can tell us what really happened. What do you say, ladies, shall we find out?"

A round of "ayuh" responses filtered around the table.

Laura worked to maintain a stern demeanor when her aunt abruptly stood. "Then this calls for a séance. Maudie, you know where the candles and matches are. We'll use Nadia's cookies as the physical nourishment to entice the spirit. Everyone join hands while I turn out the lights." She made a quick count. "We are six, which is divisible by three." She gave a little squeal. "Oh, I'm so excited."

"Aunt Philly…really?"

"Yes, really! If nothing else, indulge us for a bit of fun in our otherwise humdrum daily routines."

Feeling a bit chagrined at her aunt's scolding,

Laura glanced around the table. The flickering candles cast eerie glows about the room and added an ominous element to the mood. She wanted to laugh at the serious expressions masking the older women's faces. The thought of calling forth the spirit of an accidental drowning victim seemed sheer absurdity. Nonetheless, she joined hands with Phyllis on one side and Maudie on the other.

Phyllis kept her voice soft. "Nadia will act as our medium. First, we will offer a prayer of protection for all of us against any uninvited spirits." After the prayer, a circle of amens filtered around the table.

Laura glanced at the elfin-like woman who wore her hair in a crown of braids and whose dark eyes and complexion reflected a gypsy quality.

Nadia nodded, closed her eyes, and chanted, "Spirits of the past, move among us. Be guided by the light of this world and visit upon us. Doctor McMahon, we bring you gifts from life into death. Be guided by the light of this world and visit upon us."

Stillness filled the room. Laura continued to silently ridicule the idea of evoking spirits.

Her eyes shut, Nadia's voice quavered. "There is a nonbeliever among us. The spirit will not come."

It wasn't ghosts squeezing her hands until they cramped and caused Laura to wince. Without speaking words, both Phyllis and Maudie's tight grips singled her out as the doubter. She squeezed back.

When nothing happened, Nadia repeated the chant, and ended with, "We mean you no harm."

An icy chill settled over the room. Laura wanted to break the circle to rub away the goose bumps prickling her arms. She had been warned that breaking the circle might end the séance and send the spirit back to the netherworld.

Nadia whispered, "If you are with us, spirit, let us know. Rap one time for 'yes' and two times for 'no.' Do you understand?"

Laura gripped the two hands that held hers. It was evident that Philly and Maudie were also nervous.

One timid rap sounded on the wall behind Laura.

Nadia continued. "Thank you. Are you the spirit of Dr. McMahon?"

Two raps signaled 'no.'

"Are you a male spirit?"

Two raps.

Nadia whispered, "Thank you." She continued. "Are you a young woman?"

One rap.

Laura looked around the table at the graphically outlined faces. She wondered if the same skeptical wonderment showed on her own face.

"Are you a happy spirit?"

The frigid temperature increased, and sobbing filled the room. Nadia's voice remained hushed, her expression serious as she spoke to the group. "If things get out of control, break the circle immediately, one of you blow out the candles, and someone turn on the lights. Don't hesitate. Be quick."

When the sobbing continued, Nadia said, "We apologize for your sadness but thank you for visiting us. Can you tell us who you are?"

Laura noticed a change in the atmosphere. She looked down at the hands that gripped hers, and discovered they were twisted together so forcefully, the knuckles were white. Vapor filled the room. A hazy form materialized and drifted across the table, leaving in its wake a stifling odor of dank earth and moldy leaves. A silver aura settled at Laura, and hands appeared to lace around her throat.

Maudie shrieked, "Break the circle!"

Laura tried to stand. Her hip cramped like a vise grip clamping her to the chair, and she cried, "Aunt Philly, blow out the candles. Someone turn on the light."

Nadia stood at the head of the table and reached out her hands, an urgency filling her voice. "Quick, we must close the séance." When all hands had reunited, she spoke in a quiet monotone. "Goodbye, spirit. Thank you for visiting us. You may leave now. We ask that you go in peace and do us no harm."

And then she offered a small blessing over the group to assure the specter didn't attach itself to any of them. "Even though we have officially ended the séance, some spirits like to hang around. If this one does, I believe we have nothing to fear."

She turned her attention to Laura. "It seemed as if she were reaching out to you. Maybe she was just curious. She might even return to visit you later in the evening during a dream sequence."

Laura took a moment to collect her wits. "Yeah, well, this is just too weird. I'm not sure I'd want a dead person attaching itself to me."

One of the ladies gasped and pointed. "Look!"

All eyes riveted on the mirror over Maudie's priceless antique buffet. Leaking into obscure lines were the letters *l* and *y*.

Maudie grabbed one of the linen napkins from the table and rushed to wipe away the moisture. "This mirror and sideboard have been in my family for two hundred years. Spirit or no spirit, I'll not be the one who allows it to be damaged."

After a moment, Phyllis asked, "What do you think the letters mean, Nadia?"

The old woman shrugged, spreading her hands wide. She cut an eye toward Maudie. "The beginning of a name, or someone's initials, perhaps. Unless we call upon the spirit to visit again, we may never know."

Maudie's voice was contrite. "I'm sorry. If I hadn't panicked, the spirit would have told us who she was."

Laura snatched a cookie from the plate. She had stood in the face of danger many times, had experienced knee-knocking fear, but the people she'd encountered were flesh, bone, and blood. She didn't like situations she couldn't control. Although her hand trembled as she shoved the wafer inside her mouth, a healthy dose of curiosity filled her.

One of the ladies opened the drapes to allow light into the dining room. Laura glanced at her watch. "There's probably thirty minutes of daylight left. If anyone is afraid to walk home, Aunt Philly and I will escort you."

Maudie sidled closer to Phyllis. "Nadia, how do I know the spirit is gone and won't return? I've lived alone in this old house for fifty years and never had cause to be fearful."

The old woman patted her friend on the arm. "You have nothing to fear except your imagination. Shall I spend the night with you?"

At Nadia's suggestion, Laura noted the relief reflected in both women's faces.

Chapter Six

At the rear entrance of the library, Laura suggested her aunt go upstairs to the living quarters without her. "I won't be long, Aunt Philly. After what we've just experienced, I'm curious to look through Dan's old morgue books to see if I can find an article about anyone who died under mysterious circumstances—"

Phyllis finished the sentence. "And whose name has the initials: L and Y?"

Laura's stomach rumbled. "Exactly." Then, at her aunt's obvious hesitation to let her go, she asked, "How about a sandwich and a beer when I get back? In all the excitement, Maudie forgot to feed us. I'll get as many books as I can carry up the stairs. It's okay—nothing is going to happen."

"Ayuh. By Godfrey, me and my big mouth. Suggesting a séance. From now on, I'm keeping my fat trap shut."

Laura laughed. "If I'm not back in ten minutes, call the deputy."

Phyllis gave her a mutinous stare. "Not funny. Not funny in the least. Don't forget to lock the door before you come up."

Laura reached into her pocket for the key chain. In less than a minute she stood at the back door of her office. She shoved the key into the lock and turned the knob. Darkness and silence greeted her. Standing on the top step, she reached inside and groped the wall for the light switch. Her eyes swept the room before entering. Grumbling aloud, she said, "This is ridiculous. A grown woman, jumping at shadows, and all because of a stupid séance."

Nonetheless, she turned the deadbolt in place, then hurried to the closet where she had stored the morgue books. Not wanting to worry her aunt, she lifted the top eight volumes and almost buckled under the weight. She returned three neatly to their stack. Taking comfort in her own voice, she said aloud, "These will do for now."

The oversized scrapbooks fit awkwardly in her arms. After locking the door, she shifted the weight to keep the books from sliding, placed her chin on the top book to stabilize it, and wondered how, with a bum hip, she would manage the steep stairs to her aunt's upstairs living quarters carrying this load. She smiled when she spotted Phyllis standing on the library's stoop, holding the door ajar. "Figured you might need some help."

Once upstairs, with the apartment door secured, Laura said, "It's a beautiful evening. Let's spread out in the summer room."

"You go ahead. I'll whip up our snack."

The glassed-in porch ran the length of the upstairs suite. Phyllis and Laura's bedrooms were separated by the living-dining area and kitchen. Sliding glass doors from the bedrooms and from the living room provided private entries to the porch, where a cooling breeze filtered through the open screened windows. Laura set the morgue books on a long coffee table. Before switching on a lamp, she looked out across the main part of the town and thought it picturesque enough to be a Thomas Kinkade painting. She remained silent, considering the evening's events and the wisdom of believing the ghost of a young woman had actually appeared during the séance.

She switched on the lamp between the two glider rockers and propped her feet on an ottoman. The scrapbook in her lap was labeled with dates from the current year to five years past. As messy and unorganized as Dan had left the office, she gave him credit for the neatly clipped articles and the orderly way he'd adhered them to the pages.

She'd lost track of time when her aunt said, "Anything?"

Setting the book aside, Laura accepted the offering of a tuna sandwich, chips, and a bottle of beer. "Nothing of importance. Andrew Grubber ticketed for disorderly conduct, Edward Harvey for driving with an expired license. Limon pie wins contest for most unusual taste."

Phyllis heaved an exaggerated sigh. "Maybe our spirit is an old spirit. Cole Harbor has a history that dates way before the American Revolution, after all. There's even a little bit of history about witchcraft, though I don't think anyone was ever hanged or burned at the stake."

The next hour was spent with exclamations over various articles, or with Phyllis filling in details. It was when she huffed out, "Oh, my!" that hope sparked in Laura.

"What is it…what did you find?"

Phyllis' face puckered in a sad expression. "Not what we're looking for. Oh, I'll never forget the day Ardelia Stovall stood along the beach calling and

calling for her son, Lydel. He was only six years old."
Phyllis pulled the shawl a little closer around her
shoulders as she stood to look out across the bay. "All
my life I swam in the cove and never once feared
sharks. It wasn't natural for them to come into the inlet.
Days later, Amos Gilman was searching along the
island banks when he found what was left of little
Lydel. Just like it says in the article, every fisherman
for miles around went on a shark hunt. I can't
remember how many sharks or what kind were brought
in and gutted. Not one held evidence of having fed on a
child, or a human for that matter. The town almost died
for lack of tourism. I don't think I've ever felt
comfortable swimming since, and that happened ten
years ago. You know what's odd? There's never been
another attack or a shark spotted in the cove since."

Laura commiserated about the child. She closed the
book she held and set it on the stack, then stood and
stretched. "Let's call it a night, Aunt Philly. Maybe
tomorrow something will turn up in one of the other
volumes."

Later, in the bathroom, Laura turned off the shower
with a rusty clank. She reached to towel the mist from
the mirror. Instead, she used her finger to write the
letters: *ly*. "Who are you?"

Settled against the pillow, the last thing she
remembered was looking at the clock. As she slept, her
usual anxiety dream visited. Herself running, running,
running down a long endless alley, dark. A small,
bobbing light at the end, beckoning her. Explosions,
deafening. All around. Her labored breathing. No
matter how fast she ran, the distance between her and
the light lengthened, making it impossible to reach the

light.

Like most nights, she awoke biting back weary screams, drenched in sweat, the sheet tangled around her legs. On other nights, she simply lay there and tried to will away the painful throbs in her right hip.

The doctor had called it post traumatic stress disorder.

She climbed from the bed and limped to the bathroom, where she used the moon's light to guide her to the medicine cabinet. This time, she didn't silence the scream.

To control her trembling, she leaned forward to clutch the sides of the sink. The cold porcelain felt good to her warm hands. She gulped deep breaths to control the retch rolling up her throat.

Phyllis fairly skidded into the room, her voice in a high crescendo saying, "By Godfrey, Laura, you look as if you've seen a ghost."

"I did. I mean, I think I did. See a ghost, that is. She…um…It was staring over my shoulder. I saw her in the mirror." Laura lifted her hands to her face. Her shoulders shook as she sobbed. "Maybe the doctor was right. Maybe I am suffering from PTSD, or maybe I'm ready for a stint in the loony bin."

Phyllis wet a washcloth, wrung out the excess water, and handed it to her niece. "Or maybe you really did see a ghost. Remember, what Nadia said—sometimes, after a séance, the spirit will attach itself to a person."

Aggravation laced Laura's voice. "Yeah, well, the séance was in Maudie's house. So how would the spirit know to find me here, and why me?"

"I don't know. Unless—" Phyllis's face scrunched

into a thoughtful frown. "Was the woman young or old?"

"Young. Maybe in her twenties. What's your point?"

"Can the sarcasm. I'm merely trying to help. You are the only one at the séance younger than sixty. That's my point. The spirit is reaching out to you because she can relate to you. What else do you remember about her?"

"I don't know, Aunt Philly. It all happened in a split second. Maybe I imagined it. I awoke from a bad dream. Maybe I was still a little shaken, and the only thing I saw in the mirror was my own reflection."

"I'm certain you saw what you saw. A spirit is trying to reach out to you. The question is who, and why?"

"Oh, great. Maybe I need to wear a sachet of garlic or wolf bane around my neck for protection."

Phyllis laughed as she hugged her niece. "That's for vampires and werewolves, which is the one thing Cole Harbor doesn't have. Let's go back to bed. I don't think your ghost will visit again tonight."

Chapter Seven

Other than a flowering garden, the setting sun was his favorite sight. Tonight the sky fired the horizon and reminded him of a campfire's glowing embers. Benjamin wished he'd inherited his mother's artistic skills, for only an artist could wash the sky in iridescent hues of purple and pink. The feathery clouds reminded him of lace. He remained on the porch until the red globe slid behind the horizon, erasing the colors and replacing them with pitch black.

He liked sunsets. He had vague memories of standing with his mother on a porch every evening before bedtime. They would lean against the railing and watch the sun sink. No words were ever spoken between him and his mother. It was the only time he felt close to her. Sometimes she would lightly ruffle the top of his hair. It was the only time he ever saw the tenseness in her shoulders relax. When the sun had disappeared and turned out the lights of the world, she would sigh, deep and forlorn, as if she carried the weight of the world, but first, for brief moments, he got to see the worry lines in her face disappear. She was beautiful.

His last remembrance of her had been the ear-piercing screaming. His mother's screams. He remembered hiding behind the old floral sofa, crouched in a ball, hands over his ears to shut out the never-ending shrieks. Her name was Florence, but she had called herself Rose. It was her favorite flower.

He'd been four years old when his mother went away. His grandfather said she was never coming back.

"Why isn't she coming back, Grandpa?"

"She couldn't quiet the screams inside her head, and I couldn't quiet the screams from her mouth. You don't like screaming. That's why you hide behind the couch."

Ben hadn't fully understood what his grandfather had meant about quieting his mother's untimely and uncontrollable shrieks.

"Where did she go?"

"She's sleeping with the sharks. Don't ever scream, Benjamin. We don't like screaming."

As punishment when Benjamin committed the least infraction, his grandfather would yell and accuse him of being just like his mother, slapping Benjamin's hands when he tried to cover his ears.

Tonight, like every night, he watched the sun tuck itself away and silenced the world from the sounds that often made his brain hurt. Gulls with their incessant cries reminded him of his mother's ear-piercing wails. Chattering in the park, down at the docks, in the bars. Chattering, chattering until the noises roiled inside his head, until he wanted to…to what? He knew, and the thought frightened him.

Medicine. He must not forget to take his medication. The thing inside him was growing. It'd been ten years since he'd killed anyone, but he knew when the urge had started—when *she* came to town.

He was shivering with the need of it. Even the cool breeze against his skin aroused him. This energy had him pacing the length of the porch and back. It wasn't time. He needed to plan. To think.

Like an unshackled animal, he bounded down the steps. Walking soundless through the woods, he envisioned himself a hunter, stalking his prey. Not just any prey, like a deer. No, something more dangerous. He was the great white hunter ready to take down a charging rhino. And then he smiled. There was nothing more dangerous than—man. He was far more intelligent, more cunning, than any predatory jungle animal.

He remembered every detail of her face. He remembered her scream—and her death. He'd held her, feeling the life drain from her body. It was as vivid as if it had happened yesterday. The compulsion built inside him. Like a fire that needed cooling.

He stood at the edge of the national park campground. A shadow among shadows, he watched a young woman sitting by the campfire. She used a long stick to poke the embers. He imagined her smiling as she looked up to watch the glittering ash float into nothingness.

He, too, watched the glowing cinders, twisting in a spiraling dance with winking red eyes. Evil eyes. He drew in a somber breath and touched a hand to his heart.

His grandfather had told him about the twin that had died at birth. Grandfather said the twin died because it was evil.

"Where does the twin live, Grandpa?" Benjamin had asked.

Grandfather had touched an index finger against Benjamin's heart. "His spirit lives in here."

Sometimes, Benjamin imagined the twin was inside him. He tried hard to control the malevolence. Tonight he felt that dark, hungry spirit awakening. He closed his eyes and reminded himself that he was *Benjamin*. He needed to keep Bennie asleep. Bennie enjoyed hurting women. Bennie was evil.

A man's voice called, "Amber?"

She answered, "Coming," and rose from the log, brushed the back of her jeans, and walked into the RV.

Benjamin stepped back deeper into the shadows.

The voice inside his head said, *It's been ten years. You've missed me, Benjamin. Admit it.*

No! Go away, Bennie. Leave me alone.

By the time he returned to the cabin, his heart was pumping, his breathing labored, his sweat-soaked shirt clung to him like a second skin, and he trembled. He needed to control himself.

Bennie whispered in his ear. *We need to plan, to get the time and place of meeting just right.*

Benjamin had learned from his mistakes. This time, he would woo her. She would love him; she wouldn't scream.

His clothes bound him. He stripped down naked and stepped into the shower, allowing cold water to slowly, cell by cell, cool his brain.

Chapter Eight

The bell over the entry door alerted Laura. She stepped from the back room, her arms loaded with morgue books. "Good morning, Deputy Carter." She gave a nod toward the coffeepot. "Fresh coffee. Help yourself."

He held a bag forward. "Peace offering. I didn't exactly exude good manners the second time we met."

Laura set the large books on the desk. She accepted the sack, opened it, and smiled. "How does a deputy from Texas know that a certain girl reporter is nuts for cream cheese Danish?" She used a napkin to lift one out, then offered the bag back to Mitch.

"I'm sworn to secrecy."

"If I guess, will you be breaking the law or anything like that to tell me?"

He poured his coffee, then sat across the desk from Laura. "Maybe."

Laura took a bite of the still-warm confection. Although she knew the conspirator, she took her time before answering. "The person who makes the best ever desserts of any kind is Maudie Perry, and her best friend since childhood is Phyllis Friday, and since Aunt Philly has always been a sucker for a guy in uniform, I'll lay my money on her being the inside informant."

Mitch chuckled. "Like I said before, I'm not a betting man. But you win."

They passed the next few minutes with pleasantries before Mitch grew serious. "I wanted to let you know that the medical examiner's report came in last night. Official cause of Victor Forgione's death—arsenic poisoning. Had it not been for you detecting the garlic odor, his beautiful bride of six months would be living on some exotic island and spending his billions instead of standing trial for murder. In a few months, she'll trade her bikini for prison coveralls. Good call, Friday."

Laura exaggerated the fluttering of her eyelids. "Why, shucks, deputy, I was just doing my job." She offered her hand across the desk. "Truce?"

He accepted it. "You stepped on my ego, Friday. That's pretty dang tough on a Texan."

Setting her mug aside, she leaned forward, arms crossed on the desk. "Sorry. Hope we can be friends, especially since we'll be working together."

Mitch looked around, then back at Laura. "Did I miss something? Working together?"

"Yeah, you know, sheriff's office, newspaper office, exchanging facts, clues. I scratch your back, you scratch mine." She hastened to correct the last bit. "Well, scratch the scratching. I didn't mean that literally. By the way, you have a mole in your office."

Mitch scrunched his brows together. "Mole…as in…snitch?"

"Yes. Louise Highland is the biggest gossip in town. She couldn't keep a secret if her life depended on it. The woman thrives on telling tales, and with embellishment. Not to knock a dent in your ego armor, but I already knew about the medical examiner's report. I thought it professional courtesy to wait until you told me."

"You're not telling me anything I don't already know, Friday. Thing is, Louise worked for Sheriff Gilman's father. After he died and Roberta filled his position, she kept Louise on, saying she didn't know how to fire a woman who had worked for her dad for over twenty years. I'm not in charge of personnel; I'm just the deputy."

Laura washed down the remaining bit of pastry with the last of her coffee. She was on a roll and decided to go for broke. "So, what's your story, Mitch? What brings a Texas cowboy lawman to a small seaside community like Cole Harbor? We've got no night life, the sidewalks roll up at dark-thirty, and except for the fireworks on Fourth of July, the most exciting thing that might happen is you climbing up a tree to rescue Nadia Cruex's cat."

She watched his hesitation. The agitated way his jaw worked. Everyone was entitled to their secrets. Lord knows, she had her own. "I'd rather hear it from you than from Louise."

His eyes narrowed. She thought she saw a hint of anger. He banked it fast. "After a stint in the Army, I got my old job back with the border patrol at Fort Stockton Station. Sometimes it wasn't much different than being on patrol when I was deployed in Iraq or Afghanistan. Pulling the trigger was getting too easy. I didn't like the person I was becoming, so I asked for a transfer as far away from crime as possible. Cole Harbor seemed like a good fit."

"Aw, disappointing. I expected a love-gone-wrong story." Though subtle, she didn't miss the flinch, or the tic under his eye. She knew emotional pain when she saw it. Now wasn't the time to push. "Is it a good fit?"

Mitch shrugged one broad shoulder. "Six months on the job, and all is well. Okay, since we're playing twenty questions, it's your turn. What's your story?"

Laura looped her fingers through the handle of her coffee cup as she stood to replenish it. "Like you, nothing newsworthy. Although I was born in Cole Harbor, my parents moved to New York when I was five. My mother and Aunt Philly were sisters. We visited a few times. Not often enough. After my father's death, ten years ago, my mom returned. The last time I came was for her funeral, about five years ago."

Now it was her time to shrug. "Running the *Harbor Gazette* seemed like a prime opportunity. Not getting any younger…planning for the future. You know, logical reasoning."

He scoffed. "C'mon, Friday. What are you? Twenty-eight? Thirty, at the most? Surely you can come up with a better line. That day at the docks, you said you were an investigative reporter from New York. Though when I Googled Laura Friday, she didn't come up, but a Laura Schofield did. Odd, the striking resemblance between the two of you."

She inwardly cringed. As much as she wanted to tell Mitch about Elio Casper, she didn't trust him to keep her confidence. The last thing she needed was Louise posting gossip on some social media site that would point Casper's boss to Cole Harbor.

"Coincidence. They say everyone has a twin. I guess you found mine." She grabbed a note pad and pencil. "Let's change the subject. Anything new on Dr. McMahon's cause of death? He was wearing a life jacket when his boat flipped."

"The eyes are the windows to the soul, Laura.

59

Yours hold a secret that frightens you. Whatever it is, you can trust me."

She laughed. "A cowboy, a lawman, and a psychic. You are full of surprises, Mitch Carter. Now, about Dr. McMahon?"

He stood and placed his hat on his head. "No mystery. Medical records show Dr. McMahon had a weak heart and had suffered several heart attacks. When the boat flipped, apparently the combination of stress and frigid water was too great. Official cause of death—acute myocardial infarction. See you later, Friday. I need to make rounds. Someone's cat may need rescuing."

She laughed. "I'll make sure it's front page news. Thanks for the chat, and the Danish."

She took a second to think about the upcoming headlines for the paper's next issue. Opening her laptop, she typed: *Garlic Lands Bride in the Soup.* For the next few hours she concentrated on writing her articles.

At noon, her aunt entered. "All work and no play makes for a dull reporter. Let's walk over to the Silly Lobstah for lunch."

"You don't have to ask twice. I'm starved."

Engrossed in conversation, it was yelps that drew their attention in time to see Benjamin Noone flail a dog with a shovel before he yelled and gave chase. "I catch you digging in my flowers again, and the next time it'll be more than a whack with a shovel."

Phyllis's voice was stern and commanding. "Stop it. Don't hurt that poor animal."

Benjamin stood still, the shovel held in mid-air. He glowered at her. "Dog can find someplace else to bury its bones. So mind your business, 'cause keeping this square beautiful is my business."

Phyllis linked arms with her niece, and gave a tug. "C'mon, Laura."

"Aunt Philly, did you see the expression on his face? He looked almost…demented."

"I told you he was a strange duck. By the way, I don't recognize the dog. Maybe it belongs to one of the campers visiting the national park. I'll put in a call to Bryan Cole, the park ranger, to ask if anyone is missing a pet."

Over a dish of baked sea scallops marinated in garlic butter, Phyllis made a suggestion. "I can't believe how fast time has flown. You've been here almost a month. I say, let's have an adventure."

Laura dabbed a piece of crusty bread in the savory sauce and plopped it into her mouth. Between chews, she said, "What do you have in mind?"

"Pine Island is one of my favorite spots. I'll make sure Harmon Taylor has the skiff in good running order. What about a day of exploration, with a picnic, next Saturday?"

"Sounds like fun, but won't the owner get upset if strangers tromp all over the island without permission?"

Phyllis smiled over the rim of her iced tea glass. "Since I'm personal friends with the owner, I don't think she'll mind."

"Who? Maudie? Nadia? One of your other friends?"

"You're looking at her. Me. Several years ago, I got wind of a speculator interested in developing the island. The last thing I wanted to see was those beautiful trees and the wildlife displaced by a hotel and a bunch of littering tourists. I pulled a few strings to buy it out from under him. I've willed it to the government to become a sanctuary when I die, so the island will remain a natural habitat permanently, for all to enjoy."

"Aunt Philly, you are one in a million. I'm sorry I've stayed away for such a long time. I have a feeling I've missed out on many special times with you. And, yes to Saturday. It's a date."

What Laura really wanted after the meal was a nap, but work called. In the office, she wrote her next *Tidings* article and then turned her attention to the morgue books stacked on the end of her desk.

The first two books held nothing she felt related to the spirit that had visited her. By six o'clock, she had decided to leave the next volume for the morning, but curiosity won out, and she opened it. On page five, a headline caught her attention, an article about a teenage girl named Brenda Alligood, whose neck had been broken. The boy who killed her, Bennie Weiner, had been sent to a mental institution. She searched her memory. Neither Brenda's nor Bennie's name came up.

Laura grabbed another morgue book from the closet. She locked the office and walked to the private entrance that led to the living quarters above the library. A familiar excitement filled her. The kind of excitement that happened before a big story broke. She wondered if there was a connection between the spirit and the murdered girl.

Chapter Nine

After supper, Laura plumped two pillows and used the headboard as support, a cup of tea in her hand, the scrapbook propped against her knees. Before long, her eyes growing heavy with sleep, she yawned and almost—almost—overlooked the article about a young nurse who had gone missing from Cole Harbor.

After reading it, and with a moment's hesitation, she opened her door and peered across the living room. A light shone from beneath her aunt's bedroom door. She padded across the area and lightly rapped. "Aunt Philly?"

"Come in." Phyllis looked up from the mystery novel she was reading for the next Friday Sisters Book Club discussion. "You found something interesting?"

Laura sat on the edge of the bed. She opened the morgue book. "This is dated ten years ago. It says Lynnette Braswell disappeared. No evidence of foul play suspected in her disappearance. Do you remember when this happened?"

Phyllis rubbed her forehead. "Let me see. Lynnette came into the library a few times to do research during her nursing courses. Pretty little thing. Quiet. In fact, no one actually missed her until a friend, who lived in Bangor, called the hospital to see if Lynnette had left yet. She was supposed to spend her days off with the friend, but she never showed up. Someone from the hospital went to her apartment. Her car was gone. Sheriff Amos Gilman was called. He got the landlord to open Lynnette's apartment. Neat as a pin. No signs of a struggle or a robbery. Nothing seemed amiss. That was about the time Sheriff Gilman took ill. I guess he didn't have the physical or mental wherewithal to give the case the attention it deserved. He hired his daughter as a deputy, but she was fresh out of the academy, trying to learn the ropes and cover for her dad at the same time. Apparently, he didn't want anyone to know how sick he was. A couple of months after Lynnette's disappearance, her car was found by some hikers, at the bottom of the stone cliffs out by Frenchman's Bay. A body was never found. When Amos died, I guess the case slipped through the cracks. Like the article states, it was assumed the girl had accidently lost control of her car. It went over the cliffs. What happened to her body remains a mystery."

Laura placed a fingernail under the first two letters of the young woman's name. "*Ly*, Aunt Philly. I'll bet you a Nobel prize in journalism that our spirit is Lynnette, and her death was no accident."

"Hmmm. What do you suggest we do? Tell Mitch, see if he's interested in digging into a cold case?"

"And have him laugh us under the table? No way. If we have to hold another séance to contact Lynnette, we will. My guess is she'll contact us first."

Laura reached down to rub her aching leg. "Is it too late for a cup of your special amaretto hot chocolate? I'm so wired, I need something to help me relax."

Phyllis swung her legs over the side of the bed. "You don't have to ask twice."

****

The following morning, dressed in a pair of white slacks and an emerald green silk blouse, Laura dropped her keys as she bent to unlock the door to the newspaper. It was when she stooped to pick them up that she spotted the white rose lying on top of a piece of paper. She lifted the rose to her nose and inhaled the sweet aroma. It didn't miss her attention that the stem had no thorns. She opened the note. The words, written in an almost illegible scrawl, caused her to gasp.

"You gotta let it go, you know."

She frowned as she looked into Mitch's smiling face. "Let what go?"

"Whatever's putting lines on that pretty face."

Laura inhaled. She exhaled. "Funny the things that can rock your world." She glanced up and down the sidewalk and across the town square. Except for a few tourists walking into local eateries, and Benjamin sitting in his usual place inside the gazebo, nothing seemed out of the ordinary.

Merry blue eyes immediately turned dark. Mitch's expression went from teasing to all business. "You're trembling. Let's go inside so you can tell me what's upset you."

Opening the door and flipping on the lights, she dropped the large scrapbook on the desk. She held up the rose, and handed him the note. He read it aloud. "'No one loves you.' Not exactly the way you'd want to start your morning." He picked up the rose and twirled the stem between his fingers. "Is there a significance to the flower with the note?"

She went through the rote motions of making coffee. "I don't know."

"I'm a cop, Laura. You may have bested me with

the garlic-arsenic evidence, but I'm savvy enough to know when people are hiding from something. If you're in trouble, the only way I can help is for you to give me details."

Everything inside her tightened until she thought she was going to break. She opened her laptop. "Give me a sec. Before I get too tightly wound, I want to research the meaning of a white rose."

Her fingers flew over the keys. The frown on her face and her silence prompted Mitch to ask, "What does it say?"

"Suited to reverent occasions, the white rose is a fitting way to honor a friend or loved one in recognition of a new beginning"—her voice broke—"or...a farewell. White roses are often displayed at funerals."

She watched him watching her. He studied her intently, his eyes dark, expression somber. "Just breathe, Friday. It's going to be all right."

She closed her eyes, and felt as if her world had turned upside down. "Better pour a cup of coffee. If you have time, I'll give you the long version. If not, you'll have to settle for a quick sketch."

"I've got time."

"Promise, not a hint of this to Louise. If you do, I'm as good as dead. And if they've found me, it's only a matter of time."

He listened intently as Laura filled him in on the details of the night she was shot and her camera man killed. "That's why I changed my name and left New York. Even though I'm the legal owner, the *Gazette* was purchased under the ownership of a dummy corporation, for my protection. Writing tame articles isn't my style. I've been careful not to post my picture on social media sites or to write articles that would draw a flurry of outside reporters. Other than you and Aunt Philly, no one else knows. She's as close-mouthed as a clam when it comes to keeping confidences."

Laura propped her elbows on the desk and covered her face with her hands. "How could Elio Casper track me down? He's in prison."

"The Internet is the eyes and ears of the world. Nothing's private. I pulled up some of your articles, Laura. You've been responsible for ratting out a lot of dangerous thugs. With your permission, I'll do some snooping, on my personal computer, after hours. Louise won't know. If necessary, I can call in a few favors.

"In the meantime, go about your daily business. My guess is we've got a local who thinks pulling crank jokes on the new lady in town is funny. Whoever he or she is, they're probably waiting to see how much they've rattled your chain. You're a pro at these games. Don't give them what they want."

She had that feeling, that creeping pins-and-needles feeling in her spine, that told her something bad was about to happen. She blinked. "I have a permit to carry a concealed weapon. It's issued in the name of Laura Schofield."

"What's your weapon choice?"

"A Ruger LCR."

Mitch blew out a whistle. "Sweet. Small, compact, deadly. If it makes you feel safe, go for it."

Responding to the vibration at his waist, he looked down at his beeper. "It's Louise." He smiled. "Maybe she needs me to get a cat out of a tree, or a squirrel from an attic."

Laura's limp smile let him know the joke had

fallen short. He added, "I still think it's a sick prank, but as a precaution be cognizant of any out-of-the-ordinary strangers. You have enough street smarts to detect them."

She gave a little wave and watched him walk out the door. She opened a desk drawer and drew out a large manila envelope and labeled it "Prank." A good reporter always kept evidence. She closed her eyes as her head leaned against the office chair.

Chapter Ten

To Laura, Cole Harbor always smelled like a freshly mowed lawn, green, sunny, and bright. This morning was no exception. Dressed in a pair of cutoff jeans and a T-shirt, with orthopedic lift sneakers, sunglasses, and a ball cap, she followed her aunt down the wooden dock to where a man stood holding the rope to an aluminum boat.

She lifted the camera and clicked. In college her secondary major had been photo journalism. Perhaps one day she would publish some of her pictures.

Phyllis called out, "Morning, Harmon. Got 'er ready?"

"Ayuh. She's got a full tank of gas. Put a new spark plug in this mornin'. Motor purrs like a kitten. The tide's runnin' low. Stay in the channel, and you'll do fine."

Phyllis set the cooler of food and drinks on the dock. She accepted the old boatman's hand to help steady her as she stepped into the skiff. Once in, she looked up at the sky. "Fair weather. We plan to stay on the island all day. Should return before nightfall."

Laura grasped the man's hand. He was an old salt, for sure—weather-wrinkled skin, and ripcord tough. His strength surprised her. "Don't worry 'bout fallin', missy. You just take your time to get your footin', 'cause I got yah."

She found it awkward, reaching down with her shorter leg. Phyllis gripped her by the hips. Laura hoped she wasn't blushing for all the help. A grown woman who couldn't master getting into a boat was embarrassing.

"Got it. Thanks to both of you. I guess you can tell how much of a rookie I am."

"Don't you worry, young missy. I've known your auntie for nigh on her entire life. She's as good a sailor as they come. She'll teach you a thing or two."

"Oh, stop your confabbing, Harmon, and hand me the cooler and the lifejackets so we can get on our way. Laura, you sit on the bow seat." She pointed. "It swivels. You'll have a bird's eye view from all angles."

The cooler secured in the center of the boat, Phyllis fastened the buckles on her lifejacket. "Cast off."

Harmon handed her the rope. She primed the starter, gave one strong pull on the cord, and the old kicker roared to life. Laura turned and watched her aunt, hand on throttle, guide the little craft into the channel. The woman was full of surprises.

"How far, Aunt Philly?"

"About fifteen minutes, if we putz along. Keep an eye out for whales or seals. Sometimes seals will swim so close you can reach out and touch them."

"What about whales? Aren't we in danger of them capsizing our boat?"

Phyllis laughed. "If one does approach us, I'll shift into neutral gear until it surfaces and then swims clear." She abruptly stood and pointed, then reached down to idle back the motor. "Port side. Left, Laura. Off to your left. Thar she blows."

A whale breached about two hundred yards ahead

of them. Laura zoomed the lens and adjusted the camera's angles as she shot picture after picture. "Oh, man, that was awesome."

"Ayuh, awesome." Phyllis put the boat in gear.

The skiff sliced through the crystal calm water. Laura lifted her camera to click shots of a group of low-flying brown pelicans, all thoughts of spirits, gangsters, the rose, and its anonymous note forgotten. She felt as free as the wind.

Phyllis pointed. "We'll land there." She aimed the boat toward the shallow waters of the island, cutting the motor, and the boat slid up on the beach. She swung her feet over the side into ankle-deep water and grabbed the bow rope. "You sit while I pull her up a bit further on the shore." She secured the rope with a sailor's knot around a tree.

Laura waited until her aunt gave an "okay" nod. "You make getting in and out look so easy."

"Tell you what. Turn around and step out of the boat backwards, with your left leg first. Place your hands on the gunnel to steady yourself."

Laura did as she was instructed while Phyllis held the boat firm. Once both feet were on the ground, Laura grabbed the cooler. "How big is the island?"

"Twelve acres of paradise. It's populated with mostly pine, white birch, and wild blueberry bushes. Watch your step. The trail is rustic and reaches from one end of the island to the other. The highest point is in the center. We can see Cole Harbor from there."

The tunnel of growth opened into a clearing. Wild grasses dotted the winding path, thickly speckled with yellow and white flowers. Ahead of them a vast array of ferns spread out like a thick carpet. Towering oaks and birch trees waved their branches overhead, breaking the sun into a dozen pieces of gold. A Monarch butterfly darted in front of them. Laura sucked in her breath. "Beautiful. Simply beautiful. I can see why you wanted to preserve the island."

She spotted two birds playing tag in amongst the pine trees. She wasn't into the great outdoors. She was more of a city girl, used to sidewalks and tall buildings, but a woman just had to take in nature once in her lifetime.

Her hip throbbed by the time she and Phyllis arrived at a small clearing at the apex of the island. She drew in a breath and blew it out slowly—partly because of the pain and partly because of the circumference of beauty that unfolded before her.

She and Phyllis spent the morning exploring and eating the wild blueberries they picked. After a morning swim, they lay on a blanket to soak up the sun. "Thanks, Aunt Philly. Just what the doctor ordered. It's been a long time since I felt this relaxed."

Phyllis propped on an elbow. "Your mother and I used to come out here when we were children. After your dad died and she moved back to Cole Harbor, we'd spend Saturdays here." Her voice wobbled. "Then she got sick, and that was that." Phyllis wiped tears from her eyes. "Say, how about a lobstah roll and a cold beer?"

Laura's own voice seemed to hang in her throat when she tried to speak. "Sure. I'm starved."

At three o'clock Phyllis suggested they return to the harbor. "By the time we get back, shower, and dress, we'll be ready to settle down for the night. There's an old classic movie starring Gregory Peck that

I'd like to watch."

Laura patted the tops of her legs. "I think I've gotten a little more sun than I intended. Let me guess. The name of the movie is *Moby Dick*."

"You'd think, what with us living in a whaling community. But, no, give me a good western any day. Love the way that man sits a horse. And speaking of horses, there's some good trails in the national park. We could rent a couple of horses and go for a ride, if you're up to it."

Laura used her aunt's outstretched hands to help her stand. She hugged Phyllis. "You are my heroine. Is there anything you can't or won't do?"

"Give me a minute. I'm sure I can think of something."

Laura laughed at her aunt's quick wit as they prepared to retrace their steps on the trail.

With little or no warning, the sun hid behind the clouds, a wind kicked up, and the sky darkened. Phyllis glanced up, saying, "I checked the weather before we left. We're supposed to have clear skies through next weekend."

Laura rubbed both hands up and down her arms to ward off the chill bumps. "It feels like the temperature has dropped ten degrees in less than a minute. Is this usual for this time of year?"

"Not unless a storm is brewin'. Besides, Harmon would have sounded the fog horns to warn boaters to head for shore, and he hasn't. C'mon, we'd better hustle back to the boat."

It was the sobbing that stopped them. Laura was certain the puzzlement on her aunt's face was a reflection of her own. "Maybe it's the wind."

"Whatever it is, let's get the hell out of here."

Each woman grabbed an end of the cooler and ran, with Phyllis taking the lead. The ferocity of the wind grew. Trees bent almost to the ground. Phyllis tripped and fell. The sobbing grew louder.

As Laura helped her aunt stand, she looked around, then called out, "Who are you? What do you want of us?"

The sobbing continued.

"Hurry, Aunt Philly."

A tree crashed in front of them. Phyllis yelled, "We can either climb over or go around."

"Too many branches. Let's go around."

A dark thought entered Laura's mind. The beginning of an unpleasant fear. The séance had awoken a spirit. What if the spirit was evil and lived here? What if the spirit intended to punish them for invading its resting place?

Another tree uprooted and crashed, cutting off their immediate path to the boat. Phyllis grabbed Laura's hand. "Forget the cooler. This way."

Needles from pine limbs slashed at Laura's face. Shrubs grabbed her ankles and tried to pull her down. Her rubbery legs wobbled dangerously. Weeks with no exercise could do that. So could fear.

And then the earth opened up and swallowed her. Her head hit the rock-hard ground, and her breath was knocked from her body. Her lungs refused to inhale, but a door opened, yawned black and gaping.

Laura had a dream. In her dream, the air felt like velvet. She could spin round and round and see the bright pinpricks of stars. She had taken this door before. She walked toward it, unafraid. The only thing missing, of course, was her friend, Jolly.

She stepped inside the shadowy depths—

A hysterical voice beckoned her back. "Laura! For God's sake, Laura, speak to me!"

Her eyes flickered open. She struggled to sit up. She faced the sky. And then she looked to see what she was sitting on. Panic laced her voice. "It's a body. Oh, my God, I'm in a grave!" She tried to stop the screams rolling from her throat. Uncontrollable shivers caused her teeth to chatter.

"Get me out, Aunt Philly. Pleeease, get me out!"

She grasped the strong hands. Thankful the grave was shallow, she climbed out. The sky cleared. The wind calmed, and the sobbing ceased.

Laura and her aunt hugged each other as they knelt over the grave. Thoughts rushed Laura all at once as she looked at rotting remnants of a nurse's uniform. Her voice was hushed when she finally spoke. "I think we've found Lynnette Braswell."

Phyllis made the sign of the cross over her chest. "I think you're right. Be at peace, Lynnette. We won't leave you until help comes. Promise."

Laura gave her aunt a quizzical look. "Do you think she was alive when she was brought here by whoever?"

"I don't know. But let's make haste to the boat."

"We're not leaving, are we?"

"No. I'll give the distress signal—and send up a flare. We're close enough for Harmon or another boater to hear."

Laura reached into her front pocket and removed her cell phone. Two bars. She dialed the number Mitch had given her. "Answer. Please answer."

"Deputy Mitch Carter."

"Mitch, it's Laura. Come quick. There's a body. We're on Pine Is—oh, shit."

Phyllis yelled over the deafening blast of the siren. "What happened?"

Laura let forth a deep sigh. "The call dropped. I hope he was able to hear me."

Chapter Eleven

Laura was going to be sick. She tried desperately to control the reflex in her abdomen. Her stomach clenched, and her throat tightened. Bile burned up her throat, but she swallowed to force the acrid fluid down. Water rippled and surged around her ankles. She reached down and scooped a handful to cool her face.

"Shouldn't they be here by now, Aunt Philly?"

Phyllis looked at her watch. "It's only been ten minutes since Harmon signaled he'd heard our distress call." She shaded her eyes as she, too, looked expectantly toward the town.

Laura swung her good leg over the side of the boat. "I need to sit down. Actually, I need to lie down."

"You do look pale. Who can blame you? Falling on top of a pile of bones...by Godfrey!" Phyllis joined her niece in the boat.

Thirty long minutes later, Laura and her aunt heard the siren. They stepped out of the boat and waded until knee deep to wave their arms. Two loud blasts signaled the driver of the police boat had seen them.

Mitch stood on the bow. As soon as the skipper slowed the boat in the shallows, Mitch jumped in and waded ashore. "You ladies all right?"

He took a look at the zigzag welts across Laura's cheeks, forehead, and nose, and his voice revealed his concern. "Were you attacked?"

She reached up, touched her face, and tried to sound jovial. "Yeah, by tree limbs."

Laura and Phyllis both nodded. He met their eyes. "What's this about a body?"

Laura focused on Harmon Taylor as he swung his small craft alongside the police vessel. He steadied the boat while Dr. Musuyo climbed down the ladder into his craft. Two large black suitcases were handed down to the doctor. The skipper tossed out the anchor, then descended down the ladder into Harmon's skiff.

Phyllis wrung her hands as she began, "Poor Laura. One minute we were rushing back to the boat to avoid the storm—"

Harmon had joined them. He removed his signature cap, the one with a large fishhook adorning the bill, to scratch the top of his head. "Storm? What storm? Hasn't been a cloud in the sky all day. Water's smooth as a skatin' rink."

Laura gave her aunt a "let's keep this to ourselves" look. Phyllis nodded. "Well, never mind about the weather. What I meant to say is we were trying to avoid getting too much sun. A tree fell, and when we went around it, the earth opened up and Laura disappeared." She clasped her hands over her heart. "By Godfrey, I didn't know what had happened to her. Ayuh, scared the pee-waddy out of me."

Mitch touched Laura on the shoulder. He held her eyes for a moment longer. "You look a little green around the gills. Are you up to going back to the grave?"

She shrugged. "Yeah, sure. Aunt Philly knows the way. We'll follow her."

Ken Musuyo opened his medical bag and removed

a tube, which he uncapped. "Laura, this is an antibiotic cream. Let me put some on those scratches."

He wiped her face with a moist sterile pad and then administered the salve to the abrasions.

Mitch's eyebrows fired to life. "Ready? I'll scout the area for evidence while Dr. Musuyo sets up a crime scene, and while he does, Laura, I need you to photograph everything. I've already put a call in to the state police. They'll no doubt want to send a forensics team. In the meantime, we're in charge." He glanced at Phyllis, and extended his hand. "Lead the way. We're right behind you."

"Wait. Hold on a sec, Mitch." Laura's voice fell silent for a moment. "You need to know that it's a skeleton. Not a body. What we found inside the grave is a skeleton."

His expression switched to a mixture of skepticism and downright irritation. "Tell me you don't mean like ancient bones inside an Indian mound, that type of bones. The state police will have a hay day laughing themselves silly, and at my expense."

Laura's cheeks flamed red. "Lying in a shallow grave on an uninhibited island is the remains of a woman, who was probably scared witless at the time of her death. So excuse me if I don't give a damn about your precious ego getting squashed. Come on, Aunt Philly, let's get this over with."

Mitch's lips pressed into a thin line. His scowl deepened. "I deserved that. My apologies. To all of you."

Without another word, Phyllis took the lead, followed by Laura, with Mitch, the doctor, and crusty old Harmon Taylor all following in single file. After ten minutes of stomping through the brush, Phyllis stopped at the freshly uprooted tree and pointed at a hole no more than four feet wide and four feet deep. "Here it is."

Mitch immediately enlisted Harmon's help in setting up the crime scene perimeter with the yellow crime scene tape. He began his crime scene log—listing everyone present, those who would go past the perimeter and enter the crime scene, and the reason for their presence. He also did a rough sketch to show the scale and dimensions in a way photography couldn't. Later on he would turn the drawing into something better, either that or work with a forensics artist to improve the details of the sketch.

Clear evidence showed the ground had given way, probably when the tree uprooted and loosened the earth, aided by the weight of Laura's body. Inside the hole lay a fully clothed skeleton with a purse tucked neatly at its side. Mitch said, "Laura, before Dr. Musuyo examines the corpse, I'd appreciate it if you would take pictures of the crime scene."

Her voice grim, she agreed. "Fine."

She stepped close to the edge of the grave, lifted her camera, and clicked away, taking pictures at different angles, zooming in and out. "Dr. Musuyo, is there anything specific I need to home in on?"

"Let me take a closer look, first." He eased into the hole, straddling the corpse. Everyone watched while he squatted. He pulled on a pair of latex gloves and then removed a small voice-activated tape recorder from his shirt pocket. He identified himself as the Cole Harbor coroner and recited the date, time, and location. "From the purse, what's left of the victim's clothing, shoe size, the size of the skeletal bones in the hands, and with preliminary examination, our victim is female." He leaned closer. "The angle of her head suggests a broken neck. Closer examination required to confirm cause of death. Remaining remnants of clothing suggest the victim's occupation was in the medical field. Perhaps a nurse." He lifted the right hand. Then looked up, an odd expression on his face.

"What is it, Doc?" Mitch asked.

Musuyo again spoke into the recorder. "The first joint on each of the four fingers and thumb appears to have been removed. Since the body was unearthed at approximately three o'clock on the afternoon of"— again he repeated the date—"it is unlikely the removal of the metacarpal phalangeal joints was done by an animal. Further examination needed to draw a more accurate conclusion."

He asked Harmon to hand him a measuring tape. "Approximate height, five foot four inches. Age of victim, and approximate weight, inconclusive at this time."

Mitch tipped his hat back. "What kind of sick-o cuts off his victim's fingertips?"

It was a rhetorical question.

The doctor placed the skeleton's hands on the chest cavity. "Laura, zoom in and get a shot of the manus. Excuse the medical jargon...hands."

Although the weather had cooled, sweat trickled between Laura's breasts. She felt hot and cold at the same time. She didn't want to puke. She honestly did not want to puke. She sucked in deep gulps of air, lifted her camera, and snapped several more shots. She also clicked pictures of the uprooted tree and the crime scene perimeter.

After securing a plastic bag around each hand to keep the bones intact, Musuyo carefully opened the purse and read off the contents. "Wallet, notepad, pen, lipstick, perfume, small hair brush." He opened the wallet. "No driver's license, credit cards, nothing to identify the victim. Hmm, she wasn't a victim of robbery." He counted, "Two hundred dollars in twenty-dollar bills."

Mitch took a deep breath. "What about car keys or a cell phone?"

"No. Neither."

"Okay, bag it."

Musuyo placed the recorder back in his pocket. "This is off the record. Since she's fully clothed, my guess is she wasn't sexually assaulted. Of course, we'll know more once the ME does his examination."

As an investigative reporter, Laura knew the protocol. Once the remains arrived at the ME's, the body would be logged in, remains of clothing and shoes and other possessions inventoried. The skeleton would be weighed, and then the body would be tagged and given an official ID number. Given time and workload constraints, it could be a week or a month before Mitch received the ME's report.

The doctor's voice interrupted her thinking. "Deputy Carter, if you will, open that larger case and hand me the roll of plastic bags." He looked at Laura and Phyllis. "All that's left is to bag the bones so they can be transferred to the laboratory. There's nothing else for you to do here. I suggest you and your aunt return to town and get some rest. Deputy Carter and I will finish up."

Harmon's voice sounded a bit craggier than usual. "Now, Phyllis, before you go all women's lib on me, just hear me out. You and the young missy have had a shock. The tide's running high and swift. I'll tie your skiff behind my boat and tow 'er in. Let me take the two of you in my boat. 'Sides, it'll be dark in 'bout an hour."

He appeared as surprised as Laura when Phyllis said, "That's mighty kind of you, Harmon. You'll get no argument from me."

Mitch said, "I'll walk with you," but he turned back to ask, "Doc, will you be okay if I leave you alone for a few minutes?"

Ken Musuyo simply waved and continued about his business of labeling and bagging.

"Doc, I'll email the photos to you."

"Thanks, Laura. If you can't sleep, call me and I'll bring something by to help you relax. You, too, Phyllis."

At the water's edge, Harmon tied Phyllis's skiff to his boat while Mitch helped Laura and her aunt get aboard. "It may be too late to come by tonight. Tomorrow okay?"

"Sure." Laura lowered her voice. "I found an article in one of the old morgue books that might tell us who our girl is."

A strong gust of wind swept across the bay, causing waves to rock the boat. Harmon called, "Hold on, ladies. Looks like we're in for a rough ride."

Laura glanced over her shoulder, but Mitch no longer stood on the shore. Her mind was so consumed with this chance discovery that it was hours before she realized how deeply this ordeal had shaken her.

Chapter Twelve

Sunday morning, Laura helped her aunt fill the dishwasher. It was routine to partake of a large home-cooked breakfast, skip lunch, then have an early dinner at one of the local restaurants.

"Judging from the dark circles under your eyes, you didn't sleep well."

Laura swept crumbs into her hand and emptied them into the sink. "I kept thinking about that poor woman. To tell you the truth, I half expected our spirit to make another appearance to let me know if we'd found her...Lynnette."

"I thought she might, too."

Laura propped against the counter. "I used the time to write an article for the paper, which I won't publish until we hear from Mitch."

Her cell phone vibrated. She pulled it from her pocket. Her sigh was audible when she spoke. "Deputy Carter?"

"I'm at the back door. Are you up to talking?"

"Sure. Give me a sec."

Phyllis said, "Why don't you make a fresh pot of coffee. I'll go down and let him in."

"I'm not an invalid, Aunt Philly."

"I know you're not, dear. Although you mask the pain well, I can see how yesterday's activities have taken a toll on your leg."

A smile touched Laura's lips as she relented. "Okay, just know I'm making the coffee under protest."

After doing so, she went to her room and carried two morgue books out to the sun porch. She stood for a moment taking in the serenity. As soon as the news broke about finding the skeleton, Cole Harbor would become a hive of gossip and speculation—and in a perverse way would draw vulturous curiosity seekers.

"Good morning, Friday."

Deep in thought, his voice startled her. Her skin jumped, and she chided herself. "Coffee's fresh."

He nodded.

Phyllis intervened. "You two go ahead with business." She turned to the kitchen.

"The scratches on your face look better this morning. At least you no longer look like you tangled with a wild cat."

He was making small talk, and Laura knew it. What was he waiting for—coffee?

"You don't look so good yourself. Long night?"

"Yep. I phoned state police to let them know Dr. Musuyo and I were bringing in a skeleton rather than a fresh cadaver. We wanted to make sure our girl didn't get lost in the shuffle just because it's a cold case. By the time we arrived at the ME's office in Augusta, filed some reports, and talked to the ME, it was around midnight when we got home."

Her heart swelled. She wondered if yesterday's chastisement had changed his mind about the case. "What is the estimated time, or time period, of death?"

Mitch accepted a mug of coffee from Phyllis. He waved away the cream and sugar.

"We won't know for certain until the official report

comes in." He drank deep from the cup and offered his compliments on the coffee. "It's a good thing you found her when you did. All that was left were the bones. No trace tissues remained, and due to the peaty soil's acidity, the bones were beginning to dissolve. Ken put the time of death at approximately ten years, if not longer. He recorded the official cause of death as a broken hyoid bone, which is a horseshoe-shaped bone situated in the neck."

Laura shuddered as she unconsciously reached up and touched her throat. "Any speculation about why the finger joints were removed?"

Mitch set his cup aside and leaned forward. He clasped his hands between his knees. "The victim may have put up a fight, scratched or clawed the murderer. He probably feared if her body was discovered that his skin would be under her fingernails. Somehow, he may have known DNA is conclusive and would get him life in prison."

Phyllis had been sitting quietly, listening. Now her voice was indignant. "It's too bad Maine doesn't recognize the death penalty."

"I agree, Aunty Philly. Cutting off the joints is uber extreme. How would he have known to do such a horrible thing? And—here's a thought—what did he do with them? Keep them for souvenirs?"

Philly tsked. "He had enough foresight to row the body out to the island. My guess is that along the way he tossed them overboard, and the finger joints became fish food."

"There are a lot of sickos in this world, and I've seen my share of them."

"Friday…" Mitch brought the conversation

between the two women back to the present. "Yesterday, before leaving the island, you whispered something about knowing the victim's identity."

She leaned forward to lift one of the morgue books from the table. "Before I show you, and for you to understand, I need to preface this with the night of the séance."

He ran a hand over his face and peered at her through splayed fingers. "Séance."

She pierced him with a warning look. "Yes, and if you even hint at poking fun, you're out of here."

He raised his eyebrows. "I'm a lawman in pursuit of evidence. Whatever you have, I'll heed it carefully."

She watched his face as she gave him the rundown of what had happened that night at Maudie Perry's house, and then when the spirit had later appeared in her bathroom in the mirror.

He hadn't laughed. Good.

Her throat was suddenly dry. She took a swallow of coffee. "This will sound like a script from a horror movie. Even so, bear with me and keep an open mind. I decided to go through Dan Fremont's old morgue books to see if I could find a connection. Honestly, I didn't expect to find this." She opened the book and used her fingernail to tap the article. "Ten years ago, Lynnette Braswell, a young nurse, disappeared. *Our girl* was wearing a nurse's uniform. What was left of it. As Aunt Philly explained, Lynnette's disappearance was at the same time old Sheriff Gilman was ill, and then subsequently died. With the death of her father, Roberta Gilman found herself filling his position and trying to get a handle on everything at once, and apparently the case fell through the cracks. Dan did a great job of investigative reporting. He even took a picture of a picture from Lynnette's apartment."

Mitch turned the book for a better view of the yellowed photograph. "Do you mind making a copy of this? I'd like to fax the picture to the ME to see how close a forensic artist's sketch matches this picture." He stood. "Good work, Friday. I'll pull case files to see which ones remain open or unsolved. Whatever I find, I'll keep you posted."

Laura placed her phone over the girl's picture. In a few clicks she said, "Done. It should arrive on your phone in a minute."

"The miracles of technology. I can remember when we didn't have computers. Now, in the blink of an eye, we can share information from all over the world." A guitar strum notified him the email had arrived.

Phyllis stood and gathered the cups. "Mitch, I remember when that girl disappeared. Since no foul play was suspected, none of us really gave it a second thought. Amos Gilman's theory was that since she had no known family, she simply met a guy and ran off with him. It was many months later that her car was discovered by hikers. A body was never found. There was no registration, but folks at the hospital who knew Lynnette identified it as her vehicle. Amos died, and his daughter concluded the body was thrown from the vehicle, swept out to sea, and the fish took care of the rest. Case closed, and forgotten, until now."

Laura made a half wry smile. "Do you think the killer stayed in Cole Harbor?"

Mitch gave the ladies a guarded look. "It is possible he assimilated himself into the town. What better place to hide than right out in the open?"

"Then, before you leave," Laura picked up the second book and opened it to a marked page. "This is conjecture, nothing more. While I was searching, I found this article. Actually, I found it before I ran across the one about Lynnette. Twenty years ago, Brenda Alligood was murdered by Bennie Wiener. He was sixteen at the time, and declared mentally incompetent."

"Okay, what's your point?"

My point, Mitch, is that he *broke* her neck. I realize this picture was taken twenty years ago, but who does he remind you of?"

When Mitch drew a blank, Laura voiced her impatience. "Benjamin Noone."

He leaned closer. "Sorry, don't see a resemblance. But email me the article and picture. Now, if you'll excuse me, I've got work to do."

He tipped his hat and waited for Phyllis to lead him to the staircase. Half way down, he stopped and looked up. "Hey, Friday, when do you plan to put out the next edition?"

"If I have to stay up all night, a special edition will come out tomorrow. As soon as people get wind of our finding a body or a skeleton, they'll start beating my door down for details. Might as well give them a few tidbits to nibble on."

"Good. Also, print the picture of Lynnette and compare the missing girl as a possible connection to yesterday's discovery. If our perp is in Cole Harbor, we might as well make him start sweating."

Laura grabbed her laptop and the two large books and followed behind her aunt and Mitch. She needed to get to the newspaper office. There was work to do.

Chapter Thirteen

In the storage closet appropriately identified as the records and evidence room, Mitch walked up and down the twelve-by-twelve-foot square room, looking at the shelved white storage boxes until he found one labeled Lynnette Braswell. Today was Louise's day off, and he was glad. The woman had a way of grating on his nerves. Always smacking gum, filing her nails when she should be filing paperwork, nosy to a fault, and, in his opinion, had no business working in a sheriff's office, where confidentiality was highly essential. Plus the fact that the woman set her own hours. It annoyed him that Sheriff Gilman never issued a reprimand to Louise about showing up late for work, or not showing up at all.

He pulled the box from the shelf and carried it to his desk. Sundays were relatively quiet. He expected to work without interruption. After a quick trip to the bathroom to relieve himself of all the morning coffee, he settled down and drew a deep breath as he lifted the cardboard lid and set it aside. He didn't know what he had expected to find. Certainly not near to nothing. He fingered through the manila folders. Pulled one out. Ten minutes later he put down the file he was reading and picked another folder, skimmed through it, tossed it on the desk, and repeated the routine with file folder number three. These were just summary documents. He hated working a case from summary documents. Almost by definition the reports were filled with erroneous assumptions—assumptions and conclusions. For now, this was all he had, and they would have to do. He pinched the bridge of his nose. He was thinking hard and giving himself a headache.

His cell phone vibrated. He unhooked it from his belt and looked at the caller ID. The bottom nearly dropped out of his stomach. Why would the sheriff, his father's best friend, be calling from El Paso—unless? "Sheriff Juh."

"Howdy, Mitch."

"Has something happened at the ranch?"

He didn't miss the hesitation before Sheriff Alcaraz Juh spoke. "Nothing that needs your immediate attention. I think your mother's condition is beginning to take a toll on your father. But that's not why I'm calling."

Mitch relaxed his shoulders. "Dad hasn't called. You know him. He never complains."

Whatever Al Juh might have said, Mitch knew the cantankerous former Texas Ranger never interfered in one's personal affairs. Al's voice was all business when he spoke. "Let's cut to the chase. I'm retiring right after the November election. Forty years as a lawman is enough. I want you to take my place. Can you get here by the first of September?"

The first of September. This was the beginning of June. If he pushed, and pushed hard, he might be able to solve the mystery of Lynnette Braswell's murder. Sparks of indecision rapid-fired inside Mitch's brain. "My name would have to be put on the ballot, and I'd need to run for election. Besides, I've probably already missed the deadline for filing. Truth is, Al, I'm in the middle of a murder case. The current sheriff is on her honeymoon and not expected back on the job until July. There's no time for me to campaign."

"Listen, Mitch, you're multilingual. You're a decorated war vet, and your years of service with the Texas border patrol, plus whatever it is the hell you're doing up there in Yankee territory, qualifies you a helluva lot more than the jackasses already on the slate. Your daddy paid your filing fee. All I need is your signature on the application and you're on the ballot."

Aggravation flashed through him. "You and my dad sure are assuming I'll agree to this."

Alcaraz Juh's voice grew serious. "Mitch, two of the jacklegs on the ballot are as corrupt as they come. The other couldn't find his asshole with a flashlight."

Mitch laughed outright. "You must be talking about Bubba L'Roy."

"I'm ready to hit the Send button on the fax machine. I need an answer now—not tomorrow."

Mitch expelled an audible sigh. He riffled a hand through his hair. "Damn, Al. You're putting me on the spot. I-I…"

"Hesitation will get you dead. You know that. What's it gonna be? All I need is a yes or a no. If it's no, your dad and I will try not to fault you."

He was stagnating in Cole Harbor. Roberta Gilman would follow in her father's footsteps and stay sheriff until she was toted out boots first. Did he want to remain second fiddle in a small seaside tourist community and end up dying of boredom and wondering why he didn't do more with his life? Or did he want to run his own operation, busting drug mules and other nefarious criminals? He also rationalized that his sixty-five-year-old father wasn't getting any younger and would eventually need help running the ranch. The bullet his mother had taken in the spine...the same day his bride of six weeks was killed... No, he wouldn't go there, couldn't go there. He didn't save Susan. And he couldn't restore the use of his mother's legs. Wallow in it, or suck it up?

With the memory of Susan's death playing through his mind, he said, "Fax the paperwork. I'll sign it and send it back asap. Count on seeing me before Labor Day."

"I knew we could depend on you. By the way, word on the street is Navarre Àron is the one who pulled the trigger on your mother and Susie. I would've told you before, but I didn't want that to be your reason to run for sheriff. Get here, and I'll help you take him and his gang down."

A ring tone sounded. Mitch looked across the room. "Fax is coming through."

"Good. Go solve your murder and wrap up any loose ends you have in Maine. Before you leave, call me with your flight information, and I'll pick you up at the airport."

When the call disconnected, Mitch stared at the phone. "What the hell have I just done?"

He rolled his chair over to the machine and grabbed the form. Before giving himself a chance to change his mind, he signed where Sheriff Alcaraz Juh had placed an X, and faxed it back.

Reaching into his back pocket, he removed and opened his wallet to carefully slide out a picture tucked away between various business cards. He gingerly ran his thumb over the smiling image. "I'm coming home, Susie. I'll run for sheriff, and when I win, I'll make my own rules. There won't be a rock big enough for Navarre Àron or his gang to hide under."

Since the murder of his wife, all his idyllic days had died. No more sitting in the porch swing sipping cold lemonade, or slow dancing to Garth Brooks. He nestled the photo back inside its resting place, his heart wanting to turn to stone.

He took another hour skimming through folders, looking for more conclusive information that would lead to evidence surrounding the mystery of Lynnette Braswell. Finding nothing, he placed all the files back in the box, closed it, and returned it to the records room. He flipped open his phone and dialed. He thrummed his fingers on the desk. "Friday, do you think your aunt would mind answering a few questions about Lynnette?"

He detected the hint of caution. "Why, surely she isn't a suspect?"

He chuckled. "Absolutely not, but she's the one person I trust to give me solid answers to a few tough questions."

"Hold on. She's with me at the newspaper."

He heard Laura's muffled voice and guessed she was asking her aunt about answering his questions.

"Aunt Philly says, 'I'd be tickled pink.' We don't usually eat lunch on Sundays, and we treat ourselves out to supper. When did you want to do this?"

"What if I get take-out and bring it to your place? Crab cakes, baked beans, cole slaw, blueberry pie, beer?"

"Man after my own heart. We'll supply the plates.

Don't worry about the beer. We've got plenty. What about six o'clock?"

"Deal."

Mitch filled the hours filing paperwork. As much as he wanted to read the ME's report on the skeleton, to know if she was really Lynnette Braswell, he'd learned to expect a wait of a couple of weeks, closer to a month, before such reports came through. But now that he'd agreed to run for sheriff of El Paso County, his impatience to solve this case intensified. He needed to work, and work fast.

At two o'clock he received a telephone call from Park Ranger Bryan Cole.

"Got something you should see, Mitch."

"Yeah...what?"

"Think it's better you see rather than me telling you. You should also bring your crime kit."

"Body?"

"No, not exactly. Like I said, you need to see firsthand."

"Give me about half an hour."

"I'll meet you at the entrance."

Mitch notified the answering service that he was on his way to Acadia National Park. He also called the Silly Lobster to place his order. "If I'm not there to pick up by 5:45 p.m., deliver it to Phyllis Friday. Do you need the address?...No, okay...Good." He paid with his credit card.

A few minutes later found him locking the office door and unlocking the door to his blue-and-white police cruiser.

Tourist season had begun. RVs, vans, pickup trucks with campers on the back, and cars full of families and their gear all crawled single file toward the park's entrance. His impatience growing, he grabbed the bubble, set it on top of the patrol car, and turned the siren to intermittent blasts. He used caution as he passed the line of vehicles until he reached the park entrance on Loop Road.

He spotted Ranger Cole as he walked from the building and waved him toward a parking space. Cole vigorously pumped Mitch's hand.

"What you got?" Mitch hefted the black crime satchel from the back seat of the patrol car.

"Like I said over the phone, I'm not sure. Climb in. We'll take the Mule 4x4 in from here."

A ten-minute ride over rough terrain and past the wilderness campsites, the senior ranger rolled to a stop.

The air hung mild and faintly misty, and the grass was dappled green in the late afternoon sun. Another ranger jumped from her sitting position on a large rock to greet them.

"Deputy Carter, meet Ranger Jane Dorsey."

Like her boss, Dorsey was dressed in khaki walking shorts, a matching khaki shirt with the park's insignia badge sewn on the sleeve, and brogan hiking boots. A walkie-talkie was strapped to her waist.

Mitch glanced around the area, then quizzically asked, "What's the range on the walkie-talkie, Ranger Dorsey?"

"Between seven and eight miles."

A nod was his only response.

Cole extended his hand toward the woods. "We'll walk the rest of the way in. Lead the way, Dorsey."

Mitch followed. "Can you give me details of what you found?"

Jane Dorsey obliged. "Two teenagers were gathering wood. They tugged on a rotten log and unearthed a bloody bone."

Another five minutes, and Jane Dorsey held up her hand to signal a halt. She pointed to where she had marked the spot with a yellow streamer. "There."

The nub of a bone protruded from the ground. Mitch set the crime kit on the ground and opened it. He pulled out a pair of latex gloves and slid them over his hands. He handed Ranger Dorsey the crime book and instructed her to write as he squatted and put his hands into the damp soil, searching. Gingerly he brushed away debris and dirt until he brought up the remainder of the article sticking out, a small bone laced with dried blood.

"Where are the kids now, Ranger Dorsey?"

"With their parents. Pretty shook up."

"Gender, age, and names?"

"Bobby and Chris Ferrell. Ages thirteen and eleven—brothers."

"How long ago did the boys find the bone?"

"All total, it's been about an hour and half."

Senior Ranger Cole said, "What do you think it is? The bone appears too big for a bird."

"I hope it's an animal bone." Mitch offered. "Anyone report a missing dog, or a pet being sick and gone missing?"

Cole glanced at Dorsey, who nodded. "Neither. In the case of a sick animal, we would have advised the owner to contact a veterinarian. But, since we have no vet, it would have been Ken Musuyo they'd contact."

Mitch used special care brushing away more dirt. He hoped what he was about to find wasn't another human body—because this was a recent kill.

In the quiet woods came the unmistakable sound of sharply indrawn breaths. It was the gases from decomposition that caused the rangers to gag. Mitch swallowed the bile biting his throat. A veteran of many autopsies, the putrid odor of death still roiled his stomach.

He continued to gently sift soil. Relief shuddered over him when, at last, he'd exposed the dirt covered maggoty remains of a white liver-spotted spaniel. He continued sifting away dirt. A cat. Then another, until no more bodies were unearthed. The animals lay neatly side by side.

Cole leaned forward. "This looks like some kind of ritual burial."

Mitch grabbed a slender dowel from the crime bag. He lifted the head of one of the cats. "I want to take these back for Dr. Musuyo to examine. I have a hunch their necks were broken."

Ranger Dorsey grimaced. "You mean…by a person?"

"Yep."

Dorsey grimaced. "Sick. That's just plain sick."

Cole said, "What's going on, Mitch? You're not telling me something."

"You're right. I'm not." He went on to explain about the skeleton Laura had accidently stumbled across out on the island. "The bones were intact, but old. Dr. Musuyo figures about ten years, but here's the thing: The cause of death—broken neck."

A brief frown showed on Cole's face, then disappeared. "Get out of here. Unbelievable. And you think if these animals died of broken necks there might be a connection?"

"It's a long shot, but, yeah, that's my theory."

Mitch used his phone to take picture after picture of the perimeter, of the inside of the hole, of the alignment of the bodies. After bagging them, he said, "Spread out. We'll walk the area. Look for anything out of the ordinary—broken twigs, mashed-down brush, hopefully a footprint, and even better, a torn strip of clothing. Keep a sharp eye out."

Cole stood a good thirty feet away from Mitch, walking soundlessly around the fringes of the forest, with Dorsey the same approximate distance from Cole. For two hours they walked seamlessly in a grid pattern, slowly and methodically dissecting each inch of the area for that one clue which would magically connect a ten-year-old human skeleton and the recently dead animals.

If such a thing existed.

Mitch stopped and turned once more, frowning in spite of himself. He wanted to know who had buried these bodies, and if the animals' broken necks were pure coincidence. The area was sheltered, the thick canopy of trees making the path invisible at night. He gave an impatient sigh. "Nothing. Not even a broken twig."

Turning and walking back to where he had left his crime kit and the black polyurethane body bag, he picked up the bag with its contents. Cole lifted the kit, while Dorsey led the way until they reached the 4x4 utility vehicle.

At the main parking lot, Mitch thanked the two rangers. "For now, keep this under wraps. There's no need to cause a stir where one might not exist. Either way, I'll keep you updated." He placed the black bag inside the trunk.

Seated behind the steering wheel, and before leaving the parking lot, he phoned Dr. Ken Musuyo.

Chapter Fourteen

Ken Musuyo used a scalpel to slice through the black bag. He spoke into a tape recorder as he lifted the neck of each animal. "Liver-and-white spotted spaniel or spaniel-type canine, cause of death—broken neck. Calico feline—broken neck." He moved to the next cat, and felt from behind the head and down the spinal cord. "Grey striped feline—broken neck."

He looked at Mitch. "Do you recognize the calico?"

"Don't tell me it's Mrs. Cruex's old cat, the one I've twice rescued from the tree in her front yard?"

"I'm afraid so." Ken turned the tip of the cat's left ear to show the tattooed number.

"Damn."

Ken pulled back the dog's eyelid. "The dog was sick. From the lesions on the retina, I'd say distemper. Nadia Cruex's cat was about nineteen years old. Without an autopsy, my guess is all of these animals were in various stages of infirmity which would make them easy to catch. The question is—what sick and twisted motive would anyone have for killing them?"

Mitch stroked his chin. He was thoughtful for a moment. "In your medical opinion, do you think the broken necks on these animals have any connection to the broken neck of our female skeleton?"

"I can't honestly say. With a ten-year span, it's

nothing more than a morbid coincidence."

Mitch glanced at his watch. He had about forty-five minutes to get cleaned up and to the Fridays' for supper. He was glad he'd left a message to have the restaurant deliver the meal. "You're probably right—my gut instinct says different. Comb through the hair of these animals to see if you pick up any fibers, or anything unusual I might use for evidence." He spread his hands wide. "I'm grasping at straws here. Humor me, Doc."

Ken Musuyo smiled. "As you can see, I'm not exactly overrun with work, and things are slow at the clinic. That is, until Fourth of July weekend. Then I'll pray for an extra set of hands and two more nurses. I'll get my report to you stat."

As Mitch turned to leave, Ken said, "Nadia Cruex is in her nineties. She knew the cat was old. It's my opinion the most merciful thing is to let her think it went off and died."

Mitch tipped the brim of his hat. "Agreed."

Outside the lab, Mitch telephoned Laura to let her know he was running late. "I'll explain when I get there. Wanted to let you know a delivery guy from the Silly Lobster should be on his way to your place."

An hour later, he joined Laura and Phyllis on the sun porch of their apartment. He filled them in on the animals.

"By Godfrey...horrible. That's all I can say. Except thank you for not telling Nadia about her beloved cat. In her heart she believes Princess went off to die so as to spare Nadia the grief of finding her. To say otherwise would be just plain heartless."

Laura wadded her paper napkin and set it aside.

"Mitch, am I reading you wrong, or do you think there's a connection between our skeleton and the animals?"

"Right now, Friday, I'd rather not say. Whoever killed those animals is one sick SOB."

Phyllis stood to gather the empty disposable containers. Laura intervened. "I'll clean up. Mitch has a few questions to ask you about Lynnette Braswell."

"Ten years is a long time. My brain might be a bit foggy."

Mitch removed a small notebook from his shirt pocket. "Whatever you can recall is better than what we have now."

He picked up a magazine from the side table to use as a writing support. "Just start talking. I'll write."

Phyllis briefly closed her eyes as if sorting out her thoughts. "I believe in the article Dan Fremont gave her age at twenty-two. She had long blonde hair. She mostly wore it in a ponytail. She enjoyed reading romance novels—historicals—and was fond of Chai tea and scones. She was especially proud of graduating from nursing school. Even talked about becoming a physician's assistant."

"What about friends?"

"Not many young people stay in a town where employment opportunities are limited. No, I don't recall her hanging out with anyone in particular. I mostly saw her in the bookstore."

"How did she dress? Conservative, flashy—"

"When she wasn't in her nurse's uniform, she dressed like any normal young person—shorts, but not too short, flip-flops, T-shirt. Occasionally, she'd wear cute sundresses. Didn't wear very much makeup, or jewelry. I do recall she had pierced ears. The only reason I remember that is because one day she came in wearing little sailboat earrings. I'd say she was conservative."

"What about her personality? Wild...high-strung...sensitive?"

Phyllis shifted in the chair. "Ayuh. Sensitive, maybe. Wild or high-strung, neither of those. Lynnette lived in Cole Harbor for about eight years. She graduated high school, then left for a short time to attend nursing school. Seemed quite happy to do her internship here, at the clinic."

"Did she live with her parents?"

"No. Sad. Maybe that's why she was sensitive. Lynnette was a foster child. She lived with the Dentremonts. Who, by the way, loved her as if they'd given birth to her, even if they were old enough to be her grandparents."

"Where are the Dentremonts now?"

"Like most old folks, buried in the Cole Harbor cemetery. Mr. Dentremont died before Lynnette graduated from high school. Vedette's heart gave out after Lynnette's car was found."

"Who was the physician at the clinic when Lynnette worked there?"

"Dr. Gérard Babineaux. Everyone loved Dr. Jerry, but he was almost eighty when he retired. He, too, was devastated by her death."

Mitch tapped the tip of the pen against his lips. He hesitated to ask the next question. "Do you think Dr. Babineaux was responsible for Lynnette's death?"

The sharp gasp indicated Phyllis's shock. "Why, that's absurd. Be-because Dr. Jerry had a stroke shortly before Lynnette's death. He lost partial use of his left arm. There's no way he could have broken her neck, lifted her into a boat, dragged her onto the island, then dug a hole to bury her. Uh-uh, no way."

Mitch's dark brows gathered in a concerned way. "I didn't mean to upset you, Phyllis."

She shrugged. "Ayuh. It's your job to ask tough questions."

"One last question. You said she didn't hang out with any special friends, but do you know if she had a boyfriend?"

"In Dan's article, he said the friend who reported her missing lived in Bangor. I believe Amos Gilman and Roberta questioned the girl. I don't recall any mention of a boyfriend."

Mitch remembered reading the summary Amos had written about interviewing the friend in Bangor. A summary with sketchy details. A dead end.

He closed the notebook and stuck it back inside his shirt pocket. "Thanks, Phyllis."

Laura joined her aunt and Mitch. "All done?"

"Ayuh, and enough talk of morbid things. It's a lovely Sunday evening. There's no need for the two of you to squander it hanging around here when there's plenty of daylight left. Go for a stroll around the park, or down to the docks. Besides, I need some alone time. I have a good mystery novel to finish reading."

"We won't be gone long, Aunt Philly. Enjoy your book."

Once outside, Laura lifted her head and inhaled. "The air in Cole Harbor is clean and crisp. It almost makes your lungs hurt. Unlike New York."

"Yep, but I miss Texas. There's a lot to be said for

mild winters. Unlike Maine. When I left in December, it was fifty-six degrees. I thought that was cold until I arrived here to freezing rain and temperatures in the low twenties. Way too cold for this country boy."

At the gazebo, Mitch escorted Laura inside. "I do have to admit, El Paso doesn't have these views. There's something calming about the way the town's lights reflect off the bay. Even the forlorn clanging of the buoy is comforting."

"Is El Paso your home?"

"Yep. Grew up on a ranch there. My dad is a real-deal cowboy, championship bull rider, and was once a Hollywood stuntman."

"Sounds like you admire him."

"He's my hero."

While dusk fell, Mitch and Laura sat inside the gazebo and watched fireflies flicker and dart in the purple-tinged air.

"Friday…I'm leaving Cole Harbor."

She turned to stare at him through the dim light and had to close her gaping mouth. "Wh-what? When? Why?"

"Got a phone call earlier today from my dad's best friend, Sheriff Alcazar Juh. Al is one tough buzzard. Thing is, he's outlived his days as a lawman. Forty years is a long time. He's retiring after the election in November and has asked me to run. He thinks I'd be favored to win."

"I don't understand. Why did you leave the wide open spaces to move to a small coastal town thousands of miles away, only to return to what you left in the first place?"

He reached into his wallet and pulled out the photo.

"My wife, Susie. She taught kindergarten. Everyone loved her."

For a moment, Laura thought he wasn't going to continue. She caught her breath at the unexpected emotion in his eyes. "She was murdered. We were married six weeks when it happened. My mom took a bullet in the spine. A vibrant woman who'd rather ride a horse and herd cattle than cook and clean house will spend the rest of her days in a wheelchair. Months before it happened, I was instrumental in taking down a major player and busting up his human trafficking operation. The cowards waited until I was away on assignment to target my family. I came here to get away from the emotional pain, the crime, the everything. I think I was trying to find...normal. You have to understand that being sheriff gives me the opportunity to run my own department. Taking down bad guys is what I do best. I have to go home. It's the right thing to do."

A stretch of silence followed.

Dressed in navy blue slacks and a white button-down shirt, Laura wore her hair in a funky spiked style. Her blue eyes glinted steel. Skin that reminded him of peaches and cream, with a faint sprinkling of freckles across her nose. Even with little makeup she made a lot of women look plain. Laura was a natural beauty.

He ignored the zing of attraction he always seemed to get around her. Romance, attraction, whatever it was he felt when he spent time with her, was not an option.

"What about you, Friday? Any plans for marriage and a family?"

She considered his question. "In a manner of speaking I was married—to my job. For ten years, my only desire was to out-scoop the competition. I loved seeing my name in the byline. As for family, the newspaper was my family." She went quiet.

Mitch waited.

"As for losing someone close…Jolly was like my kid brother. I felt the life drain out of him, and there was nothing I could do to stop it. For the rest of my life, I'll have to live with the fact that his dying was my fault." She held up her hand to stop Mitch from speaking. "Oh, I didn't pull the trigger. Jolly was killed because of my stupidity. I came home to heal."

"What happens when you do? Will you sell the paper and move back to New York?"

"The thought has entered my head, more than once, but no." She lifted her foot, the one with the oversized orthopedic heel. Her voice soft. "Unlike your mom, I can still walk. Thing is, with a bum leg, I'm no longer able to outrun bullets. Nor do I have the desire. I'm here to stay. Plus, Aunt Philly has always wanted to visit Paris. Right now, with a monthly edition and limited special editions, I have the time to travel. Because of my self-centeredness, I've lost precious time with my only real family member. I intend to stick as close as possible."

"What about love?"

She laughed. "I'm thirty-two, and underneath this blonde from a bottle lies a beginning crop of gray hairs." She laughed again. "In the olden days, I'd be considered an old maid. Joking aside, Mitch, I'm not looking for love. If it happens, he'll have to be someone pretty darn special."

She changed the subject. "As long as we're playing twenty questions—what about our skeleton?"

"Yeah. About that. Sheriff Gilman returns from her honeymoon the end of July. Her husband is law enforcement. She may want the two of them to run the office together. If that's the case, then I'd be looking for a job anyways. As for our skeleton, I hope to solve that mystery before I leave in September."

Laura whistled. "Wow, it's already the first of June. We'd better get with it, cowboy."

Chapter Fifteen

At eight-thirty Monday morning, Maudie Perry greeted Benjamin Noone with a small coffee and a bagel with lox. She chirped her customary greeting. "Your usual, Benjamin." She glanced around. "My goodness, Cole Harbor was certainly lucky the day you were hired as the town's gardener."

He stood, gripping the sack and wishing she'd go away. He'd listened to her repeat the same phrase every day for the last three thousand one hundred and seventy days. Her chattering hurt his head. "Thank you, Mrs. Perry." He turned toward the gazebo.

"I know what a workaholic you are, so I won't keep you." She stepped closer and laid a hand on his arm. He flinched and drew back. "Did you hear the latest news?"

"Guess not. I don't own a television. Prefer books and my record player. It needs a new needle."

"Oh, yes, well, never mind that." She leaned in closer and lowered her voice. "The skeleton of a woman was found, Saturday."

The cap he wore suddenly felt too tight. He was certain his head would explode. "Where?"

She stretched her arm and pointed. "At the place you've enjoyed sitting and looking at for these last ten years. Pine Island." She smiled. "I don't blame you. We'd all like to own our own private paradise."

His temples throbbed, and he wondered if the yakking old woman could hear the thudding of his heart against his chest. He wanted to press his hands against his head to shut out her screeching. He wanted to scream, *Shut up…shut up…shut uuuup!*

"Why, Benjamin, have you taken ill? You've turned white as a ghost. Except for the weekends and holidays, I don't believe you've taken a day off since the city hired you. Perhaps you've been working too hard."

"After I eat, I'll be fine. Again, thanks for the food, Mrs. Perry. I gotta go." This time he left her standing while he entered the gazebo and sat down.

"Of course, Benjamin. You heed what I say, and go home to rest."

The clacking of her heels against the cement sidewalk kept on until he thought his ears would burst. He inhaled, deeply, and blew out a long breath. *Calm…remain calm. Eat…drink…calm. Did I take my pill this morning? Can't remember.*

He looked out across the bay toward Pine Island, and then turned to look over his shoulder, and called out, "Mrs. Perry, who found it?"

"Laura Friday and her Aunt Phyllis."

"What happened to it—the skeleton?"

She waved her hand. "You'll read all about it. Laura put out a special edition this morning."

His hand trembled when he removed the plastic cap from the cup. Without blowing to cool the steaming coffee, and with his thoughts on the skeleton, he gulped. The hot liquid slid down his throat, scalding all the way to his stomach. He coughed. His hand trembled more, this time spilling the cup's contents down the front of his shirt. He yelped as he tried to brush away the blistering liquid. *Go home. I have to go home.*

He left the sack with the untouched bagel on the bench. He gathered his rake and hoe, and the wheelbarrow, and for the first time in ten years he carelessly plowed through his precious flowers to get to the gardening shack where he kept his tools and other supplies. After securing the lock, he jumped on his bicycle and pedaled away from town. At one of the houses, he skidded to a halt long enough to snatch a newspaper from the paper box. He rolled it into a roll and stuffed it inside his shirt pocket. This time, he didn't stop until he reached the edge of the national park where his cabin sat hidden from sight, far off the road.

He was tired now. The sun, bright and strong, had kept him pedaling up the steep grade. Habit forced him to lift the bicycle up the steps to where he could lean it against the cabin's outer wall. Wiping the sweat from his brow, he sat in a chair and looked beyond to the sea. There was no sound. He closed his eyes and allowed the hush to hover over him.

Benjamin reached up to swat a stinging black fly seeking nourishment. In the process, he knocked the newspaper from his pocket. He unrolled the tabloid. His eyes darted back and forth over the page and the picture of the hole in the ground. Most of the language was too complicated for him. He stopped and went back to the beginning of the article, skipping over the hard words. He did understand the part where the earth had opened up beneath Laura Friday's feet to reveal a grave that held the skeleton of a female believed to be the long missing body of a young nurse, Lynnette Braswell.

He had a morbid need to chase death, having felt its hands crush the necks of those animals. He automatically flexed his fingers. He thought of his mother again and the sad expression she'd worn every time she watched the horizon steal the sun. She had left him. A mother should be a safe harbor. A protector.

The beginning of a headache throbbed against his temples, and he felt liquid oozing through the black holes to crowd his brain. A voice rasped, *Bennie is a bad boy...bad boy...bad boy. He killed the dog, he killed the cats. Bennie killed one girl and then another.*

He clasped his hands over his ears, and through the pulsating pain he cried, "No! Go away! Bennie is dead. I'm Benjamin. Benjamin is a good boy."

His chest heaved until his breath came out in great gasps. Tears leaked from his eyes, and he used the sleeve of his shirt to wipe away the snot dripping from his nose.

He was tired, bone-deep weary in a way that people who had never killed would find impossible to appreciate. Bennie was hungry. His need was growing stronger. He would kill again.

When Benjamin awakened, he lay on the ground. He glanced around. His bicycle lay next to him. His last memory was carrying it up the steps to the porch. Darkness crowded the thick canopy of trees. Shadows grew and lengthened, and the horizon was streaked with the vivid pinks and bright oranges of the dying sun.

He brushed leaves and dirt from the front of his shirt. Weary, he climbed the steps to the cabin, walked to the bathroom, and washed his face. The cooling water refreshed him. Returning to the bedroom, he sprawled to the floor on his stomach and removed his special box. Sitting with his back against the bed, he opened the lid, removed the papers, and the little drawstring sack. Careful not to spill any of the leaves, Benjamin rolled a joint and lit it. He inhaled deeply, held it, and then swallowed. He closed his eyes and let the devil lettuce work its magic.

Relaxed and giddy, he giggled. The voice, that hateful voice, intruded.

Bennie, I see you.

He sobered as he eyed the shadowy image that crouched near him. He hissed, "Go away. I'm Benjamin. You're Bennie." He rubbed his eyes with the heels of his hands. "You're not real."

I'm your twin. We are one. I'm tired of waiting...aren't you?

Benjamin placed his hands against his head and squeezed. Why wouldn't the pain go away? In a frenzy, he ran to the front door and locked it, then did the same to the cabin's back door. He raced into the bathroom and locked the door. He stripped down, kicked his dirty clothes aside, and climbed into the shower. With his knees drawn to his chin, he sat on the fiberglass floor under the cold spray, and bit his lip until it bled. *Don't scream. We don't like screaming.*

Chapter Sixteen

Her laptop tucked under her left arm, Laura held the handrail as she walked down the stair steps one at a time. A shooting pain in her right thigh sucked the air from her lungs. Her leg was letting her know she'd overly exerted the muscles the past few days. Unfortunately, that wasn't going to change.

At the bottom of the landing, she unlocked the back entry door and stepped outside and around the corner, just a few steps to her office. She was careful to keep her stride smooth. Several business owners called morning greetings. She waved and, with a smile, returned their good wishes.

She stood back a moment and looked at the glass-paned door. A swell of pride filled her as she mentally read her name: Laura Friday, Editor-in-Chief. The painter was scheduled to make it visible to everyone next Monday. She reached into her pants pocket and removed her keychain. It wasn't until she leaned forward to insert the key and turn the lock that she noticed it. There, on the sidewalk, resting peacefully within inches of her shoe. A rose. A white rose.

She bit against the pain as she stooped and used her fingernails to lift the stem. Shifting the laptop, she laid the bud on top of the flat surface. She didn't want to handle the flower for fear of obscuring possible fingerprints belonging to the donor.

Maudie Perry saved the day. "Let me get that. You seem to have your hands full," she gushed as she pulled the door wide. "A secret admirer leaving a rose on your doorstep? How romantic! I was always a sucker for romance. I wish Phyllis would discuss a romance novel at the book club meetings once in a while. Mysteries. Always mysteries."

Laura offered a sympathetic smile. "When it's your time to host the next meeting, simply suggest a romance novel. Do you have a favorite title in mind?"

A pink glow tinged the older woman's cheeks. She placed her hands against her heart and sighed. "I've just finished reading *Bannon's Brides*. The hero, Cordell Bannon, is every woman's dream. Oh, my, what those poor women endured while crossing the prairie." She seemed to realize she had drifted into a dreamy prattle, and fluffed herself up like a hen ruffling its feathers. "I'll take your advice, Laura. By the way, wonderful article about finding the skeleton. I can't imagine you showing up for work this morning. Falling into a grave…" She tsked. "Why, I'd be absolutely traumatized."

"We all cope in different ways. Work is my catharsis. Have a good day." Laura walked through the open door.

Maudie waved as she walked on down the sidewalk. "See you at the tourism council tonight. We're looking forward to your presentation."

Laura limped to the desk to set down the laptop. She opened the top drawer and pulled out the manila folder that held the first white rose and the note with it. She undid the metal brad and dropped the second flower inside. Then, on an index card, she wrote the date and time she'd found the second rose, and slid the card inside the envelope. A thought entered her mind. She reached inside for the note that had accompanied the first rose. Her heart thumped as she read the scrawled message, *No one loves you.* With four words the sender had scrambled her emotions all over again. Looking at her calendar, she flipped over the square piece of white paper and jotted the date she'd received the first bloom. Details like this might be important later. She dropped it into the envelope and sealed the flap with the brad, eyeing the envelope with disgust.

She waded through a mash of emotions as flashbacks of disturbing memories from that night in New York resurfaced. She lifted the land-line phone and punched in the numbers for the sheriff's office.

"Cole Harbor Sheriff's Office."

"Good morning, Louise. Is Deputy Carter available?"

Louise Highland squeed. "Laura...Laura...Laura. I am positively mesmerized by your reporting skills. In all my fifty-five years, nothing exciting has ever happened to me. Falling in a hole, and on top of a skeleton? How thrilling! I almost envy you."

Laura grimaced at the morbidity of Louise's comments. "If it's bones you'd like to dig up, I hear there are universities that offer excavation digs in Egypt for volunteers. You should check it out." She inquired, again, "If Deputy Carter is in, I'd like to speak to him."

"Sorry, kiddo, he's with Ken Musuyo. Can I have him call you?"

"Sure."

"Thanks for the tip, Laura. It's been years since I took a vacation. Digging for relics in Egypt sounds like dirty fun." Louise guffawed. "Get it—*dirt—dirty?*"

Laura lifted her eyes toward the ceiling as she cradled the receiver. She opened her laptop to work on the slide presentation she'd prepared for the tourism council on ways to promote Cole Harbor. After an hour of work, and satisfied with the power point, plus growing restless, she grabbed her camera and decided to do a leisurely walkabout, taking a few more pictures for a possible promotional brochure.

At the bookstore, she tapped on the window and waved at her aunt. Then, lost in thought, Laura headed in the direction of the gazebo. The picturesque views of the bay were postcard perfect. As she neared, she listened to a voice filled with obvious anger. She stopped. The gardener, the strange duck, as her aunt referred to him, was on his knees and appeared frantic.

Before approaching, she lifted the camera and clicked several frames. "Is something wrong?"

Benjamin squinted as he looked up. "Somebody hurt my flowers. My precious flowers! Except for the thorns, roses never harmed anyone. Every single day of their lives, all flowers do is sit and look pretty for people to admire. They give pleasure."

Still grumbling under his breath, he seemed to forget Laura's presence and bent to snip away broken stems and smooth the footprints and wheelbarrow ruts with fresh mulching.

Though she didn't see the damage that would cause him this much upset, it did look as though someone had purposely trod through a section of the colorful blooms. "Do you mind if I take a few pictures?"

He rocked back on his knees. "You're that newspaper lady, ain't you?"

She nodded.

"I 'spose if the flowers don't mind, I don't either."

The eerie intensity of his gaze unsettled her, and she searched her mind for a distraction. "The roses are lovely. I especially like the white ones."

Her breath locked inside her throat. A gust of chilling wind blew from the bay. She swallowed hard to settle the uneasy knot twisting in her stomach. *White roses.*

"Ayuh. The mayor is partial to white roses. Mostly, it's his wife who is always after me to keep up the red, white, and blue theme. Says it's patriotic. Me, I think it looks funny to have red roses, white roses, and blue geraniums, 'cause you can't get blue roses, don't yah know. But she tells the mayor what to do, and then he tells me, to keep her happy."

Laura thought she heard him mumble, almost under his breath, something that sounded like, *Fat bitch pisses me off.*

When she lifted the camera, Benjamin pulled his cap low on his forehead, and bent forward. Whether on purpose or unintentionally, he had blocked his face, which kept her from getting a clear camera shot. She wanted a close up to compare to the image in the twenty-year-old feature article Dan Fremont had written about Brenda Alligood's murder. Her gut instinct said Bennie Wiener and Benjamin Noone held a striking resemblance to one another. "Excuse me. Would you mind smiling for the camera?"

Without looking up, he said, "Don't like havin' my picture taken. 'Sides, you're keepin' me from gettin' my work done."

The camera clutched tight, she almost felt his flinty

blue eyes boring a hole in her back as she walked away. Still rattled from receiving this morning's anonymous white rose, she chastised herself for viewing everyone as a potential criminal.

Later that night, Laura stood in front of the tourism council, inside city hall's conference room. She thanked Mayor Shipley for the illustrious introduction and inwardly cringed when she spotted the white rosebud in his lapel.

Drawing in a fortifying breath, she stepped away from the portly man, who reeked of musk cologne and wore a toupee that reminded her of a nest for vermin. Her first thought—*pervert!* She shriveled inside when his clammy hand patted her on the arm. Was he the one who wrote the note and sent the roses? She scanned the audience. Her heart sank a bit. Mitch wasn't there. Her aunt gave her two thumbs up.

After the slide presentation, Laura said, "Cole Harbor has a beautiful port. We must give tourists a reason to visit and to linger in our quaint community, and in addition, give the campers in the national park a reason to come to town. Our little slice of paradise is the perfect place to hold an island lobster bake, take a romantic evening sail aboard a friendship sloop or a schooner and listen to the stories of seasoned captains from some of you who have sailed the seven seas. Our harbor bustles with fishing vessels and pleasure craft in equal numbers. Capitalize on offering excursion boats to enjoy a harbor tour, cruise out to explore any one of the public islands, or spend the day watching seals, puffins, and whales."

Martha Shipley stood. "This is all well and good, dear. How do you propose to advertise? No offense, but your little newspaper has limited circulation, and this council has equally limited funds."

Laura recalled the words she thought Benjamin had spoken under his breath—*fat bitch.* Noting the indignant scowl, and to avoid a verbal out-lash from her aunt, Laura smiled. "Raise your hand if you are a business owner and have a computer." She counted. "Websites and blogs, Mrs. Shipley. With very little expense, we can reach the world. In my spare time, I will teach all who are interested how to create a website to promote both your businesses and Cole Harbor."

Not wanting to omit the non-business owners, she ventured on. "The same offer is available to the rest of you. I'll help you set up blogs." She rubbed her hands together and waited for the onslaught of dreaded reactions—groans and grumbles.

Martha Shipley once again stood. "I, personally, don't think—"

Phyllis Friday quipped, "Sit down, Martha. If it isn't your idea, you are automatically against it. If you have a better idea, let's hear it."

Harmon Taylor from the boat yard stood and removed his cap. "I'm a crusty ole seadog. Have to say, I admire this young woman's spunk. Ayuh, for certain, I ain't the smartest fish in the sea, but sign me up, missy."

Laura wanted to kiss the spindly, bowlegged salt on his weathered cheek. Without knowing it, he'd opened the door for opportunity, and others walked through. Including Martha Shipley.

The fervor died down, and the meeting adjourned. Laura strolled with her aunt down the sidewalk leading to the back entrance of their living quarters above the bookstore. As she discussed the events of the evening, the hairs on the back of her neck prickled. She glanced over her shoulder.

"What is it, Laura?"

"Nothing. Just jumping at shadows."

After saying goodnight, Laura went to her bedroom. She opened the sliding door and stood for a moment looking out at the bay. The cool air caused a shiver to waft over her. Kicking off her orthopedic shoe, she walked tiptoe to the bathroom and changed into her pjs. Then she settled on the bed with her laptop propped against her knees. A moment later, she rubbed her eyes and yawned. A bleep-bleep interrupted her thoughts. She grabbed the cell phone from the side table and smiled at the caller's name.

"Mitch?"

"I know it's late, Friday. It's been a hectic day."

"Yeah, for me, too. What's up?"

"Ken Musuyo concluded his report on the animals. He found no unusual fibers in the hair. Analysis samples indicate soil and plants found on the bodies were native to the national park. He did a necropsy which turned up nothing unusual—no poisons or unusual chemicals. Final conclusion—all the animals died from broken necks."

"What about the boys who found the animals? Could they have killed the animals?"

"Not likely. The animals were in rapid decomposition. The family had been in the park less than forty-eight hours when the boys found the bones."

"This is like a needle in a haystack. Are you going to write it off as some sick whacko camper who is long gone, and hopefully will never return?"

"For now. Louise said you called."

"My secret admirer left another rose. Have you had a chance to find out anything about Elio Casper?"

"Damn. I'm waiting for my source to get back with me. Was there a note?"

"Not this time. Just the rose."

"Hmm. I'll put in a call to see if my contact can put a rush on the information. How are you holding up?"

She frowned. Was a half-truth really a complete lie? "Don't worry about me. We reporters have emotions thick as rhino hides."

It was as if he'd heard the hesitation in her voice. "What is it you're not telling me?"

"I'm not sure. At tonight's tourism council, the mayor and his wife both wore white roses." She related the incident at the gazebo with Benjamin Noone, and the specific request from Mrs. Shipley to plant white roses. "Do you think there's a connection?"

"Don't go jumping at conclusions, Friday. The Shipleys are a mainstay in this town. Until proven otherwise, chalk it up to coincidence."

She then told him about how upset Benjamin appeared. "There was minor damage to the garden. It looked as if someone had either stomped through the flowers or shoved a wheelbarrow or a bicycle through them. He was truly agitated. And he made it quite clear he didn't want his picture taken."

Mitch chuckled. "Don't read too much into it. Lots of people are camera shy. Doesn't mean he's hiding a deep dark secret."

Laura sighed. "I guess it's too early to hear from the ME?"

"You're an investigative reporter. You already

know the answer."

"Just curious, and impatient to know if our skeleton is Lynnette Braswell."

"How's your leg?"

"Sore. I'm not complaining."

"Good girl. I'll keep you posted."

"You said your day was hectic. Other than visiting with Dr. Musuyo, what else happened?"

Laura thrummed her fingers against the closed laptop. "I can hear you breathing, Mitch. What happened?"

"Senior Park Ranger Bryan Cole reported one of the female campers called him, hysterical. She was certain someone was watching while she was inside the public showers. An hour later, another woman reported she thought someone was peeking through the bedroom window of her RV. He called me after he'd spoken to the ladies. I drove out. By the time I got to the park it was almost too dark to see. Ranger Cole and I used flashlights hoping to find footprints. Nothing conclusive at either scene."

Revulsion rippled through her. "A peeping tom in a campground? Maybe it was a bear or a moose."

"I had the same reaction. According to Bryan, neither is likely. His ancestors settled Cole Harbor. He's lived here all his life and states there's only about fifteen bears in the park. He's never seen one near the campsites, and it'd be even more rare to see a moose. I'm going back out in the morning."

"Mind if I tag along?"

"Sure. I'll pick you up at eight."

She stared at the computer and pondered the conversation. As a reporter, she had an obligation to report the news—good, bad, or otherwise. As a citizen of Cole Harbor, what kind of uproar would this information about peeping toms create in the community once she printed it?

She hissed out a breath. News was news. She turned her attention to drafting the article.

Chapter Seventeen

The morning dawned gray and misty. Laura grabbed her rain jacket and camera case before heading downstairs. She drifted through the bookstore, noting book titles—and the lack of customers—on her way to greet her aunt. "Aunt Philly, answer me honestly. How's business?"

"Could be better. The Tea Room keeps me afloat."

Laura glanced around at the overstuffed chairs, the dark wood. The place reminded her of an English gentlemen's reading club. "I see a lot of potential to turn the bookstore into a thriving profit."

Phyllis rubbed her hands up and down her arms as if warding off the dampness. "Ayuh. Been thinking about that. Harmon Taylor isn't the only ole salt willing to make a change. I'm all ears."

Laura spotted the sheriff's car stopping in front of the store. "Mitch is here. We'll talk tonight." She pulled on the rain jacket over her khaki cargo pants and long-sleeved purple T-shirt, and lifted the jacket's hood over her head. Without waiting for Mitch to get out, she dashed into the mist, climbed inside the sheriff's car, and shut the door.

After the morning pleasantries, Laura studied Mitch before she spoke. "Tell me about El Paso."

He shifted into gear and headed toward Acadia National Park. "Except for its land mass and larger population, it's not much different from Maine. We have mountain ranges, suffer from tornados and hurricanes."

"And crime?"

Merry blue eyes turned dark, his smile from cheery to grim. "That, too."

"I'm sorry, Mitch. I didn't mean to dredge up hurtful memories."

He seemed to relax a fraction. "We all live with our ghosts, Friday. It's not your fault I can't keep mine in check."

The mist steadily increased. Small talk and silence drifted between them. By the time Mitch reached the park's entrance, the windshield wipers were working overtime.

He pulled as close to the main building's curb as possible. She knew he'd considered her inability to run for cover. Chivalry wasn't dead.

He gripped the steering wheel. "I'll meet you inside."

She nodded her appreciation. For a second the picture of his young wife floated in front of her eyes. A life and happiness cut short. She knew the ache of such feelings.

The moment she walked into the building, a willowy, freckle-faced ranger approached. "Hi, I'm Ranger Jane Dorsey."

Laura accepted the outstretched hand. "Laura Friday. Deputy Carter is parking the car."

"Days like this aren't popular with the campers."

"Can't say as I blame them. Especially for those in tents."

Mitch sprinted toward the canopied double doors.

Before entering, he brushed drops of water from his jacket and removed his cap and slapped it against his thigh. Ranger Dorsey welcomed him. "Bryan is in the office."

Laura and Mitch followed the ranger past the snack bar, the gift shop, and a left turn down a short hall which led to the administrative offices. She pointed to a coffee station. "Help yourself. It's fresh." She snagged a napkin and grabbed a glazed donut from its box. "Perfect day for doing paperwork." She waved as she strolled to her office.

Senior Ranger Bryan Cole stood. He indicated seats. "Looks like the rain isn't going to let up anytime soon. Too bad."

"Bryan, I'd like you to meet Laura Friday. She runs the *Harbor Gazette*."

The senior ranger offered his hand. "Any relation to Phyllis Friday?"

"My aunt."

"She once tweaked my ear when she caught me ogling a nude model in a girlie magazine. I was ten."

Laura laughed. "Sounds like her."

A moment passed as the trio sat and stared at each other in an awkward silence. Laura tucked her hands in her lap and fiddled with her fingers.

"Well." Ranger Cole opened a drawer and pulled out a file folder and removed two forms. "These are incident reports taken from the women. Neither could identify the alleged perpetrator." He held up one sheet. "This is the shower episode. Her story changed from someone actually watching her to 'having a feeling someone was watching her.' He shoved the form forward. "Your copy, Mitch. Now, this one, the woman states she definitely saw a pair of eyes staring through her RV window. However, she thinks it might have been some preteen boys she'd spotted earlier. She suspects the boys were having a hormonal attack at her expense. She states, 'no harm done.' And doesn't wish to pursue the issue further."

Mitch leaned forward to accept the reports. "Are we chalking this up as a wild goose chase?"

"Pretty much."

"For the record, to show that I've followed up on the complainants' concerns, how great are the chances the rain has washed away any signs of footprints or other evidence from last night's events?"

Ranger Cole shrugged. "At least ninety-nine point nine percent."

"Can we get to the showers and where the RV is parked without endangering ourselves?"

"Sure. We'll take the 4x4. What about you, Ms. Friday…game?"

Laura opened the rain jacket to reveal the camera case. "Laura, please." She smiled. "Game on."

Cole stood and grabbed his cap and jacket from the coat rack. "Let's saddle up."

Outside, claps of thunder vibrated across the mountain range. The clouds grew darker, and the rain increased. Bryan Cole said, "With this downpour, the only thing we'll find around the public showers is water and mud. Same at the RV site. It's up to you, Mitch. We'll go if you insist."

Mitch pulled the collar of his jacket up around his neck. He tucked the envelope containing the two reports into the rain jacket's inside pocket. "No need. Keep me posted if you get similar complaints, or if you see any suspicious characters lurking around."

Bryan guffawed. "That would account for about every other guest coming into the park." He shook hands with Mitch.

Then he turned his attention to Laura. "Give me a call, Laura. It'd be my pleasure to give you a personal tour of my playground. Thunder Hole is one of the more popular sites. I'll even pack a picnic lunch."

"Sounds wonderful. It will give me an opportunity to take pictures of the park and add them to the list of tourist spots to visit." She gave a brief explanation of how the town planned to rejuvenate themselves. "I'll let you know."

Once settled inside the patrol car, she side-glanced at Mitch. The truth was she liked the man. Liked being with him, liked his serious demeanor, liked bouncing the cases off him and getting his reactions.

And that worried her. Mitch Carter was easy to be around, but he was leaving Cole Harbor. In his eyes there was pain that never went away. She knew why, plus she'd made it clear they had no future together. She'd not put a crimp in his plans to return to Texas, or in hers by falling in love with him.

"You okay, Friday?"

He pulled her out of her meandering thoughts and she nodded, turning to stare out the window. "Just thinking."

"Yeah, I know what you mean."

The winding road was void of traffic; the drive to town didn't take long. Laura kept her gaze glued to the scenery while Mitch drove with practiced ease. He pulled up in front of the bookstore, and she stared for a moment at the building that had become her home.

As she opened the door and climbed out of the vehicle, Mitch leaned away from the steering wheel to look at her. "Bryan Cole is a nice guy."

She jerked in surprise. A longing filled her. What would it be like to find that one person she could feel comfortable with to share her life? "Yeah, so what's your point?"

He frowned. "Nothing. Nothing at all."

Silence echoed for a brief moment. "I'll call when I hear anything about Elio Casper or from the ME."

She smiled. A quick twist of the lips. "I hope it's soon." She turned away and limped toward the bookstore door.

Chapter Eighteen

Benjamin stood at the porch railing and watched the storm. He covered his ears to shut out the rumbles of thunder and the sharp cracks of lightning. The noise vibrated painfully through his skull.

His inner-twin stood next to him. *A perfect day for killing.*

"Go away, Bennie. I'm not listening to you."

Benjamin stepped inside the cabin, and though he knew nothing could keep his dark nemesis out, he locked the door. He turned on a lamp and then, selecting several of his favorite records, switched on the old-fashioned record player and settled on the sofa. He shut his eyes and allowed the slow, sweet music to soothe the persistent throbbing in his temples.

He didn't remember falling asleep. At first he thought the pounding was inside his head, before he realized someone was beating against the cabin door.

His heart lurched. No one ever visited. Never. Maybe he was hallucinating. Maybe Bennie was playing a trick on him.

The thumping continued. A woman's voice called, "Hello…hello…Is anyone in there?"

Benjamin stumbled to his feet. Rubbing the sleep from his eyes, he was uncertain about answering the door. He clasped his hands in a wringing motion as he fretted over what to do.

Answer the door, stupid.

He willed his feet to move, and crossed the small area to release the lock.

On the other side of the screened door a vision stood leaking all over his porch. She pushed a mop of sodden brown hair from her face. She wore a pair of cutoff denim jeans. Threads clung to her long slender legs like thin worms. The white T-shirt molded to her frame, outlining her bare breasts. His eyes riveted to the strutted nipples, and he felt flushed. She held a pair of flip-flops in her hand.

Her teeth chattered as she spoke without drawing a breath. "D-do you have a phone? I was hiking, and then the rain and fog came, and I got lost. Oh, I'm so thankful I saw your cabin! I need to call my friends. They're probably sitting in the tent trading tequila shots while I'm wandering around in the wilderness freezing my ass off. Oh, sorry." She extended her hand. "My name is Daisy Fuller."

She's a Daisy, Bennie. We like flowers.

He hissed. "Go away!"

The girl corked her face into a frown. "Son of a bitch! I'm wet, I have to pee, and you're telling me to go away—in this weather?"

Frustration rolled over him. "No…I-I wasn't talking to you. Never mind. Come in." Keeping his gaze riveted to the floor, he held the door wide. "The bathroom is over there, on the left."

The way she bounded across the room reminded him of a frightened doe. For the first time in ten years, he saw the shabbiness of his open-concept grand room. When his mother went away, his grandfather had kept everything in the house the same. Then the old man died, and Benjamin had returned to live in the cabin. He saw no reason to make changes. The sofa, its brown floral design worn threadbare, stuck out like an advertisement for ugly furniture. The once-white lace curtains wore coats of gray dust. Rust spackled the side of the antiquated refrigerator. He'd placed folded cardboard under one of the legs of the dining table to keep it from wobbling. He didn't like that this woman…this intruder…made him feel uncomfortable in his own home.

"Hell," he mumbled.

He stood in the middle of the room. Waiting. Remembering. Remembering every detail of Lynnette Braswell's face. And of her death—the way the snap of her neck echoed in his ears.

Ben…ja…min. Did you see her tits and tight ass? I bet she wouldn't make fun of Beenie with the little weenie.

The voice inside his head hushed when the girl walked out of the bathroom. He gawked. Daisy Fuller had changed out of her wet clothes and was wearing a red-and-black checkered flannel shirt that hung to her knees.

"Whew! My kidney's were 'bout ready to explode." She dried her hair with a towel. "Hey, I hope you don't mind me borrowing this. It was hanging from a hook behind the bathroom door. Besides, it's better than dripping all over your floor. I hung my clothes over the shower stall to dry."

He nodded, searching his muddled mind for a response.

"What's your name, sweetie?"

"Ben…Benjamin."

She smiled. "Well, Bennie, I dropped my cell phone, and it slid inside a rock crevice. I heard a splash, so it's probably floating in the bay by now. Mind if I use your phone to call my friends?"

The shout rolled out before he could draw it back. "Don't call me, Bennie! I told you my name is—Benjamin."

She held her hands forward. "Hey, no sweat, sweetie. Now about the telephone—"

"Don't have one. Never saw a need."

She blinked. He watched her hands flitter around her waist, drawing the flannel shirt around her body as if it were protective armor. He'd frightened her.

"S-sorry. Didn't mean to yell at you. I don't get much company."

"Sure, sweetie. Whatever."

A glow spread through his veins. The raspy cry in her voice reminded him of his favorite blues singer, Etta James. "I could heat water and make a cup of tea to help warm you up." He indicated the sofa. "Won't you be seated? It's old, but comfortable."

She sat down and drew her legs under her. "Hot tea...cool. I'm starved, too. Haven't eaten all day."

"Mostly I eat in town. Would a peanut-butter-and-jelly sandwich do you?"

She licked her lips and huffed a little snigger. "Hey, beggars can't be choosers, right?"

He busied himself in the kitchen—filling a pot with water, opening a cabinet to get a cup, and placing a teabag in it, getting the bread and jelly from the refrigerator, rummaging in a cabinet for the peanut butter. He wanted to look at her, to see those long legs that seemed to go on forever under the shirt. Hell, he wanted to see beneath the shirt.

He finished his preparation and willed his hands to stop shaking long enough to hand her a plate with the sandwich. "I don't use sugar. You'll have to drink the tea black."

"No pro-blame-o. Girl's got to watch her figure." Daisy spoke between chews. "Do you know the way back to the Blackwoods campground, where the tent campers stay?"

He gave a little shrug. "Ayuh. But it's stormin' and not safe to be out this late at night. In the morning, I'll show you the way before I leave for work. I had to miss today because of the storm. Not tomorrow, though. The weather will clear, and we'll have cloudless skies."

He didn't like the incredulous way she stared at him. His inner sense knew she mocked him. "What are you, some kind of meteorologist that you can forecast the weather? I've never met a freakin' genius before."

"Why are you making fun of me? I don't like it when people do that."

"It's a joke, sweetie. Honest, I'm joking. Can't you take a joke?"

Bennie whispered in his ear. *We don't like Daisy. She's not a nice flower. Tell her she isn't nice, Bennie.*

Benjamin sprang from the kitchen chair, knocking it over. The black holes in his head had opened. Electrical conduits were short circuiting. He pressed a hand against his temple to ease the white flashes of pain.

"Do your friends like your sarcasm? I don't like it when people make fun of me! And if you d-do it again"—he pointed toward the door—"storm or not, you can leave, and if you slip on the rocks and break

136

your neck, I won't cry over you."

Daisy scooted against the corner of the couch as if she were trying to wedge herself to safety. "Whoa, sweetie. I didn't mean to light your fuse. I'm a waitress—well, actually a barmaid—and tend to forget not everyone appreciates my dry sense of humor."

Without a further word, he strode to the bedroom and returned with a quilt. He tossed it to her. "I gotta work tomorrow. Be up and ready by the time I leave."

"What time is that?"

"You'll know when I wake you. Don't expect breakfast. I eat in town."

He turned out the lights and walked to his bedroom in the dark.

****

The dream came the way it always did when he was stressed. Benjamin didn't like this dream and fought to wake himself. The blankets covering him scalded his body. He thrashed and kicked them aside.

The dream persisted, sucking him into a deep abyss. He was at a funeral. The day was unbearably hot in the graveyard. His mother gripped his hand until the life drained from his fingers. He was a little boy. He was three. The priest droned on and on. Benjamin inhaled the offensive odors of sweating bodies. His little legs hurt. He wanted to sit down. There were no chairs.

His mother rocked from side to side, keening piteously, while he struggled to keep her standing upright. Finally, the priest shut up, and the sweaty gravediggers walked forward with their shovels. His mother cried out, "Wait. Not yet."

She yanked on Benjamin's arm, dragging him

closer to the casket. Her bloodless lips and her lifeless eyes turned vibrant and frightening. She bent to face him. "Your twin is in there. Why didn't you die, too?"

He drew back. "No, Mommy. I a good boy."

He had backed against the casket. He snatched his hand from her grasp to cover his ears as she screeched venomous words. "You are a bad boy. You are a filthy boy. You are a selfish, rotten little bastard."

An older man, his grandfather, reached out and slapped her hard across the face. "Stop that incessant screaming, Rose. It isn't Benjamin's fault his twin died. The lad slipped and fell from the cliff. He couldn't survive a broken neck. It was an accident."

Benjamin lowered his hands from his ears. He kept his hands at his side. His mother's cheeks filled with color. Her vibrant blue eyes snapped fire. "What did I do to deserve a boy as evil as you?"

The dream turned. Benjamin's fingers fished for the quilt to cover his shivering body. The next memory was strong. His grandfather lifted him into a boat. "Hold tight to the lantern, Benjamin."

"Why, Grandfather?"

"Never you mind. Be a good boy and do as I say."

The old man pushed the small skiff from the shoreline until he stood knee deep. Then, climbing inside, he took up the oars. The boat lumbered against the roiling water. Lightning coursed across the sky enough for Benjamin to see the whitecaps cresting the waves. He was afraid. "Are we fishing, Grandfather?"

"In a manner of speaking."

There were no stars to light the way. The sound of waves slapping the side of the craft frightened Benjamin. He gripped the lantern's wire handle. And then the boat stopped moving forward. The gentle to-and-fro motion lulled Benjamin. He wanted to sleep.

"Don't drop the lantern, Benjamin. We need it to find our way home."

He watched the old man use a sailor's knife to slice open a plastic bag. "Sit on the bow and hold the lantern high, lad, and watch for sharks."

"Why did Bennett die, Grandfather? Wasn't he a good boy too?"

"Don't talk, Benjamin, and don't look at me. Watch for sharks."

He heard a splash, and then another, and another. The metallic odor of blood assailed his nostrils. In the lantern light, he watched fins slice through the water. Another splash. More sharks. The boat rocked dangerously on its side as the killers fought for the prize grandfather was tossing overboard. Benjamin was afraid and wanted to shriek. A voice inside his head warned, *Shh...mustn't scream.*

At home, his grandfather instructed him to go into the house. "Go to bed. I'll hear your prayers as soon as I wash up."

The dream continued in a mist of surrealism. The bed sagged as the old man sat on the mattress.

"Where is Mama?"

"She's sleeping with the sharks."

That night was the first time Bennie visited him. *Don't scream. Don't ever scream. It will get you dead.*

And at the tender age of five years, Benjamin still believed he'd killed his twin.

A woman's voice beckoned him. Not his mother's. "Hey...hey! Wake up."

Benjamin slapped away the hands shaking him.

The black holes in his brain closed, the pain subsided, and the dream faded. He blinked in the darkness. "Why are you in my room?"

Daisy hovered over him. "Hey, dude, that must have been some freakin' scary nightmare. You were screamin' your head off."

He swung his legs over the side of the bed and stumbled to the bathroom. "Get out of my room, and close the door."

After relieving his bladder, he opened the door and peered out to make sure she had obeyed his command.

The clock's fluorescent hands read two a.m. He lay back and stared at the ceiling. The darkness gathered at the fringes of his mind. Pressure grew at the back of his skull. He felt it with another tendril running up his spine and pressing against the back of his eyes.

He knew the black holes had opened and had begun feasting on his brain. *Wake up, Bennie.*

No, I'm Benjamin. You're Bennie.

Who the hell cares? We're twins, and our flower waits.

He eased out of bed and slipped from the bedroom. He wasn't sweating or shivering. His heart pumped a little faster. Bennie came alive inside him.

Benjamin stilled. He closed his eyes and reminded himself that he was Bennie, and Bennie was him.

The storm outside had calmed. The storm inside Benjamin roared to life. Moonlight spilled through the kitchen window, flooding the open space with shadowy light.

Gently, he eased back the quilt from Daisy's supine body. The flannel shirt had ridden over her thighs to reveal her nakedness. He almost roared with delight.

The snickering inside his head stopped him when he reached down to touch her. *Daisy is a pretty flower. We like pretty flowers.*

She was sound asleep and beautiful. In the moonlight, her skin appeared pale and flawless. Her brown hair was long, straight, and sleek.

She's here for us, Bennie. I brought her to you. Go ahead. I want to watch.

His hands trembled as he traced fingers up her inner thigh. He sighed. It felt good to touch a woman again. He quivered as he gently unbuttoned the flannel shirt. His crotch ached. He needed to relieve himself. He carefully folded back the top to reveal the fullness of each breast. She released a breathless sigh. His hand hovered.

Daisy's voluptuous frame stiffened. She came awake fast, sat up, and scooted away from him. "What the hell are you doing, you freakin' pervert?"

He drew back. "Don't…don't scream."

In the dim light, her nostrils flared, and her brow knotted into a fierce frown. She pushed to a standing position, the cushion sagging under her weight. With her hands balled into fists, she snarled, "Touch me, and I'll kick your brains out."

"No…no…it's a mistake. I only wanted to love you." He grabbed his head. "It's Bennie. He's the bad boy."

It's been a long time, Bennie. Ten years. Don't chicken out. You deserve to be loved.

"I deserve to be loved."

She blinked owlishly. "I've stepped into a freakin' insane asylum. Stay away from me. Just let me leave and no one will know what's happened here." She made a little motion against her mouth as if turning a lock. "My lips are sealed."

His hand snaked out and grabbed her ankle. He pulled her down. She lashed out with the other foot—landing a resounding blow to the side of his head.

For a moment, colored sparkles floated before his eyes. He shook his head to clear his vision. He yanked again. Her back bumped the edge of the couch as he dragged her to the floor. She fought as he straddled her, and she screamed. She pummeled his back with her fists, and she screamed louder.

He placed his hand over her mouth and squeezed her cheeks. "Shh…shh. I don't like screaming. P-please don't scream."

She forced her mouth open and clamped down on the soft part between his thumb and forefinger. She thrashed beneath him. He fell to one side. Daisy rolled to her knees and struggled to crawl to the front door. He grabbed her legs and pulled her back. He lifted her to a standing position, and held her in a bear hug.

She inhaled deeply, and spoke in a calm, rational voice. "Sweetie, if it's sex you want, I'll give it to you for free. Just…don't hurt me."

He groaned against the pain. The tempo inside his brain was reaching a crescendo. Each word she spoke sounded like nails scratching down a chalkboard.

His hands wrapped around her throat. He squeezed. A rush of ecstasy washed through his body like a wave of warm sea water. Her eyelids fluttered rapidly. She opened her mouth wide. He saw the constriction moving up and down her throat and knew he had to stop the sound.

"This is the last time I'll ask you not to scream."

With a sharp jerk, he twisted with all his might. He was aware of the moment Daisy Fuller died, and with it came a rush of release that made an ordinary orgasm pale in comparison. It lit him up. Every nerve in his body tingled with delicious sensitivity and sent quivering aftershocks into his convulsing muscles.

Ah, Bennie, you're a good boy...a good boy.

Slowly, cell by cell, Benjamin's brain reawakened. The pleasure ebbed and delight receded as rationality returned. His hands trembled as he looked at the limp body crumpled at his feet.

He sank to his knees and lifted her into his arms. He sobbed, "Go away, Bennie. This is all your fault."

Chapter Nineteen

Prior to leaving New York, disturbing dreams had plagued Laura. A psychiatrist had diagnosed her with post traumatic stress syndrome.

The panic attack that hit a few minutes before three in the morning left her drenched in sweat. She lay in bed, thinking about all of it—Jolly's death, Elio Casper's threat, falling in a grave and landing on top of a skeleton, the white roses—and at the same time trying not to think about any of it.

Her skin was on fire. She peeled off her pjs, stepped into the shower, and scrubbed herself from head to toe. For a full thirty minutes she stood there letting the warm water flow over her skin. She brushed her teeth, gargled with mouthwash, put on a fresh set of pajamas, and crawled back into bed.

She fought against the urge to do it all over again. This time she was cold and shivery, and the clothes touching her body felt scratchy and irritating. She struggled to ward off the panic. She got out of bed and paced the length of the room and back. She walked out to the sun porch. The monotonous clanging of the buoy escalated her tension. She turned to go back to bed and stubbed her little toe against the coffee table leg. "Ouch! Shit!"

A light went on from the other side of the porch. She had awakened her aunt.

"Laura?"

"Go back to bed, Aunt Philly. I'm okay." And the tears came.

Phyllis folded Laura into her arms. She soothed her with cooing sounds. "How about a cup of my special hot chocolate?"

Laura nodded against her aunt's shoulder. "Make mine with a double shot of amaretto."

At four in the morning, she sat on the bed, shivering, cradling the mug of chocolate. "I hate not being able to control these attacks. It comes over me like a storm. I feel weak and out of control."

"Listen to me, Laura Friday. You've had a trauma that most women will never experience in their entire lifetime. It's barely been four months since you were shot. You lost your best friend, and you came close to losing your own life. Then you uprooted from everything familiar, moved here, and dove right into running a newspaper. Healing, both physically and mentally, takes time—months, maybe years."

Phyllis scooted to the edge of the chair. She tucked the blanket tighter around Laura's body. "It's been eons since I've had a real vacation. Never had a reason to take one. It will do us both good to get away. So, when fall comes, I propose we take ourselves a Mediterranean cruise. Instead of mooning over the travel brochures collecting dust on my bedside table, I say let's make it a reality. We both need a change of scenery. What do you say to that?"

Laura swiped the tears from her cheeks. "Works for me."

Phyllis looked at the clock. She gathered the mugs. "Try to get some rest."

When the shivering subsided, tiredness overtook Laura. She drifted off and slept.

The sound of birds tweeting jerked her awake. She opened her eyes to bright sunlight streaming through the open mini-blinds. The clock read eight forty-five. Two hours past her usual rising time. She awoke with the awareness that she was alive, and all she had to do was put one foot in front of the other. She felt shattered. Completely exhausted. She forced herself to stand up and stretch. Limping to the kitchen, she poured a cup of coffee, and took the cup onto the sun porch so she could see the trees. The branches swayed in the wind, dancing, the puffy white clouds behind them scudding along at a merry pace—the promise of a pleasant day.

She watched Benjamin Noone with his hedge clippers trimming the topiaries, and then Maudie Perry approached him with the usual morning cup of coffee and the little white sack, which Laura knew contained a bagel with cream cheese and lox. The odd relationship between Maudie and Benjamin stymied her.

Her cell phone chimed. She half hopped, half limped to the bedroom. Mitch's cell number. She answered on the fourth ring.

Her voice was breathless when she spoke. "Mitch?"

"Good morning, Friday. Thought you'd like to know the ME faxed his report to me this morning."

Her heart quickened. "And?"

"Dental analysis confirms our skeleton is definitely Lynnette Braswell. He also faxed a copy of the forensic artist's composite, which is a close match to the photo in the newspaper article. Exact cause of death—cervical fracture."

"What happens now?"

"The ME will put out the usual seventy-two-hour search for family members. If no one claims the body, he'll see to the cremation."

"Was there anything in the report to point a finger toward who might have killed her?"

"Ten years is a long time. The ME's report was thorough. Unfortunately, nothing. At least our girl is no longer a Jane Doe."

Laura sat on the bed to take the pressure off her leg. She sighed. "It's too bad she remains a cold case. Guess we can be thankful part of the mystery is solved. Anything more about the peeping tom?"

"Case closed. But, Friday…I do have another piece of news. It's about Elio Casper."

Unease rippled over her. Bitter bile from the coffee rose in her throat. She swallowed, closed her eyes, forced herself to take slow breaths.

"Okay." Her voice came out in a gravelly whisper.

She listened, uncertain she'd heard his words correctly.

"Do you want to talk about it?"

She thought for a minute, then shook her head. "I don't think I can, Mitch."

"Gotta go. Louise is signaling that I have a call on the office line. We'll talk later."

A queasy discomfort gurgled in Laura's stomach, like when she'd had one too many gin and tonics. Placing both hands over her mouth, she swallowed the scream. Her heart pounded in her throat. Her legs felt rubbery, and she wasn't sure she could make it to the bathroom.

Shrugging out of her pajamas, Laura cranked on

the shower taps and stepped under the spray. She stood there with her head hanging down and Mitch's words sifting through her mind. Elio Casper was dead. Stabbed during an exercise session in the prison yard. And Mario Gombiani, drug lord? Gunned down in a feud over territories.

Her entire body trembled, her breaths weren't breaths at all but hiccup-like sobs. And then she felt something amazing. Peace.

Chapter Twenty

"Mitch, line one. It's Bryan Cole. Sounds urgent."

He pushed the button. "Ranger Cole?"

"Got an emergency at Thunder Hole, and it's a hellish nightmare."

Mitch stopped smiling and listened. "Close off the area to spectators. We don't need a panic. Don't touch anything. Try to preserve the scene as much as possible. As for witnesses, isolate them from each other. It will keep them from feeding off each other's recollections. Get them coffee, and pencil and paper to write down everything they can remember. I'll get there asap!"

"Will do."

As Mitch hung up the phone, he issued instructions to Louise. "Call Dr. Musuyo, tell him he'll need his forensics kit, an EMT, and the ambulance, and to meet me at the main entrance of the national park. Musuyo is to ask for Ranger Jane Dorsey. She'll direct him to the scene."

Louise adjusted the eyeglasses that had slipped down on her nose. "What is it, Mitch? What's happened?"

His voice brooked no nonsense. "In a minute, Louise. Right now, do as I've asked."

He punched auto-dial for Laura's number and was relieved when she answered on the first ring.

"Hey, Mitch, I've been meaning to call and thank

you for telling me about Elio—"

He didn't have time for platitudes. He glanced at his watch. Eleven fifteen. "Friday, I'll pick you up in fifteen minutes. Bring your camera."

"Don't tell me. Another peeping tom report from an overly excited woman who will probably change her story like the last two did?"

She heard his impatient sigh. "Worse. We have a body."

"Oh, crap. I'll meet you outside."

"Friday, keep this under wraps until we have more facts."

Mitch grabbed his cap and jacket from the coat rack. He stared hard at the secretary. He'd noted how she had hung onto the word *body*. He stood with his legs apart. "Louise, if you breathe one word of this before I've given clearance, I can guarantee you a place in the unemployment line. My report will state that you willingly and unlawfully breached the confidence of your position in this office and jeopardized the investigation of a possible murder case by spreading false information. Do you understand me?"

She crossed her arms over her breasts. The cocked eyebrow added to her smugness. "Ayuh, sure. You don't have to bite my head off. But you don't have the authority to fire me. Only Roberta. Her father hired me, and I've known her since she was a child."

He narrowed his eyes. "Sheriff Gilman's influence doesn't extend all the way to the State Attorney's office."

He didn't care about the surprised, pouty look on her face. He cared about how the effects of her premature and embellished gossip would affect this case, and the possible panic it might create in the town—and worse, what would happen if the killer was hanging around. He stepped closer to the desk and leaned forward with his hands splayed on the surface so he was eye level with her. The bane of her incessant, arrogant attitude had pushed him to the limit. "I'm not joking, Louise."

Snugging the cap on his head, he expelled a tense breath as he strode across the room and out the door.

****

Laura tugged on the neckline of her V-cut lavender pullover. Jeans and a T-shirt would be more appropriate for this assignment. She worried about the climbing and how it would affect her bad leg. Flipping the strap of her camera over her head and shoulder, she walked outside and locked the door. Cool June air infused with the rich smells of salt air fanned Laura's skin and hair as she stood in front of the newspaper office.

Music floated from one of the outdoor cafés, mingling with the aroma of grilled onions. Laura's mouth watered. A young couple with a small white dog on the end of a leash walked down the steps leading to the beach. The peaceful scene was a contrast to the phone call from Mitch.

A body...male or female? She thought about the small tidbit of information Mitch had given her. Would he have called her if a mere accident was the cause of death? A shiver rippled over her.

The ambulance drove past, its siren screaming. She stretched her neck to watch it moving cautiously through the narrow streets. People on the sidewalks and in the shops seemed to pay little attention to the red flashing lights and the whirring warning signal.

Accidents inside the national park or on one of the islands was a common occurrence during tourist season.

After Mitch phoned, she'd called her aunt.

From experience, she knew to preserve the confidentiality of a story's content until all the facts were verified. "Aunt Philly, I'm riding to the park with Mitch. I've got a lead on a story. Probably nothing real newsworthy. I might be a little late and wanted to let you know not to worry about supper. I'll grab a sandwich later."

"Not to worry, dear. It's our Friday Sisters Book Club night. Maudie has pestered the daylights out of me to discuss a historical romance."

"And you gave in?"

"I have to admit, there was plenty of mystery in the one she chose. *Bannon's Brides* was a real page turner. I'm looking forward to the discussion, and what the other ladies think of the book."

"I'm proud of you, Aunt Philly. It was nice of you to bend the rules a little."

"Ayuh, but next month we'll read another mystery, *Séance on a Wet Afternoon*, in which an unstable medium convinces her husband to kidnap a child so she can help the police solve the crime and achieve renown for her abilities. Maybe we'll hold another séance."

Laura imagined the excited grin on her aunt's face at the prospect of calling forth another spirit. "Gotta go. Mitch is here." She disconnected the call and slid the phone inside her pocket.

She opened the patrol car door, climbed in, and buckled the seatbelt. She pulled out her notepad and pen. "Did Bryan give you any details about the body?"

"He said it was too complicated to explain over the

phone."

Laura closed her eyes and breathed deep. "Male or female?"

Mitch kept his hands tight on the steering wheel and his eyes on the road. "Female."

As soon as he cleared town limits, he turned on the siren and increased the vehicle's speed. She decided it best to let Mitch concentrate on maneuvering the hairpin curves along the skyline drive while she practiced the art of silence.

Mitch glanced over, his eyebrows shifting with his amused smile. "Not scaring you, am I?"

She hoped her face was a blank mask of calm. "No. I read somewhere that talking distracts the driver. I prefer you give the road your full attention."

"Uh-huh. There's the ambulance."

She glanced forward to see the vehicle a distance ahead of them as it rounded an outside curve.

Mitch said, "We should arrive in about fifteen minutes. And Friday, be prepared. I don't know what condition the body is in. I'll need you to take pictures for Dr. Musuyo while he performs his preliminary exam. We'll also needs shots of the scene where the body was found."

She stared down at her hands as she tapped the pad with the tip of the pen. "You think I can handle all of this?"

"You're an investigative reporter. That's what you do, remember?"

She simply looked at him and blinked back the vision of Jolly and the helpless look on his face when he knew he was dying. She hoped a little bit of that gutsy fortitude she'd lost still lurked inside her.

"I remember."

Mitch punched the accelerator. "Hold on."

She massaged her temples. She would not give in to self-pity.

The squeal of tires turning into the parking lot drew her back to earth. Mitch parked the car behind the ambulance. Opening the door, Laura watched Ranger Dorsey waving them toward the 4x4. She moved toward the vehicle as quickly as her leg would allow. The muscles tended to seize up whenever she sat for more than fifteen minutes, and they hurt like the dickens when she first stretched the leg out afterwards.

She hit that point where bending roiled her stomach when the sharp pain hit. She was thankful Mitch gripped her arm to keep her from collapsing. "I'm good. It just takes a couple of minutes to get going."

Nonetheless, she was keenly aware of his strong hands around her waist assisting her into the ATV.

Ken Musuyo hefted his forensics kit into the back of the off-road vehicle. "We'll need the gurney, Ranger."

Jane Dorsey nodded. She glanced at the EMT. "Follow me, and watch for my signal. I'll wave when you can't go any further."

Mitch climbed in next to Jane, with the doctor and Laura in the back seat. "Ranger Dorsey, who found the body?"

Laura flipped open the pad she held, pen ready, and scribbled as the vehicle jostled along a gravel cut. "An elderly couple, with their son and daughter-in-law. The Yeomans from Vermont. They're plenty shaken. Can't say that I blame them."

"Where are they now?"

"With Senior Ranger Cole's secretary, Carol Brennan. She put them in the conference room and is sitting with them."

"Good. Any other witnesses?"

"None. I can't believe that in this day and age not everyone owns a cell phone. The Yeomans didn't, so the son raced all the way to the main building. He refused to talk to anyone except a senior ranger. Senior Ranger Cole called me and Ranger Tony Klopper. He and Cole are at the scene."

Ranger Dorsey stuck her arm out and waved to signal the EMT to pull over. She waited for him to approach. "Hang tight. As soon as I deliver these folks, I'll come back to get you and the gurney." She sped off.

Within minutes, she said, "There's Senior Ranger Cole."

The area had already been cordoned off, including a sign stating the area was temporarily closed.

Mitch assisted Laura while Dr. Musuyo retrieved his kit. Together the group walked the short distance to the stone steps leading to Thunder Hole. Laura held the rail for balance. "Don't wait on me. I'll catch up."

Going down, she knew, would be easier on her muscles than the trip back to the top. At least these were gradual steps and not like the steep stairs in her aunt's apartment.

She watched Mitch and the doctor climb over the metal railing and jump to a rugged table of red clay stones where Bryan Cole and another park ranger stood. She lifted her camera and clicked.

As she approached the same spot, Dr. Musuyo looked at her. "Don't try to climb over. Use your zoom lens to get the preliminary shots I need." He removed the voice-activated tape recorder and spoke into it, giving the date and time, before he stooped and lifted back the canvas covering.

Laura gasped. Tiny bumps pebbled her skin. She hadn't expected to see the body of a fully naked female corpse sprawled like a broken doll on a pile of rocks. She took a step forward to get closer. Not satisfied, she lifted her good leg to the bottom rail, pulled herself upright, and leaned forward. Laura lifted the camera and zoomed in. A mass of tangled brown hair covered the corpse's face.

Mitch drew on a pair of clear plastic gloves as he squatted. "This is where the body was found?"

Ranger Cole huffed out his acknowledgment. "Ayuh. Except it wasn't exactly found. According to the Yeomans, they were standing there"—he pointed—"at the end of the observation deck waiting to see if the water spout would happen today. It did. Water shot out of the hole, and the next thing they see is a body flying through the air to land where we're standing."

Laura hastily scribbled down Bryan Cole's statement. Startled and intrigued, she spoke over the din of waves crashing against the stone barriers. "How would such a thing happen?"

Ranger Cole shrugged. "Not to get too technical, Thunder Hole is a small inlet, naturally carved out of the rocks, and the waves roll in. At the end of this inlet, down low, is a small cavern where, when the rush of the wave arrives, air and water is forced out like a clap of thunder. Water might spout as high as forty feet."

"Interesting. Like a geyser. Does this happen every day?" She shifted slightly to take pictures of a particularly large wave that crashed over the observation point.

Cole shouted over the noise. "Depends on how the tides are running. It's more apt to happen during high tide or after a storm."

Laura clicked away where Dr. Musuyo indicated, and all the while she kept an eye on Mitch's expressions. He asked, "What do you think, Doc? Did the victim drown, and then possibly the body washed into the cavern, then got tossed out the blow hole?"

Musuyo held up each of the victim's hands for Laura to photograph before he placed bags over them to preserve possible DNA. He appeared to mull the question. "Not likely. Two critical questions require resolution: Was the victim alive or dead when she entered the water? And is the cause of death drowning, and if not, what is the cause of death?"

"What's your best guess?"

"The body has taken quite a beating. Possibly from the wave action of slamming it against the walls of the cavern. Corpses in water always lie with the face down and with the head hanging. Buffeting in the water commonly produces post-mortem head injuries, which may be difficult to distinguish from injuries sustained during life. The presence of bleeding usually distinguishes ante-mortem from post-mortem injuries. However, the head-down position of a floating corpse causes passive congestion of the head with blood, so that post-mortem injuries tend to bleed, creating diagnostic confusion."

"I'm just a country boy, Doc. Can you put that in simpler terms?"

Musuyo rolled the body to its side. He lifted the

hair from the base of the neck and used the end of his pen to point to a bruise. "Without a complete autopsy to confirm my suspicions, I'd say our victim died of a cervical fracture."

"A broken neck?"

"That's what I said."

"Okay, our victim decides to take a moonlight swim in the buff. She dives off one of the cliffs, hits her head, snaps her neck.".

Musuyo studied the back of the victim's shoulders, along the spine and buttocks. "Bruising at the base of the spine above the waistline, and on both buttocks. These may or may not be consistent with diving off a cliff or being slammed against rocks. She would have had to land in a sitting position, which does not explain a possible broken neck."

"How long do you think she's been in the water?"

Musuyo glanced up at Laura and instructed her to get close-ups of the eyes, nose, and lips. "The time it takes for a body to decompose in water varies depending on temperature. In cold water, it will take longer for the body to decompose because the body will fill with gas. However, there are no signs of bacterial growth, and there are minor signs of feeding from crabs and small fish around the eyes and lips. Thankfully, the sharks didn't get to her."

Laura gasped. "Sharks feed on dead bodies?"

Musuyo smiled up Laura. "Sharks, like any predator, are opportunistic feeders, and they'll take advantage of any resource that's given to them."

He redirected his attention to Mitch. "Again, without an autopsy, my best guess is death occurred approximately forty-eight to seventy-two hours ago."

He sighed. "I've done all I can do on location. Okay to release the body so I can take it to the lab?"

Mitch nodded. He looked at Ranger Cole. "Any idea who she is?"

Cole shrugged his shoulders. "With all the visitors who pass through, it's impossible to recall faces. Most of the time, I'm not in direct contact with the people."

His walkie-talkie squawked. He lifted it from the case at his waist. "Cole. Go ahead." He listened. "Do whatever is necessary to hold them there, Ranger Dorsey. Don't let them out of your sight. We're on our way." He turned to the deputy. "Mitch, that was Jane. Some campers from the Blackwater site are at the office. They're looking for a friend who disappeared four days ago."

Mitch's smile was grim. "Four days? What kind of people wait four days to report a missing friend? This had better be good. Lead the way, Ranger Cole."

Mitch followed the senior ranger over the rail, while Laura snapped shots of the EMT helping to zip the cadaver inside the body bag. With the help of Ranger Klopper, the two men lifted the cadaver pouch onto the gurney. She photographed the entire process of hoisting the collapsed bed on wheels over the railing and up the stone steps to where the ATV waited, biting back the grunts of exertion as she labored behind the EMT. Dr. Musuyo brought up the rear in case she stumbled.

Chapter Twenty-One

Mitch followed Ranger Dorsey to an office where four people sat close together. Jane Dorsey said, "Excuse me, folks, I'd like you to meet Deputy Sheriff Mitch Carter. Deputy Carter, this is the Yeoman family. In a manner of speaking, they found the body."

He thanked the ranger and asked if she would stay. He observed the anxious faces—an elderly couple, perhaps in their late seventies, and a younger couple, estimated in the late forties. Cameras around their necks. Sensible walking shoes. The older gentleman's head bobbled, and his hands trembled as he gripped a metal cane. Mitch surmised the man might suffer from Parkinson's Disease. That definitely ruled him out as a suspect. These were ordinary people whose happy day had turned into an unexpected nightmare.

He pointed to Laura. "I'd like you to meet Laura Friday. She runs the *Harbor Gazette* and would like to take a photo of you."

She smiled as she stepped forward, clicked a couple of times, then stepped into the background to take a seat. "For the record, where are you staying?"

The older man said, "At the Lighthouse B&B."

Mitch pulled two chairs closer and sat down. He placed a small tape recorder on the other chair. "I appreciate you folks waiting patiently. If you don't mind, I'd like to record this session. It will save you a trip to my office. I imagine this has been a trying experience and you'd like to return to the B&B so you can relax."

All four of the people nodded. The younger Mr. Yeoman said, "Thanks, Deputy. You can count on our cooperation."

Mitch pushed the Record button and looked at the older man. "Beginning with you, sir, then going down the line, please state your full name, address, and relationship to each other."

"Richard Yeoman, Senior, 2453 Lone Pond Road, Island Pond, Vermont. This is my wife, Alaina."

The man's son and daughter-in-law gave their information.

"Were you at the scene together?"

All nodded, and Mitch reminded them to speak their answers into the recorder.

"I need one person to relate what you saw at the observation deck, and the approximate time."

The father looked at his son. "I don't think I have the heart to speak of this dreadful thing, and your poor mama is too upset."

The son scooted to the edge of his seat. He cleared his throat as he patted his father on the shoulder. "We, the four of us, arrived at the Thunder Hole observation point about ten a.m. There were probably six other people there. About a half hour later, they left because the hole hadn't erupted. We decided to wait another few minutes. I remember looking at my watch just as I heard the loud clap, like thunder. It was exactly ten forty-five. We didn't expect the large gush of water. It was like a tidal wave rushing over us. We were laughing with excitement, and then we laughed harder, and we were all pointing. At first we thought it was a joke, that someone had thrown a mannequin, you know, like one of those store mannequins, down the hole, as a sick prank to scare the tourists when it spewed out. We all rushed to the other side of the railing to see where it would land.

"After the geyser stopped flowing and the water receded, I climbed over the railing. My plan was to get the thing and take it to the ranger's shack so it wouldn't get washed out to sea."

At this point he lowered his face into his hands and shuddered. Mitch gave the man time to collect himself.

"Only…it wasn't a doll. And we were laughing."

Alaina Yeoman spoke in a reverent voice. "She was just lying there. I told my son to remove his jacket and cover her up. It seemed indecent to leave her exposed to the world."

The son said, "I'm a college professor. I teach math. I don't know about forensics, but from watching cop shows, I knew not to contaminate the scene. I asked my parents and my wife to stay, in case other tourists showed up, while I ran to get a ranger."

He spread his hands wide. "That's it, Deputy. That's all we can tell you."

Mitch's gaze drifted over the pale, haggard faces. "Did you happen to notice anyone out of the ordinary hanging around the area, someone who might have shown an unusual interest in the cadaver?"

A second of silence. It was as if the Yeomans were of one mind when whispering, "No," as their answer.

Mitch pressed the Off button on the recorder. He stood and extended his hand to both the father and the son. He touched the bill of his cap to acknowledge the ladies. "Thank you for your cooperation. You're free to go." He reached into his shirt pocket for a business card. "Before you leave Cole Harbor, I'd appreciate a call…in case I have further questions."

****

Mitch cricked his lips into a smile. "Ranger Dorsey, lead us to where you've contained the three people who wanted to file the missing person report."

"Mind if I sit in, Mitch?"

"Sure, come along, Friday."

Laura followed behind Mitch and Jane Dorsey. The ranger pushed through a pair of double doors. "This is the mini-theater. We often show short films about the wildlife native to the park."

"Ranger Dorsey, ask Dr. Musuyo and the ambulance driver to hang around. I may ask these people to identify the corpse."

"Yes, sir. Will do."

Senior Ranger Bryan Cole stepped forward and whispered, "Glad you're here." He indicated the three huddled together. "Natives are getting antsy. Claim they're being held against their will."

"Hmm, sounds like a guilt trip coming on." Mitch raised his voice. "Folks, I'm Deputy Sheriff Mitchell Carter. I understand you're here to file a missing person report."

A tall man with a scraggly beard and curly brown hair, and wearing a tie-dyed T-shirt and jeans cut off at the knees, said, "Yeah. She went missing four days ago."

Mitch handed the recorder to Laura with instructions to turn it on.

"Hey, man, you can't record any of us. We know

our rights."

Mitch and Bryan Cole exchanged glances. The second man in the group said, "Ain't that an invasion of privacy or somethin'?"

Mitch appeared to mull over the comment. His voice was curt. "Your privacy is only invaded if you've committed a crime and are trying to hide it. Would that be the case?"

The woman of the group, her hair slicked back into a pink-and-purple ponytail, reached to scratch a rash on her bare leg. She had an annoying rasp to her voice that sounded as if she needed to clear her throat. "The two of you cut the crap and let the man do his job. Sorry, Deputy. Mutt and Jeff there are really Louis Castle and Joe Manfred. I'm Sybella Dauzat. We're from Bangor and came to spend a few days primitive camping. We don't have nothing to hide."

"Thank you, ma'am. What is your missing friend's name?"

"Daisy Fuller."

"What is Ms. Fuller's age, and would you supply a description of her?"

"Ayuh. Daisy tells everyone she's twenty-five, but she's closer to thirty-five. About five foot six, brown eyes, brown hair. Built like a brick shit house." Sybella placed her hand against her mouth and giggled. "Pardon my French."

"What's your relation to Ms. Fuller?"

"None. We're friends. Both work together as hostesses at the Thirsty Frog."

Louis Castle sniggered. "Fancy name for a barmaid who scalps drinks and does a little boom-boom business on the side."

Sybella cut him a mean eye. "Shut your damn hole."

Mitch interceded. "Settle down. Sparring with each other won't help us find your friend. You told Ranger Dorsey you hadn't seen Ms. Fuller in four days. Why did you wait until today to report her missing?"

Joe Manfred said, "You don't know Daisy. When she gets a notion in her head, there's no changing her mind."

"What notion did she get in her head the night she went missing?"

The three friends looked at each other. To Mitch's mind they wore that "guilty as sin and we're busted" expression.

Sybella said, "Ah, hell, it ain't no big whoop. We were smoking a little combustible love, and knocking back tequila shooters, and…well…you know…doin' the nasty boom-boom, if you catch my drift." She tsked and shot a wink toward Mitch.

"Anyhow, Daisy said she needed some fresh air. We told her it was gonna rain. She said it was okay 'cause she needed a bath anyhow. With all the dopin' and drinkin', we were all visiting la-la land. You know…passed out. When the buzz finally wore off and we woke up, she was gone. We went looking for her, and called her cell phone. Didn't get an answer. Figured it was 'cause there's no reception up here."

"When was that, Ms. Dauzat?"

"Day before yesterday. I think. I don't know. My mind is still…you know, fuzzy."

"How would you describe Ms. Fuller? Rational? Would she commit suicide?"

Louis Castle chortled. "Suicide, nah! Daisy's okay

when she isn't messed up. 'Sides, she ain't afraid of nothing. If she run up on a bear, she'd ball up her fist and challenge it to a fight. She's got a wicked right jab." He waggled his jaw as if he'd been hit.

Mitch stared at him sharply. "Uh-huh. Let me get this straight. It wasn't until today that you got worried about your friend?"

Joe Manfred scratched through his limp purple Mohawk. "Yeah, like, you know, we all have jobs. Vacation over. Time to get back to livin' real, until the next time."

Mitch looked at each of the friends. Were they suspects? Did they kill Daisy Fuller and dump her body inside the cavern?

"Did the three of you visit Thunder Hole this morning?"

Louis said, "Nah, man, we spent the morning packing our gear, then taking another look around for Daisy. I'm really pissed at that bitch. We'll have to leave her and hope she can hitch a ride back to Bangor."

Mitch glanced at Laura, then to Bryan Cole. "I think we're about finished here."

He gave each of Daisy's friends one of his business cards. "I'd like all of you to accompany me outside."

Sybella reached down and scratched the rash on her leg again. Mitch noted the redness had spread, and water blisters had formed. "Ms Dauzat, there's a doctor waiting outside with an ambulance. I'm sure Dr. Musuyo will agree that you've been exposed to poison ivy."

"Oh, shit. Just wait 'til I see Daisy. It's her fault I went traispin' around trying to find her. If I have to go to the hospital, she's gonna foot the bill."

Louis Castle and Joe Manfred stood. Louis said, "Is that stuff contagious? I can't afford to lose any days off work."

Joe stepped away from Sybella. "Yeah, me neither."

Mitch shot Laura and Bryan an impatient glance. "The three of you are true friends. You're more concerned about yourselves than what happened to Daisy Fuller. It's possible we've found her, and she's dead."

Sybella managed to stop scratching. Her voice rose to a squeaky octave. "What is this, some kind of sick joke? If so, it ain't funny, and we're not laughing."

"I never joke, Ms. Dauzat, especially about murder. Now if all of you will follow me, I'd like one of you to take a look at the body and tell me if it's Daisy Fuller."

Outside, Laura acknowledged Mitch's slight nod. She stood back and focused her camera on the three possible suspects.

Mitch motioned for the EMT to open the ambulance's rear doors. "Dr. Musuyo, if you'll open the cadaver bag."

Mitch waved the three forward. "Which one wants to see if you can identify the body?"

No one volunteered.

"If I have to drag you over, I will."

Sybella sighed. "What if we all looked together? C'mon, guys. Don't make me do this by myself."

The EMT scooted the gurney to the edge of the ambulance. Bryan Cole helped lower it to the ground, while Dr. Musuyo unzipped the bag and folded the sides away to expose the corpse's face.

Louis Castle's eyes rolled upward. His knees sagged, and he slumped to the driveway in a dead faint. Joe Manfred clasped both hands over his mouth and raced toward the grassy area, where he bent forward and retched.

Sybella sobbed. "Oh, m'god…oh, m'god. It's her. It's Daisy. What the hell happened?"

Mitch nodded, and Dr. Musuyo closed the bag.

"You are verifying that the body you've just seen is that of Daisy Fuller?"

Sybella flailed her hands up and down like a bird trying to fly. "Yes. I've known Daisy for three years. It's her, all right."

"Thank you, Ms. Dauzat. Dr. Musuyo, this young lady appears to have poison ivy. Would you mind looking after her, once you've awakened Mr. Macho from his faint?" Mitch added, to Sybella again, "For now, you and your friends are free to return to Bangor. I'll notify local law enforcement that you're part of a murder investigation. My suggestion is not to plan any sudden out-of-town trips."

"Wait, are you saying we're suspects? That's just plain bullshit."

Mitch looked intently at the woman. "Ms. Dauzat, if you were suspects, you and your two buddies would be in handcuffs and on the way to my jail."

Chapter Twenty-Two

Ranger Dorsey approached Mitch to hand him three clear bags, each containing a plastic coffee cup. "I did as you asked and labeled each cup with a separate name." She grinned. "Makes me feel like a super sleuth."

"Good job, Ranger." Mitch in turn handed the bags to Dr. Musuyo.

The doctor choked on his laughter. "You know obtaining DNA without permission isn't legal."

"You think those three would have willingly volunteered? If DNA points fingers at any of them, we'll plead forgiveness later."

"You're my kind of lawman, Mitch. I'll call you when I'm ready to perform the autopsy."

Mitch watched Sybella Dauzat herd Louis and Joe to an old beat-up hippie camper van. He turned to Bryan Cole. "If one or all of them murdered Daisy Fuller, how would they have dumped the body in the blow hole without being seen or without the waves washing it out to sea before the geyser erupted?"

"If they'd dumped the body, it would have floated, and you're correct, the waves would have washed it out to sea." Bryan extended his arm and pointed. "There's a long oceanside walking trail. It's about a mile and a half directly north from the parking lot—from their campsite an easy three-mile round-trip hike. The trails are rustic, but easy traveling. Like I said before, there's a small cavern inside Thunder Hole's inlet. Anyone familiar with getting to the beach area might risk going inside the cavern on calm days. But with the storm we had a few nights ago, the waves against the rocks would be treacherous. I seriously doubt the yokels who just left would have had that kind of balls."

"Uh-huh, I have to agree with you." Mitch thought for a moment. "What about locals familiar with the cavern? You ever have to chase them away?"

"Honestly, we recommend our guests do the walk along the coast because of its beauty. As for locals, on a calm day, there's always the daredevils. We do our best to keep everyone safe."

Mitch said, "What else is on your mind, Ranger Cole?"

"Just a theory. It she was murdered, it is possible the killer rowed the body out to sea, hoping the sharks would destroy the evidence. But, with the storm, waves could have actually washed the body toward shore and inside the cavern. The tides were right for that type of action to take place."

Mitch shook hands with the senior ranger. "It's a theory worth considering. I don't envy you the paperwork that's ahead of you. 'Preciate your help today. And, if you notice anything out of the ordinary, keep me posted."

Bryan Cole nodded his agreement. He turned his attention to Laura. "Good seeing you again, Laura. My offer to show you the park, with a picnic lunch, still stands."

She glanced at Mitch, who winked his approval. She patted her leg. "I'm not much good with hikes."

Bryan opened the patrol car's door for Laura. "Hey, not a problem. That's why we have ATVs. If the park's not in your near future, how about dinner? Restaurant of your choice."

Mitch looked over Bryan's shoulder to waggle his eyebrows at her.

She climbed inside and grabbed the seatbelt. "Sure, give me a call, and we'll figure it out."

Bryan shut the door and stepped back. She waved as Mitch walked around the car and got into the driver's seat. He turned the ignition, shifted into gear, and pulled away from the curb.

Sitting in silence until they cleared the entrance gate, Laura frowned over at Mitch. "Why are you playing matchmaker?"

He faked surprise. "Me? Matchmaking? Never."

"Then, what was up with the snarky grin and waggling eyebrows?"

"Bryan is a nice guy, and you are a beautiful, workaholic woman who needs a little fun in your life."

"Can we change the subject? Do you really think someone from Cole Harbor killed Daisy Fuller?"

Mitch removed his cap and set it on the console. "Right now, I'm not ruling out the possibility. How well does your aunt know locals who live on the fringes of the park?"

"It's a small town. Everyone knows everyone else's business. Do you have a specific person in mind?"

"Just those who live on the fringes of the park, and in close proximity to the oceanside walking trail."

"Tonight is the Friday Sisters Book Club meeting. When those ladies get together, they gabble for hours.

I'll ask tomorrow to see when it's convenient for you to come over."

He nodded. The rest of the drive was in silence. Laura determined from the working of his jaw and the serious expression on his face that he was thinking about the case.

****

Laura thought about Bryan Cole. A man with ancestral ties to Cole Harbor, he'd left for a while to do a stint in the Navy, then returned to pursue a career that kept him close to home. He didn't have the same rugged handsomeness as Mitch. With Mitch there was an element of danger which excited her. She'd only met Bryan twice, but he appeared cool under fire. Slightly bland. A nice smile, kind eyes. Steady. Maybe too steady.

Comparing Mitch to Bryan was like comparing a stallion to a carriage horse. She dismissed this ridiculous train of thought. There was no way she was falling for either one, because she'd never met a man who made her feel worthy of being loved. She was destined to live alone. And that was that.

"How's your leg?"

Lost in thought, she hadn't realized how fast the ride had gone. "Huh? Oh, we're here. My leg… It's okay."

"We missed lunch. Let's grab a bite before I take you home. My treat."

She didn't want to admit how badly her leg ached. All she wanted was to prop it up with an ice pack. "How about a rain check? I need to get the pictures to Dr. Musuyo, and I'd like to transcribe my notes before they get cold. Is there any information in the news

172

article you want me to hold back?"

He reached over to squeeze her hand. "We won't know for certain if Daisy Fuller was murdered or if she committed suicide until Doc performs the autopsy. You're a good reporter. I trust you to keep it neutral. Print a few pictures. Nothing like seeing a dead body to rattle a perp's cage."

"So you're about ninety-five percent certain it's murder?"

"Pretty close, Friday."

Mitch slowed the car. He pulled in front of the bookstore. "It's dark inside. I thought you said there was a meeting tonight."

"A different member hosts each month. Tonight it's at Maudie's house."

"I'll walk with you to the back entrance to make sure you're safe."

A chill rippled over her as they went around the corner. "Mitch, as farfetched as this might sound, is it possible that after a ten-year hiatus the person who killed Lynnette Braswell also murdered Daisy?"

"Our thoughts are running on the same track, Friday. It's possible."

"Are you attending the autopsy?"

"Part of my job. You?"

"Umm, no. Not even if you were to approve me as a civilian to observe. I'm tough, but my stomach isn't."

Mitch laughed. "I'll call you when the report is in. G'night."

She opened the door and switched on the outside light. "I think I'll have a motion detector light installed. I don't like the idea of Aunt Philly in a dark alley, either."

"I'm not leaving until you shut the door and I hear the lock click."

She smiled as she turned the lock.

Chapter Twenty-Three

A week had passed since the discovery of the body at the park. The fervor over pictures of Daisy Fuller inside a body bag, with the article that also included a story about the identity of the skeleton, had died down. Laura immersed herself in the campaign of launching Cole Harbor beyond the borders of Maine.

The chime over the office door caused her to look up from the computer. "Good morning, may I help you?"

A teenager stood just inside the door as if unsure whether or not to enter the office. With a smile, Laura prompted, "It's okay. I don't bite."

Taking cautious steps, the teen came to stand in front of Laura's desk. "How much to place an ad in your paper?"

Tall, skinny, short wispy blonde hair, overly large eyes against a gaunt face—except for the imperceptible breasts, Laura almost mistook her for a young boy. "It depends on the number of words." She offered the girl a seat. "What's your name?"

"Amy Osmond. I want to place an ad for a handyman job for the summer. I've looked everywhere. No one wants to hire a kid."

"How old are you?

"Sixteen."

"School is out. Shouldn't you be enjoying the

summer?"

A loud rumble from her stomach caused a blush to redden the girl's cheeks. Laura pushed from her chair. She glanced at her watch and indicated the corner of the office. "Why don't you pour us a cup of coffee. I take two creams in mine. If you'll excuse me, I'll be right back."

Before Amy could react, Laura hurried out the door and to her aunt's bookstore. "Aunt Philly, what can you tell me about the Osmond family?"

Phyllis raised her eyebrows in curiosity. "Yves Osmond was a crabber. The boat he was working on went down in a storm about three years ago. He drowned and left a wife and four children. Helen is a waitress at the Silly Lobster. I believe it's all she can do to make ends meet. Why?"

"Amy Osmond is in my office wanting to place an ad in the paper for a handyman job. Says no one is hiring."

Phyllis tsked. "That's why the young people leave Cole Harbor. There's no job base. Shame."

"I've got to get back." She walked to the tea room section of the bookstore and bought two blueberry muffins. "See you, later, Maudie. Bye, Aunt Philly."

Back at her office, Laura placed one of the muffins in front of her young customer. "It's about time for my morning snack. While we eat, tell me what kinds of jobs you're willing to do."

She was correct in her assessment. The girl was hungry. Amy apologized for wolfing down the muffin. "Sorry. I missed breakfast this morning." She continued, "I'll do most anything—mow yards, clean gutters, wash windows, pull weeds. That sort of thing. I have three brothers and a sister, all younger than me. Now that I'm old enough, I want to help take the strain off my mama." She hesitated. "I'm stronger than I look, and I'm not lazy."

Laura opened a desk drawer and removed the phone book. She flipped through the pages until she found the number for the National Park's office, then dialed. "Senior Ranger Bryan Cole, please. Laura Friday calling."

When he answered, Laura explained her reason for contacting him. "I'm hoping you have a position available for my young friend."

"I might have, that is, if you're willing to do me a favor in return."

Laura wasn't sure she liked the mischievous tone in his voice. "And what would that be?"

"Lunch or dinner, your choice, this Friday. My treat."

Looking at the desperation on Amy's face, Laura tapped her fingers against the desk. She supposed it was a small price to pay for helping the teen. "Make it lunch. I've promised Aunt Philly to attend her book club meeting."

She listened to the details. "Hold a minute, and let me ask."

"Amy, Senior Ranger Cole has a part-time position working in the park's concession. It's yours if you have transportation."

The girl's face brightened. She clasped her hands together. "Ayuh. I know a shortcut to the park."

Laura spoke into the phone. She didn't smile. "Done deal. Pick me up at noon."

The chime over the door drew their attention.

Laura smiled at Mitch. "Amy, this is Deputy Sheriff Mitch Carter. Mitch, congratulate Amy. She begins work at the park on Monday."

Before Mitch could say anything, Laura turned a concerned frown toward the girl. "Amy, it's a long ride to the park on a bicycle, and longer if you're walking. Are you sure you can get to work by 8 a.m.? I can call Ranger Cole back to see if he's willing to let you come in at eight-thirty or even nine."

"Yes, ma'am, eight is okay. You see, I live on the fringe of the park. If I take the shortcut up the trail to the skyline, it's an easy fifteen-minute walk. If we're not on our bicycles, we Osmonds walk everywhere. One day, I'm gonna own a car."

She rose and thanked Laura for the muffin, and for the job. "Nice meetin' ya, Deputy. I gotta go tell mama the good news."

Mitch offered a dazzling smile. "Congratulations, Amy. Let me ask, do you know most of the people who live on the mountain and close to the park?"

"Sure do. I mean, don't know 'em personally, just who they are."

He glanced over to Laura, who returned a knowing look.

"Would you mind pointing out the ones whose houses are visible? I'd sure appreciate it."

Amy said, "Sure. C'mon."

Mitch and Laura followed the girl outside and across the street to the grassy area. She pointed. "There's the Lighthouse B&B, the yellow house is where the Robbinses live, and over there where you can barely see the tip of the roof is the Quincys. They're summer people. Rich, too. You can't see my house. It's

178

hidden in the trees more to the north." She named off several other people and pointed to their homes. "That's about it."

"Thanks, Amy."

She waved goodbye and walked toward the Silly Lobster. Just as Mitch and Laura crossed the street back toward the newspaper, Amy shouted, and trotted toward them. "I almost forgot until I saw him." She pointed to where Benjamin Noone squatted. "He lives closest to the fringe of the park. Can't see his cabin from here, and none of us go near it. He's weird."

A faint breeze crinkled through the trees. A bird chirped happily, and another answered.

Laura asked, "Weird in what way, Amy?"

She shrugged. "I dunno know…just weird. Got lots of junk all around. Yells at anybody who comes in his yard. You know…creepy."

Mitch thanked the girl again.

Inside the office, Laura asked Mitch what prompted his visit.

"Dr. Musuyo is doing the autopsy today. I know you don't plan to attend, but I thought I'd ask in case you changed your mind."

"Huh-uh, no way. I've been to one, and that one is enough to last me a lifetime. Change of subject. I asked Aunty Philly about the people who live close to Acadia's boundary lines. Amy verified everything she said, except according to Aunt Philly there are a couple of abandoned cabins up there, too. You think the killer might be hiding in one of them?"

Mitch merely shrugged. "Won't know until I check it out." He touched the bill of his cap. "Have you noted any unusual activity since you printed the articles about the dead woman and Lynnette Braswell?"

Laura mimicked his shrug. "I think the most outrage came from Aunt Philly's group of Friday Sisters. They're all a-twitter about holding a séance to see if they can conjure forth another spirit that might lead them to the killer."

Mitch offered a "spare me" shake of his head. "They are an interesting group of ladies. I'll miss them when I return to Texas. Catch you later, Friday."

"Mitch, when you check out the houses on the fringes of the park, can I go with you? I'd love to take a few pictures."

"Sure. I'll pick you up Saturday morning."

"If you're not busy, come by tonight and fill me in on the autopsy report."

"Only if I can bring a pizza."

Laura grimaced. "How can you think of food and autopsy in the same sentence?"

"Never gave it much thought."

Without another word, Mitch walked out of the office.

****

Mitch pressed the heels of his hands to his eyes. He hadn't slept well since the discovery of Daisy Fuller's body at the park. He'd considered Laura's suggestion that the killer had taken a ten-year hiatus before committing another murder. If this was the case, what had triggered the motivation to take another life? The other part of him wanted to believe Daisy Fuller's murder was in no way connected to Lynnette Braswell's.

He bit back a bitter smile as he walked down the long, sterile hall. Most autopsies were scheduled days after the discovery of a body. Not much call for such a thing in a small town. He pushed through the morgue's double doors. Inside, the odor hit him at once. Too antiseptic. Too disinfected.

Dressed in a blue gown and cap, Ken Musuyo motioned to the cabinet. "Extra cap, gown, and gloves are in the cupboard. Help yourself."

Mitch walked over and snagged the gear and covered himself. Then he stood back as an observer.

Ken Musuyo introduced Mitch. "This is James Hirsch. He's the morgue attendant/diener and will assist me." Mitch and Hirsch acknowledged each other with a nod.

The diener unwrapped the body while Dr. Musuyo looked up at the microphone suspended from the ceiling. "Testing...testing." Satisfied it was working, he proceeded with business. "Unwrapping the body now."

Hirsch pulled back the external layer of heavy duty plastic. Next he unfolded a plain white sheet. Then he unpeeled the internal layer of plastic, much like a dry cleaning bag, from the corpse's body. Each layer was folded down around the gurney's legs.

While Musuyo prepped the body, the diener said, "Because the body was nude when found, there is no inventory of clothing or jewelry. Sand and seaweed samples were collected from the victim's hair. White particles from the hair and body test positive for sodium chloride."

Afterward the body was weighed and measured and placed on the autopsy table. The diener photographed the inside of the evidence bag for any debris that might have fallen from the body. The cadaver was placed face up on the table, and a rubber body block was placed under the patient's back. "We're ready, Dr. Musuyo."

Hirsch wheeled the gurney over to the cutting table. It was obvious to Mitch the two had done this several times before. Musuyo moved to the head of the table. Hirsch moved to the feet. On the count of three they slid the naked corpse from the gurney to the metal slab, then Hirsch wheeled the table away.

First, Musuyo cataloged the victim's naked body. "Daisy Fuller, female, approximate age thirty-five, five foot six, one hundred twenty-five pounds." He gave her hair and eye color, and also commented that she appeared to be in good health.

He used the words "victim" and "deceased" a lot. Raising her right arm, he noted a brown mole on the inside of her right breast.

Musuyo moved on to identify perceived injuries, stating that multiple contusions to the exterior were possibly due to the ocean's waves battering the body against the interior walls of the cavern. "No apparent defensive wounds on the right or left arm. No bruising on the facial areas."

He moved to the outsides of each leg and noted multiple scratches before moving to the inside of each leg. At the left leg he bent for a closer observation. "Mitch, take a look at this."

Mitch also leaned in. "Green and yellow tinges around the ankle." He glanced at the doctor. "Looks like someone grabbed our victim around the ankle."

Musuyo nodded as he lifted the left leg. He used a magnifying glass to examine the perceived injury. He frowned, studying the abrasion, and placed his fingers around the ankle. "Bruising on outer side of the ankle is indicative of a thumb print."

He used his gloved hand to poke and prod the waxy skin. He rolled the body to its stomach, and lifted the long brown hair to note the bruising along the neck region of the spine. X-rays had verified a cervical fracture between the C1 and C7 vertebrae. Moving his attention down the spine, he said, "Large blue butterfly tattoo on right shoulder approximately two inches in diameter. Bruising at the lower lumbar region."

He reached up and pulled the magnifying glass closer to the buttocks. "Bruising on the right and left glutes." He then finished his initial exam by narrating the condition of the bottoms of the feet. "From the bruises and superficial wounds to the soles, it appears the victim was not wearing shoes." He used a scalpel to open an inch-long cut on the sole. He scraped the area onto a slide and handed it to Hirsch with instruction to examine the contents.

Hirsch placed the slide under a smaller microscope and reported, "The debris appears to be pieces of pine needle, crushed leaves, and dirt."

Mitch's voice was low and deep. "This definitely places the victim in the national park."

Musuyo nodded as he recorded the evidence. He removed the plastic bags from her hands. Both he and the diener leaned close while Musuyo scraped each fingernail. Hirsch collected the samples. Next Dr. Musuyo swabbed each nail with a cotton swab, testing for traces of blood. He looked at Mitch. "Nothing. It appears she didn't put up a fight. No skin, no blood."

Musuyo instructed Hirsch to bring over the inkpad and fingerprint the victim. This took a few minutes, due to full rigor mortis. They worked methodically, the doctor popping each finger to release the joints while Hirsch did the inking and fingerprinting.

With the printing done, Musuyo moved down the body to examine between the victim's legs. Although the corpse was nude when found, and in the water for approximately seventy-two hours prior to being washed ashore, he still had to examine the interior of the body.

"No bruising on the inner thighs, no lacerations of the labia majora or labia minora," Dr. Musuyo recorded. He combed the pubic hairs and Hirsch collected the strands in a plastic bag. Musuyo then picked up several long-stemmed cotton swabs. After the internal exam he handed them to Hirsch with instruction to match the spermatazoa with the DNA from the coffee cups that Ranger Dorsey had bagged and identified as Louis Castle and Joe Manfred.

Dr. Musuyo again narrated, "For the external examination, I have concluded there is no evidence of sexual assault. However, there is evidence of non-motil spermatazoa in the cervix." He shut the mic off and looked at Mitch. "This concurs with what her friends stated at the park. My guess is the semen will match with either Castle or Manfred, or both."

"How long will it take to determine the DNA matches?"

"It's modern day, Mitch. Shouldn't take Hirsch more than thirty minutes."

Mitch wanted to shoot the clock. The ticking seemed to grow louder with every second while he waited and observed Dr. Musuyo continuing to examine the body for clues. Twenty-nine minutes and thirteen seconds passed before the diener returned.

Hirsch reported. "Semen matches are ninety-nine

percent positive for Castle and ninety-six point nine percent for Manfred."

Musuyo shrugged. "Rules out rape. Okay, let's turn her on her back and clean her up."

Hirsch turned on a hose. He and the doctor hosed down the body. This was routine procedure prior to making the first incision. It was important that factors from the outside—dirt, algae, microscopic crustaceans, sea salt, and other debris—not contaminate the internal organs.

Dr. Musuyo matter-of-factly turned off the hose. "The outside has told its story. Now we will see what the inside reveals."

This was the part Mitch hated the most. He sucked in a deep breath and slowly exhaled. No matter how many autopsies he attended, his stomach always felt queasy. He pulled the surgical mask over his mouth and nose as he watched Musuyo make a small puncture to release the body gases. Depending on the rate of decomposition, the odor could be overwhelming, and sometimes the bodies splattered. With precision, the doctor made the initial incision.

While Musuyo probed the organs, he said, "Toxicology came back positive for both alcohol and cannabis, as well as tannic acid, which means that at some point in time she drank tea." He turned off the mic and spoke to Mitch. "Which confirms what the victim's friends stated. By the way, her friends didn't say anything about eating a meal, did they?"

Mitch frowned at the question. "I'd have to go through my notes to confirm, but I'm positive none of them mentioned food. Why? What did you find?"

Mursuyo's brow furrowed as he reached up to turn

on the microphone. "What do we have here?" He used a pair of needle-nosed tweezers to pluck a brown object from the stomach. He held it closer to the microscope. "A partially undigested peanut. It appears the victim may have either eaten peanuts or a crunchy type of peanut butter not too far prior to death. With tannic acid in the urine analysis, a strong conclusion is that she had a peanut butter sandwich and tea as her last meal."

They both lapsed into silence as Mitch continued to observe. He sighed heavily. "Ken, how soon will you know whether she died from a broken neck or if she drowned?"

Musuyo didn't crack a smile as he narrated into the microphone. "No sea water evident in the lungs, which draws the conclusion the victim did not drown. Official cause of death—cervical fracture."

Mitch roused himself. "Damn. I don't wish anyone dead, but I was hoping evidence would confirm suicide. Since there's no substantiation pointing to the victim's friends, it's safe to say we can rule them out as suspects. As much as I hate to think we have a murderer in Cole Harbor, it appears that may be the case."

Dr. Musuyo removed his gloves. "What are the chances the killer poses as a camper, picks out a victim, then moves on, and that Daisy Fuller just happened to be in the wrong place at the wrong time?"

"Where murder is concerned, anything is possible. Send me your report as soon as it's ready."

Mitch removed the disposable gown and gloves and dumped them inside the hazardous waste bin. He bid the doctor a good afternoon and crossed the room, closed the door behind him, and exited the morgue the same way he entered. Outside in the sunshine, he sucked in the fresh air to clear his lungs of the smell of chemicals and death.

He walked the short distance to his office to spend the rest of the afternoon filling out forms and writing his report, and to formulate a plan of investigation. He wanted this mystery solved before Sheriff Gilman's return. This was his watch, and he had no intention of leaving Cole Harbor with an unsolved murder on the books.

Chapter Twenty-Four

Bryan frowned at the hard knot that had settled in his gut. He stood in front of the newspaper's large glass door and read Laura's name and title. His body hummed with the feel of her presence as he watched her sitting with her full attention to the computer screen. *Bryan, old boy, all you have to do is convince her that she likes you.* So why did he feel like he was about to approach a man-eating shark? The two sandwich bags he held suddenly felt like lead weights, and he regretted his idea of a picnic lunch rather than taking her to a restaurant. Before he could abandon the idea and ditch the sacks in a public waste receptacle, Laura looked up, offered a smile, and motioned him inside.

She closed the laptop. "Right on time. I'm starved."

He held forth the two white bags labeled with large red lobsters wearing chef's hats. To his chagrin, she was not smiling. "I thought a picnic at the gazebo might be fun. Can I entice you with lobster rolls?"

When she didn't give an immediate response, he said, "Or…not."

The discomfort of his smile echoed in his blue eyes. She definitely wasn't dressed for eating outdoors. "Listen, bad idea. I can see I'm not scoring any points here."

Laura's own blue eyes narrowed. She arched a

brow. "Had you warned me, I would have dressed for a picnic." And then she smiled. "But a girl has to eat, and I never turn down lobster rolls from the Silly Lobster."

Bryan smiled. His pulse raced from the faint scent of the vanilla she wore. He kicked himself six ways to Sunday for not thinking through his idea of wooing her. At his age he should know that a reporter from New York might prefer flowers and dinner by candlelight.

He switched the bags both to one hand and rushed to open the door for her. "After you."

She headed off down the sidewalk for the short walk to the gazebo. Bryan fell in step beside her, resisting the urge to cup her elbow. He shook his head. *Damn.* What was wrong with him? No woman had ever had this effect on him, and he fought the urge to touch her.

Sun glistened off the bay's teal liquid surface as Laura and Bryan neared a group of trees that shaded the gazebo. Birds chirped their revelry from the tops of overhanging limbs. Nearby, Benjamin walked about with a trash grabber and placed debris in the sack that hung at his side.

Laura spoke to him. "Lovely flowers, Benjamin."

He simply offered his usual dullard stare and a slight nod.

Bryan touched Laura's elbow as she stepped inside the gazebo, and she lifted her head as if to catch the breeze. He placed the lunch bags between them as she sat on the bench seat and hunched her shoulders, closing her eyes. A puff of air ruffled several short strands of hair against her cheek. Bryan noticed the tenseness in her shoulders. "Laura?"

She slowly opened her eyes, a guarded glint

hovering in their blue depths. "It seems only yesterday when I looked at Pine Island and all I saw was its rustic beauty. Looking at it now reminds me of what Lynnette Braswell must have suffered."

"I'm sorry, Laura. Truly sorry. It was callous of me not to remember that you'd suffered a trauma on the island. Would you like to go back to your office?"

She reached for a sack, opened it, and was about to speak when a cheery voice said, "Hi, Ranger Cole, here's the iced teas you ordered." The young waitress winked as she handed him a cup carrier and a small white box. "And here's the gingerbread with a container of fresh whipped cream. I waited 'til I saw you, just like you said. Enjoy your lunch."

Bryan blushed all the way to his ears. The odds for a pleasurable hour or two with the woman of his dreams seemed stacked against him. To add to his frustration, Mayor Shipley strolled up. "Pleasure seeing you, Bryan…Laura. A picture perfect day, don't you think?"

He removed a small pen knife from his pocket and bent to cut the stem of a white rose. With methodical care, he stripped away the thorns before presenting it to Bryan. "A man should always give his lady a beautiful flower."

Laura was lovely, all right. Soft and tempting. Bryan shook his head to clear his wayward wanderings. "Your thoughtfulness goes without question, Mayor."

Shipley leaned forward and sniffed. "You've given me an idea for lunch." He waved as he proceeded down the sidewalk.

Laura's grimace didn't go unnoticed. Bryan's hopeful expression faded. "What is it, Laura?"

"Look at the scowl on Benjamin's face. If looks

could kill, the mayor would..." Her voice drifted off without finishing the sentence.

Bryan helped himself to a large bite of the lobster roll. He wiped his mouth with a napkin. "Guess he doesn't like anyone messing with his flowers. Although, technically, they aren't his, since the city pays for the plants and fertilizer."

Laura pinched crumbs from the roll, tossed them to the ground, and watched the gulls swoop in to feed. "Bryan, I have something I need to tell you, and please don't interrupt until I'm finished."

He took another bite. "Sounds serious."

She stuck a straw inside the plastic tea mug and drank as if to quench a parched throat. She rewrapped the lobster roll and placed it back in the sack. Her voice soft and quivering with emotion, she related to Bryan about being shot, the death of her best friend, and the overwhelming relief she'd experienced when Mitch had informed her that her life was no longer in danger. She followed up with falling into the grave and finding the skeleton.

"A lot has happened in these four months, Bryan. I came home to pull my life together. You seem like a really nice guy, and under different circumstances, maybe—" She spread her hands and shrugged. "In small degrees, life is beginning to stabilize, and I've almost stopped jumping at sounds that remind me of gunshots."

She placed her hand on top of his. "And, because you are a nice guy, I don't think it would be fair of me to lead you to believe that we can be anything more than friends. In the best way I can, I'm asking you not to push me into a relationship. I'm not ready."

Bryan nodded his appreciation for her straightforwardness. "I understand all you've been through, and I admire the way you've taken charge of your life." He hesitated. "An honest question deserves an honest answer, right?"

"I'm always honest."

"Is Mitch Carter my competition? He's a good-looking guy, but I'm willing to give him a run for his money."

Laura's face tightened. It didn't take a mind reader to interpret the angry glow in her blue eyes. "Did you not hear what I said? There is no Mitch, there is no competition, and if you don't respect my feelings, there is no friendship with *you,* either."

She stepped from the gazebo. Then, as if seeing the rose she held for the first time, she tossed it to the sidewalk and squashed it under the toe of her shoe.

Bryan caught up to her. "Laura, what I said was stupid. I hope you'll accept my apology for being totally out of line."

She held her hand up as if telling him to leave her alone. Crossing the street to her office, she unlocked the door and stepped inside. Within seconds, the "Closed" sign faced the street, and the mini-blinds were snapped shut.

Bryan bent and lifted the mangled rose from the sidewalk. A hot flood of shame washed over him. He was a grown man acting like a stupid high school jerk. He hadn't meant to speak his thoughts about Mitch. No smile graced his lips for his lack of respect for the small request Laura had asked of him and his lack of compassion for what she'd suffered.

He pulled the ranger cap from his back pocket and

jammed it on his head. He pivoted on his heel—and nearly collided with the groundskeeper.

Benjamin frowned down at the rose Bryan held. "That reporter lady shouldna done that. Flowers don't hurt nobody."

Bryan gathered up the sandwich bags and plastic cups and tossed them into the trash container. He handed the small white box holding the gingerbread to Benjamin. "No sense letting it go to waste."

Long strides took him to where he'd parked his truck. The memory of the tears clouding Laura's eyes twisted his gut. On the drive back to his office, he chastised himself and tried to think of a way to make things right with her.

****

Laura locked the back door to her office. She walked the short distance to the rear of the bookstore, inserted the key into the apartment's entrance, and, with quiet determination, climbed the stairs. The last thing she desired was for either her aunt or Maudie to know she was home.

Walking straight to the bedroom, she sagged onto the bed like a flower that had wilted from too much sun. She pulled the pillow over her face, trying to dismiss the sight of the white rose and the mayor's leering grin as he'd used the knife to strip the thorns from the long stem.

As far as she was concerned, Shipley was a fat, pompous pervert.

She was furious. Furious at Bryan for his oafishness, at Benjamin because he gave her the creeps, at the mayor because she suspected he was the anonymous admirer leaving the white roses, and especially angry at herself for the way she had acted toward Bryan. She wanted to scream. When she'd stopped complaining to herself, exasperation rolled over her. Stripping out of her clothes, she donned an oversized T-shirt and, with a mutter of disgust, walked to the kitchen, opened the freezer, grabbed the carton of chocolate ice cream, and went to sit on the sun porch. Whatever articles she had planned to write could wait until later.

Lord, she was embarrassed, and she owed Bryan an apology.

Chapter Twenty-Five

Mitch punched the alarm. His gaze traced to the numbers on the clock's face. He rolled out of bed, stretched, and yawned as he headed for the shower. Standing under the steaming spray, he did a mental count of how many weeks he'd worked without a holiday. He wasn't complaining about the fifteen-hour days and always being on call seven days a week. One sheriff, one deputy, one secretary to man the office. Sheriff Gilman had taken a three-month leave of absence. A person needed time for pleasure and relaxation...a do-nothing day...and his body and mental attitude were talking to him.

With a towel wrapped around his waist, he stood at the kitchen window and looked out. The town was waking up. Saturday, and businesses were in full swing. Laura's campaign to open the doors of Cole Harbor seemed to be working. Vehicles lined the sidewalk along Front Street, filling all available parking spaces.

Laura. Beautiful, compelling blue eyes, and no one had a claim on her. If he allowed his mind to drift in that direction, she was his only regret for not remaining in Cole Harbor. There was an unspoken attraction between them. He knew she felt it as much as he did. Pondering the talk they'd had several weeks back, both had admitted there was no room in their lives for love. He closed his eyes and allowed his wife's image to fill his mind. He gripped the edges of the sink. His body responded with an aching need that had remained unfulfilled since the day he'd buried her. He turned and walked back to the shower, this time to stand under a steady stream of cold water.

He was Texas born, and Texas was where he belonged. Under different circumstances, he would have given Bryan Cole plenty of competition where Laura was concerned.

He rubbed the towel briskly across his body and was reaching for his uniform when his cell phone rang. He picked up the phone from the nightstand. A smile crinkled his eyes when he spied the caller ID.

"G' morning, Friday."

"Aunt Philly's making waffles. How about coming for breakfast? We'll need hearty fortification to see us through while we're looking for evidence at the park."

"Give me ten minutes."

During the meal, Phyllis bemoaned her disappointment that the Friday night séance was a bust. "We followed the same procedure as the first one we performed, and not one spirit visited. I just don't know what we did wrong. Maybe it's because you didn't attend, Laura."

"That's quite all right, Aunt Philly. I've had my fill of dead people following me around." She gathered the plates and set them in the sink. "I'm ready if you are, Mitch."

She kissed her aunt on the cheek. "I don't need a crystal ball to predict you'll have a busy day with all the tourists in town. We'll order dinner in."

She grabbed two bottles of water, sandwiches, and candy bars from the refrigerator and zipped them inside a small backpack hanging from one of the dining chairs. She smiled at Mitch. "Never hurts to be prepared."

"I'm impressed." He grabbed the olive drab bag and followed her downstairs and out to the patrol car.

Once settled inside, she said, "I have an embarrassing confession." Without great detail, she explained about her miserable lunch with Bryan and the encounter with the mayor. "I hope today is Bryan's day off. I'm not up to seeing him. As for the mayor, I'm still certain he's the one leaving the white roses. The question is—why?"

Mitch put the car in gear. He studied her for a second. "No need to worry about bumping into Bryan. I have it on good authority that he's attending a weekend seminar in Bangor. Something about first-responder recertification."

Laura stole a sidelong look at Mitch's lighthearted expression. "I did a story once on first-responders. They go through rigorous training."

"Yep. Bryan's up to the challenge. Anyhow, Ranger Dorsey has agreed to drive us to the campsite where Daisy Fuller and her friends pitched their tent. About Shipley. You're a beautiful woman. Chalk it up to him being a secret admirer. Unless it gets out of hand, I think he's harmless." Mitch laughed. "I wouldn't want to be in his shoes if Martha catches him."

Laura also laughed.

He watched the worried frown crinkling Laura's forehead relax. "Friday…give Bryan a chance. He's a steady guy. I happen to know he's crazy about you."

"I don't know, Mitch. He's nice enough, it's just that I'm not ready to be involved with anyone. There are things I want to do with Aunt Philly—like travel. For years I put my job and the next assignment ahead of everyone important, including my mother. You have no idea how much I regret not spending more time with her. I don't intend to make that same mistake with my aunt. Bryan doesn't seem to understand that I don't want a relationship. Besides, he thinks you're his competition. Which is ridiculous—right?"

It was a rhetorical question. Mitch could see the debate in her expression. He kept the answer to himself. "You set the pace on how slow or fast you want to proceed with the friendship. He'll understand."

Mitch drove through the large entrance and pointed the car toward the visitor's center, where he parked. Laura grabbed the backpack, unzipped a pocket, and removed her camera, placing the strap around her neck.

When he opened the car's trunk, he said, "Here's a small gift for you."

A puzzled look on her face, Laura accepted the two red-and-white rods. "What are they?"

He pushed the release button to telescope the poles to their length. "Trekking poles, to help stabilize you over the rough terrain, and to ease the strain on your leg."

The look she gave him as she placed the straps around her wrists was reward enough. Before the moment blossomed into awkwardness, Ranger Jane Dorsey approached. She smiled at Laura. "Hey, nice sticks." She smacked her hands together and beckoned. "Ready if you are. The 4x4 is this way."

Mitch reached to adjust his walkie-talkie. "Ranger Dorsey, what channel are you on?"

"We're always on nine. If you find yourself in

trouble, every ranger in the park is on the same channel. Smart. Most people tend to forget the cell phone reception up here is slim to none."

During the ride, Dorsey pointed out different points of interest while Laura snapped pictures. At the campsite, the ranger said, "As you can see, Blackwater is fairly remote. We get a few campers who like the semi-roughing-it experience." She pointed to the bathroom designed to resemble a log cabin. "Two composting toilets. No showers. Unless they swapped out sites for some reason, Daisy Fuller and her friends were there. Spot number thirteen. As you can see, it backs up to the forested area and is a distance from the bathroom."

Mitch merely nodded at her explanation. "Give us a layout of the area, Ranger Dorsey."

She pointed. "All of the trails are rustic. There are a few boardwalk areas, but most are covered with leaves. Every trail loops into each other, and all are visibly marked with a number and arrows, so campers don't have to guess which path leads back to their campsite, or the visitor's center, the beach area, and even to the higher elevations for the veteran hikers."

Laura and the ranger followed Mitch to the vacant area. He used the toe of his boot to sift through fallen leaves and dirt. "How likely is it for someone to get lost?"

Dorsey thought for a moment. "I'm not saying getting lost wouldn't happen, but the trails are marked exceptionally well." She shrugged. "Wandering off in the dark without a flashlight adds to the possibility. Even though we don't allow alcohol or drugs in the park, unless we searched every vehicle, people can slip it in. If Daisy Fuller was inebriated, and wandered off without a flashlight, then, yeah, she could have easily gotten off the trail and gotten lost. Conditions for the night she disappeared would have aided in losing her way. Don't forget it was storming, and then fog set in. Thing is, if she'd hunkered down and stayed put until daylight, she'd have found her way back to her friends." She shook her head in disgust. "Amateurs."

Mitch thanked the ranger for her help. He glanced at his watch. Nine a.m. "Unless you get a distress call, don't worry about us."

Dorsey climbed into the off-road vehicle and turned the key. "Good luck. Hope you find what you're looking for." She waved and drove off.

"All right. Let's look at the facts, Friday. We have a group who admitted they're dopers. If the tent was backed up to this wooded area, it's possible Daisy was stoned enough to lose her bearings and went tromping through the weeds instead of heading in that direction toward the restroom." He pointed. "Let's take the trail that parallels where the rear of the tent should have faced, and see where it leads us."

Laura nodded. She lifted the trekking poles. "Lead the way."

"We've got all day. You stroll on the trail. I'll go through the brush to see if I can spot where Daisy may have walked. Don't push beyond your comfort level. If your leg gets tired, tell me."

After a mile, a bench looked inviting. Laura sat, stretching her leg.

Mitch waded out of the thick brush to join Laura. "How is it?"

"The trekking poles really work. My leg is tired,

but not as much as I'd expected. I guess you're not having much luck with spotting evidence, huh?"

Mitch slapped his hand against his thigh. "This is damned frustrating. Not even a broken twig, or a piece of torn clothing."

They sat, neither of them speaking. Mitch lifted a finger to his lips to signal quiet as he pointed. Laura followed the angle of his arm. She lifted her camera and clicked. A doe with a fawn stood in the high brush. Laura offered Mitch a wide-eyed grin. "It's beautiful here. Nothing like New York, where the only animals you see are the pampered pets at the end of a leash or police horses and carriage horses."

"Do you ever think of returning to your old job?"

She turned toward him and sighed. "Once in a while, part of me gets an itch for the limelight. A small part. The rest of me likes my new life. It'd take a mighty big offer, with lots of money behind it, to entice me back to overpriced restaurants, shoulder-to-shoulder crowded sidewalks, noxious fumes, yelling, rudeness."

She lifted the camera again and adjusted the zoom lens.

"Another deer?"

"Mmm, no. How far are we from where the park property ends and the residential area begins?"

"I'm not quite sure. Why?"

She removed the camera strap from around her neck and offered it to Mitch. She showed him how to look through the display screen. "I see a rooftop." She pointed to a button. "This controls the zoom."

Mitch moved the camera around until he spotted the barest view of a rusted metal roof. He zoomed in. "It's off the path, and the going could get tough…"

She interrupted his sentence, slipped her hands through the pole straps, and, gritting her teeth, stood. "I'm okay. Let's go."

Wild blackberry bushes tore at their trouser legs. Mitch watched the ground as he walked. After a half hour, he held up his hand as a signal to halt. He stooped down and pointed. "Get a shot of this before I pick it up." He reached in his front pants pocket and removed a pocket knife and a plastic evidence bag.

Laura focused from three different angles. Mitch used the tip of his pocket knife to brush the leaves away and then to lift the blue rubber stub. He held it up. "What is it?"

Laura snapped more shots before he dropped it into the bag. "May I?"

She scrutinized the piece of rubber. "I'm not completely certain, but this looks like a toe post from a flip-flop."

A grin spread across Mitch's face. "Good work, Friday. Sybella Dauzat said the victim was wearing flip-flops. If the shoes broke, that accounts for the cuts on the bottoms of her feet, and wading through this thick brush explains the multiple scratches on her legs."

"Maybe she spotted the rooftop and hoped to seek shelter from the storm. I wonder who lives there?"

"We'll soon find out."

The distance was farther than it looked through the camera lens. The park's trail led away from the area Mitch and Laura traversed. After an hour of stepping over fallen logs, and wading through bushes that threatened to trap and hold them captive, Mitch and Laura stood at the edge of the woods and looked down at a small cabin. An old wooden boat with peeling blue and white paint lay keel up on two rickety sawhorses. The yard was littered with rusting appliances, car tires, and a bicycle frame. Other than junk and weeds, the place appeared abandoned.

Mitch removed the backpack and unzipped it. He pulled out both bottles of water and handed one to Laura. He watched her drink deep and then stand as if trying to catch her breath. "How's the leg?"

When she didn't answer, he said, "Your eyes tell me all I need to know. Let's head back."

"No, Mitch. Give me a few minutes and I'll be okay. The trekking poles help more than you'll ever know. We've come this far. Besides, I want to know who lives in that cabin."

"Tell you what. You stay put. Rest your leg. Your aunt said there were several abandoned cabins up here. This could be one. If it's occupied, let me check it out first. I'll signal if it's safe. Deal?"

He read the relief in her expression. She drew in a long breath and released it. "Deal."

****

The minute Mitch turned toward the dilapidated structure, Laura allowed her shoulders to sag. She bit her lip against the throbbing white-hot pain that seemed to permeate her entire right side. Thankful for the support, she allowed the trekking poles to bear the brunt of her weight. She watched Mitch as he descended the slope and approached the cabin with caution. One hand on his service revolver, he walked to a window and stood on tiptoes to peer inside. From a distance, he fit the visual image of a dangerous cowboy. Mesmerized, she caught herself staring at him.

A stab of anxiety pierced Laura when he

disappeared around the front of the house. She clenched her hands around the poles. The air suddenly felt heavy. Heavy and damp and full of promise for rain. The weather, the pain—this entire situation made her edgy. She drew a deep, fortifying breath and reminded herself that she was fine, and that Mitch knew how to take care of himself.

Relief washed over her when she heard him call her name, and spotted him climbing up the hill toward her.

"Anything?"

"Nope. Place looks like it's been abandoned for years. No sign of any recent activity. In fact, all the floorboards have either rotted away or someone pulled them up." He touched her on the arm. "How're you holding up?"

"Great. Where to from here?"

"I see a trail marker. We'll head toward it and hope it leads us to Ocean Path, and then on to the beach area at Thunder Hole. I'd like to get a look around the area and the cavern."

"You lead. I'll follow."

"Friday, I can call and have Ranger Dorsey come get you."

She didn't speak right away. She was tired, but in a different sort of way. This was physical fatigue, unlike being exhausted after too many sleepless nights from battered emotions. She liked this kind of tired better. She was pushing her body and knew she'd pay the consequences tonight and maybe tomorrow.

He reached over and squeezed her shoulder. After a moment, she touched his hand. "Thanks for caring, Mitch."

He gave a nod and led the way up the steep incline. To take her mind off the ache, she said, "Have you created a profile of the killer?"

She could almost see the muscles rippling through the back of his tan uniform shirt, and the way his glutes tightened as he strained up the incline fluttered her insides. She reminded herself he was leaving. He was running for sheriff in El Paso, and he needed to exact restitution on the men who had harmed his family. This thought solidified her resolve to remain detached emotionally. His voice interrupted her meandering thoughts.

"We know his favorite kill method is to break the victim's neck. He's not a flashy killer or a serial killer, yet he certainly gets the job done. With the recent discovery of the animals, all with cervical fractures, this indicates our perp's desire for taking lives is most likely increasing.

"There was no evidence of sexual assault. This could mean the crime itself gives him orgasmic gratification, or he gets caught in a megalomaniacal fantasy which possibly means that if he was abused as a child, he's punishing the person who harmed him, most likely a female relative. He is strategic and canny, intelligent and confident, but he might struggle with reacting appropriately to other people's emotion-driven social cues.

"The one thing I don't want to happen is for the trail to grow cold. Every lawman knows the more time that passes, the more difficult it becomes to find a suspect. Also, is there a connection between Lynnette Braswell and Daisy Fuller?"

Behind his back, Laura frowned. "Then this person

could be a sociopath, living right under our noses, and we'd never know it."

Mitch grunted his response. "Exactly."

She huffed as she spoke. "I guess every case is like a jigsaw puzzle. It's a matter of making all the pieces fit together to solve the crime."

He darted a quick glance over his shoulder. "Not altogether different from what a good investigative reporter does."

Laura smiled through gritted teeth. She tried not to think about the sweat pooling under her arms or trickling between her breasts. Then, one moment she was using the poles as stability and the next moment the tip of one of the rods slipped on a rock and her foot slid out from under her. She teetered precariously before she grimly fell forward. She squealed as she reached for a handful of bushes and dirt to keep from sliding backwards.

Chapter Twenty-Six

Laura was aware of Mitch calling her name. A buzzing roared in her ears, and sparklers burst in front of her eyes. She blinked and took a moment to regain her senses. The metallic taste of blood filled her mouth where she had bitten her bottom lip. "Oh, damn."

Mitch came crashing down in front of her. Before she realized he'd grabbed her, she was sitting next to him. Her chest heaved. She was hot. Her legs trembled. He removed a bottle of water from the backpack and wet his handkerchief to wipe the blood from her lips and chin. He handed her the bottle. "Here, swish some around and spit it out so I can see if you need stitches."

The water was tepid. She did as instructed. He gently folded her bottom lip down. "You'll need some ice to reduce the swelling, and to be on the safe side, let's get you to a doctor."

She ran a hand through her short-cropped hair. "I must look a total mess."

He merely grinned. "I haven't seen a girl with a fat lip and dirt on the tip of her nose and cheek in a while. Kinda cute."

She offered him a lopsided smirk. "You're a real pal."

After another moment she brought the water bottle back up and drank a long, deep swallow. "What time is it?"

"A little past noon."

"Where are we?"

"We're about a hundred yards from the marked trail. Can you stand?"

He placed his arms around her to help her upright. She took a step, only to have her right leg fold beneath her. "Stay put while I check the trail number."

Something scuffled in the underbrush not far away. Her attention snapped into gear. Nothing appeared. It was broad daylight and she was jumping at shadows. She thought about how Daisy Fuller must have felt wandering around at night…sopping wet…lost.

Mitch stood before her, holding out his hands. "Ranger Dorsey is on her way."

****

Mitch knelt down and lifted Laura in his arms. He stilled with the strange feeling her simple contact stirred within him. He hadn't been touched intimately by a female since his wife died.

Laura nestled against him. Her supple body invited thoughts he hadn't entertained in a long time. Like how much he missed spending the night in a soft bed with a woman he could devote hours to pleasuring. Warnings inside his head reminded him that she needed a man who wasn't as cold and dead inside as he was.

He hadn't realized until this moment how much he'd missed that connection with a woman. The sound of the four-wheeler approaching jerked his mind back on track. He stepped out of the brush and onto the trail, and set Laura on her feet.

"So what are we going to do now?"

He turned his thoughts inward to shake away those feelings and to focus on what was important. "You need a doctor. We'll call it a day and return to town."

He lifted his hand and waved as Ranger Dorsey pulled to a stop. She handed Laura a small package. "I brought the ice pack Mitch requested for your lip. Looks like a whale of a bruise is forming on your cheek, too."

Laura groaned. "Great. Just great. Every person I see will ask what doorknob I ran into, or some such idiotic remark."

As soon as Mitch had Laura settled in the front seat, Dorsey put the vehicle in gear. "Sorry about your fall, Ms. Friday."

"Yeah, it's a bummer. I hate cutting the day short, but Mitch insists I get medical attention."

Keeping her eyes on the trail, the ranger said, "My shift ends in about twenty minutes. I'd planned to do a bit of shopping in town, and I'd be happy to drive you to the doctor."

Laura didn't answer at first. Shifting around to look at Mitch, an aching pain bit her hard in the hip. "Mitch, as much as I'd like to explore the beach and cavern with you, it's not going to happen today. Besides, you said the more time an investigation takes, the colder the evidence gets. I won't have you wasting any more time on me when it can be better spent searching for more clues."

Mitch watched her with an assessing gaze. He nodded, accepting her offer with mixed feelings. "Ranger Dorsey, how far to the beach area?"

She pointed as she braked to a stop. Then she glanced at her watch. "We're at low tide. High tide at four fifty-four p.m. Don't linger, Deputy. There's a storm brewing, which means the tide will roll in fast.

Predictions are for eighteen feet."

Mitch stepped out of the vehicle. He thanked Ranger Dorsey for driving Laura to town, then lifted his hand in a wave. "I'll check on you later, Laura."

"Be careful, Mitch."

He stared as the 4x4 disappeared, then followed the short path to the coastline area. For several moments, he stood taking in the serene beauty of gentle waves lapping against the pebble-strewn beach and, in the distance, colorful sails of bobbing boats. At the bottom step his boots sank into the sand. He walked along the pebbly shore area in a grid pattern, scouring the sand and clumps of seaweed for any unusual objects, and when the beach ended he climbed atop a craggy table of rocks. Careful not to slip and fall, he searched crevices and found nothing of importance. He continued along the granite ledges until he reached the sheer stone walls of Thunder Hole and could go no further.

Standing with hands on hips, frustration rode him like the wild waves washing in and out of the cavern and sending bursts of foamy spray skyward. Whoever killed Daisy Fuller knew the area. He had to agree with Bryan Cole's assumption that the killer's intention was to dump her body in the ocean and let the predators destroy the evidence. Except the waves had turned the tides on him.

A small ball of fire sparked in front of him, followed by a vibrating boom of thunder. The electrified air caused the hairs on his arms to stand on end. He looked at the leaden sky. It was time to heed Ranger Dorsey's warning. With a storm approaching and the way the waves were kicking up, he needed to make tracks to higher ground.

He raced along the surface of uneven rocks. At the rate the tide was rolling in, if he didn't get across the beach area soon, he'd have to risk battling the current in order to swim to safety.

A splat of rain hit his shoulder. The breath was sucked from his lungs when an unexpectedly large wave crashed over him. His boots slipped on the boulders' wet surface. He scrambled to maintain his balance, and fell to one knee. Another wave rushed at him. He dug his fingers into small crevices and held tight. The force of the breaking surf felt as if it were a beast trying to swallow him. Unable to regain his balance, he called on the strength in his arms and legs to pull himself across the slippery stone.

A thundering roar warned him that another cascade of water was approaching. The knees of his pants ripped as he scrambled to the rocky rim. What had been an easy climb thirty minutes ago had become a life-and-death struggle. The wave washed him off the ledge and dragged him into the frigid water. Beneath the roiling surf, he held his breath, worrying he might be caught in a riptide. At the moment he feared the air had run out, his lungs near exploding, a wave lifted him up and spit him out. Gasping for air, he managed to stand. Running through waist-deep water was no easy task. He moved his arms back and forth in a swimming motion to help propel himself forward. The tide continued to rise; it reached his chest now.

He struggled. The steps to safety were within fingertip reach. He leaned forward and stretched. Another wave crested, grabbed hold, and sucked him under. His boots and service gear weighed him down.

He fought until he surfaced. Salt burned his eyes.

He sucked in large gulps of air and then heard his name.

"Mitch...Deputy Carter...Here."

The water had reached his chin and was inching toward his nose. He swirled around to see Ranger Klopper standing with a life ring tied to the end of a rope.

"Grab hold."

Mitch prayed the current wouldn't sweep the lifeline out of his reach. Watching the white ring sail through the air, he crouched on his knees and used the force of the water to surge his body upward as he jumped—and landed with a splash, face down in the briny sea. His last thought was how glad he was that Laura wasn't with him.

And then he was skimming through the water, his right arm hooked through the ring. Strong hands pulled him to safety.

Mitch coughed and gasped his thanks. "How did you know I was here?"

"Ranger Dorsey reported that you had come to the area to do some investigating. I got worried when you didn't answer your walkie-talkie. Sure hoped you weren't in trouble but thought I'd better check."

Mitch accepted the blanket the ranger handed him, and wrapped it around his shivering body. "You saved my bacon, Ranger. I won't forget it."

Chapter Twenty-Seven

Laura labored up the stairs. The apartment was quiet. That worked for her. She wasn't in the mood for conversation. She carried the camera case and trekking poles to her bedroom and dropped everything on the floor, then turned to look in the mirror and stood there not believing the course of the day's events. The laugh that escaped her came out as a disgusted snort.

Glad to be home and thankful no stitches were needed to close the inside of her lip, Laura touched her tender cheek, which was rapidly developing into a black eye, and then peeled off her clothes. Aunt Philly would understand if she didn't watch television with her tonight. A soak in a hot shower and a glass of wine cured many ills when all else failed.

In the kitchen, she grabbed a bottle of merlot from the cabinet and poured a glass, then headed back to the bedroom to finish undressing, cranked up the hot and cold knobs, and settled on the shower seat, her legs stretched forward and her head resting against the tiled wall.

Steamy water gushed over her battered body as she sipped, grimacing when the wine stung the cut inside her lip. The alcohol would have to wait for another night. She closed her eyes and allowed the last vestiges of stress to drain away.

She stepped from the shower and snagged a towel

to wrap around her body, tucking the corners in at her breasts, then bit back a moan from the pain in her hip. She gritted her teeth to walk without a limp to the bed. Ahh, the bed. It crooned her name. What she needed at this moment was a pain pill. She grabbed a clean baggy T-shirt, pulled it over her head, and hobbled to the kitchen, Ken Musuyo's scowl and words still fresh in her mind. *If you don't allow your hip to heal, I can guarantee another surgery in your future, and this time the outcome might not be as successful as the first.*

After a feast of potato chips, peanut butter slathered on graham crackers, a large glass of cola, and three scoops of chocolate ice cream, she sighed. There was nothing like a healthy dose of junk food to bolster a girl's fortitude.

She fell back on the bed and used a pillow to support her bad leg, grabbed a romance novel from the bedside table, and opened it to the marked spot. Her eyes had a mind of their own, and drifted shut.

The cell phone vibrated and hummed against the nightstand. Turning on her side and wrapping her arms around a pillow, she let the message go to voicemail.

****

A week later, Bryan Cole strolled into the newspaper office holding a vase filled with a variety of colorful flowers. Laura closed the top to her computer. She greeted him with a smile and extended a hand, offering him a chair. He set the container in front of her. "Peace offering."

She lifted the flowers to her nose and sniffed. "It's me who should apologize to you for spoiling the picnic lunch at the gazebo. I could offer you a thousand reasons for my rude behavior, and yet none of them can excuse the way I acted."

She liked the way his eyes crinkled at the corners when he smiled. "You didn't seem fond of roses, white ones, especially. So I chose wildflowers. These are from my garden. Hope we can be friends."

Friends. His voice reverberated through her with a lazy sensuality. Perhaps she had been too quick in her judgment of him. "The flowers are lovely."

An awkward moment of silence passed as if each of them were searching for something to say. It was Bryan who interrupted the moment. "How does owning your own newspaper in a small town compare to being a big city reporter?"

Laura realized with a start that with recent events, she hadn't given much thought to her life in New York. She stared at Bryan, recalling Mitch's words about giving the friendship a chance to grow but to go at her own pace.

Bryan chuckled. "If it takes this long to compare your city life to this, you must be trying hard to be tactful."

"Not at all...but it's not what I expected. It's beautiful."

He looked at her, meeting her gaze. "And deadly boring."

She gave a shout of laughter. "Is it, really? You mean after all that's happened since I arrived?"

"So, tell me." His voice was soft and low. "What do you miss about being an investigative reporter consistently appearing on the nightly news?"

The moment of camaraderie shattered as her memories flooded back. In an instant, she was sitting on the sidewalk, soaked in blood, cradling Jolly's head in her lap.

"It was my life for ten years. Every time a drug ring was busted up, or a serial rapist put behind bars, it made me feel needed, as if I were helping keep the streets clean. Plus, the adrenalin rush of danger and excitement becomes addictive."

Bryan shrugged his shoulders and smiled. "You seem to have brought some of the big city drama with you. Dead bodies popping up all over the place."

Laura shuffled the papers on her desk. She studied him for a moment, the teasing glimmer in his eyes fading.

"I've done it again, haven't I?"

"What?"

"Insulted you." He stood and paced around in a circle as if looking for something he had lost. He huffed out a breath. "I'm not usually a bumbling idiot. It seems whenever I'm around you, it's open mouth, insert foot. I...I..."

She stared at the papers in her hand. Swallowed. A little part of her liked having this effect on him. Before she could get the words out of her mouth, the chime over the door pealed, and Mitch walked in.

Laura watched Bryan quickly mask his disappointment. Apparently, he still thought of Mitch as competition. Well, all that romantic love crap be damned.

Mitch and Bryan shook hands. After the pleasantries were over, Mitch gave Laura a half smile. There was no humor in his eyes. "Three calls this morning, each one to report a missing dog, and all of the dogs were old, so it would make them easy to catch."

Laura's eyes widened. She placed a hand to her cheek. "You don't think he's struck again?"

"That's my first thought." Mitch cut his attention to Bryan. "What time does Amy Osmond usually get to work?"

"Always early. Around seven-thirty. Good worker. Visitors and staff love her. Why?"

"She takes a shortcut from her house to the edge of the forest until she gets to a marked trail in the park. Are there any employees who live in town that might give her a ride?"

"I'm not in charge of the civilian workers. Laura, okay to use your phone?"

She nodded. "What's happened, Mitch?"

He blew out a breath. "Might not be anything. I stopped by the Silly Lobster for dinner, and Amy's mother asked to speak to me in private. She didn't want anyone to hear her concern that a couple of times Amy was certain someone was in the woods watching her. At one point, she thought she was being followed. She even called out. When no one answered, Amy chalked it up as a deer rustling the bushes. Naturally, her mother is concerned, and so am I."

Bryan pursed his lips as he disconnected the call. "All the locals work different part-time shifts."

"I'd take it as a personal favor if you changed her hours…maybe ten to two. That way anyone who lives along the rim is already at work and still at work when Amy leaves for home."

Icy fingers shuddered down Laura's spine. "You've got a suspect in mind—someone who lives near the park?"

Mitch's voice sounded tired. "I wish I did. This is

merely a precaution." He looked at Bryan. "My gut tells me the missing dogs are buried in the park. Notify your rangers to keep an eye out for any freshly disturbed earth."

Bryan straightened to his full height. "With thousands of acres, that's a big request, but anything to catch this pissah, all you need do is ask." He smiled at Laura. "Duty calls. Enjoy the flowers."

She tilted her head and thanked him again for the bouquet.

Before the ranger walked out the door, Mitch said, "Hey, Bryan, don't you own a small sloop sailboat?"

"Ayuh. You want to go out sometime?"

Mitch chuckled and shook his head. "I'm a landlubber, like to see what's under my feet. Give me a horse and saddle any day over a boat and water." He winked at Laura. "Actually, I was thinking you might invite Friday to go sailing. It's not nearly as strenuous as hiking trails. Whadda you say, Friday?"

A wobbly smile cut across Laura's face. "Well—" Damn Mitch Carter for putting her on the spot. The expectant look in Bryan's eyes reminded her of a little boy waiting to hear if he'd won a prize. Hell. "Sure. What about Saturday morning, at nine? This time, I'll pack the lunch."

"I'm on call the entire weekend. Monday?"

She was her own boss and could set her own hours, yet she didn't want to get into the habit of allowing pleasure to interfere with work. "Just this once, I'll take a work day off."

The expectant frown on Bryan's face softened into a smile. "My boat's name is *Not for Sail*. She's red with white trim. Slip number five."

He waved and walked out the door.

Laura scowled at Mitch. "You put me at a distinct disadvantage. How could I possibly say no?"

Mitch shrugged, spreading his hands wide. "By the looks the two of you wore when I walked in, it was obvious I had disturbed an *about to happen* important moment. I'm just makin' amends."

Not wishing to pursue the romance subject, Laura switched gears. "Seriously, Mitch. Do you have any leads on who killed Daisy Fuller?"

"Nothing. Her body was squeaky clean. No DNA, not a hair or a fiber. But he's here, and he'll mess up. When he does, I'll nail the jack-off."

"Shall I write an article about the missing pets?"

"Yep, and if the owners have pictures, post 'em." He rattled off the list of names.

"By the way, care for a bit of gossip?"

He narrowed his eyes. "Let me guess—Louise."

"Told Aunt Philly you threatened to fire her, and with great embellishment said she told you a thing or two."

He offered a sardonic smile. "Louise is a real prize. Embellishment or not, I meant every word I said."

Laura hesitated. "Are you still planning to run for sheriff in El Paso?"

He waited a heartbeat, then pivoted on his heel. "Yes."

She watched as he disappeared through the door.

Chapter Twenty-Eight

Mitch spent the rest of the day knocking on doors and asking questions of the various residents along Cole Drive. No one had seen or heard anything out of the ordinary the night of Daisy Fuller's murder. He garnered the same responses from those who lived along Atlantic Avenue. Everyone expressed concern for their own safety, some more vocally than others.

He drove to the highest point of Lighthouse Road. Except for the Osmond family, and a few of the fisher families, the remaining structures were abandoned. It wasn't until he headed back to town that he noticed a dirt road made nearly invisible by the overgrowth of trees. He turned onto the narrow lane and followed it to a rundown dwelling. An aging beauty with a sweeping front porch. Whoever resided here took little pride in the property's upkeep.

Mitch exited the patrol car. The hairs on the back of his neck prickled. Taking precaution, he used his door as a shield. "Hello, the house."

No answer.

He called again. "Deputy Sheriff Mitch Carter. Anybody home?"

He scanned each window fronting the house and saw no sign of anyone peering out at him. Feeling relatively safe, he approached and walked up the steps. He rapped on the door and called out once again, identifying himself.

Stepping to a window, he placed his hands on either side of his face and peered inside. The interior showed signs of being lived in. One large space consisting of kitchen, eating area, and living room. A shirt draped over a dining chair. Pots sitting on a drain board. From what he could see, the inside was neat and orderly.

As he turned to leave, he felt as if he had stepped into a painting and was part of the scenery. The blue-hued panoramic vista of the bay was beyond description. He doubted if an artist could capture the beauty and bring it alive on canvas.

Reminding himself he was here to work, he walked down the steps and around the side of the dwelling. A greenhouse drew his attention. Inside, long wooden planks atop cinderblocks formed neat rows of potted plants, lined the length and width of the structure, with pruning shears, plastic gloves, fertilizer, sacks of peat and potting soil all visible.

He didn't recall seeing a mailbox as he entered the drive, which wasn't unusual. Most people received their mail at the Cole Harbor Post Office. At the rear of the house, a footpath led from the yard up an incline. Mitch followed it. He wasn't surprised when he spotted a trail marker. The path definitely led to the national park's interior.

Glancing around, he did a mental calculation of how far this dwelling was from the abandoned structure he and Laura had investigated a few days ago. An easy mile along the paved road. He searched for signs of a path that ran along this property to join the other. If there was one, it wasn't visible in the day's fading light.

He checked his watch. He didn't want to get caught off guard should the owner return and find his patrol car. His cop instinct warned this property belonged to Benjamin Noone. Mitch mentally questioned if Noone fit the profile of a murderer.

In the evening's quiet dusk, a roaring sound caught his attention…the crash of waves spewing through a blow hole. Sprinting along the park's path, he estimated he was no more than a half mile from the scenic area where, just two days ago, the tide had almost swept him out to sea.

Mitch turned and jogged back to the trail and skittered down the path to the yard. He stooped to look beneath the house. Uncertain of what he was searching for, he used his cell phone to take pictures. What was it he was missing? An elusive detail teased his mind. He couldn't quite call the information forward.

Placing his hands on his hips, the yard was much the way Amy Osmond had described it: weedy, littered with bits and pieces of lawnmower parts, a wheelbarrow. He checked for signs of freshly dug dirt that resembled small graves. Nothing.

Mitch returned to the porch. He jammed a business card between the door and the frame. Maybe Benjamin Noone was exactly who he was. An eccentric loner who enjoyed gardening.

****

Weary from helping string lights and getting the town ready for its annual Fourth of July bash, Benjamin's headache increased when he removed the card from the doorjamb and read Deputy Sheriff Mitchell Carter's name. Anxiety race through him like a dose of medicine attacking his bowels. His afternoon sandwich roiled up his throat, and he gagged. Whimpers echoed in his ears as he reached for the key lying inside a rusted birdcage.

His hand trembled as he unlocked the weathered front door, flung it wide, and stumbled inside. Slamming it shut, he collapsed to the floor, curling into a ball, his knees drawn to his stomach. He closed his eyes and allowed the black tomb of darkness to engulf him.

"Bennie, that deputy sheriff was here. What should I do?"

Only the thrumming inside his head answered.

He pleaded, "Where are you when I need you?" Benjamin balled his fist and slammed the floor. "Sniveling bastard! I hope you burn in hell."

Shadows gathered at the fringes of his mind.

A voice mocked him. *You always were the weaker twin. Stop whining. Deputy...smeputy. He's got nothing on you.*

Snickering. Whose? Benjamin wasn't certain who made the sound.

I know what will make you feel better.

"What?"

This time his mind filled with teasing laughter. *A...woman. Bennie needs a woman.*

Benjamin placed his hands over his ears and pressed. "How many times do I have to tell you...I am...not...you?"

He was tired. So very tired. His eyes closed of their own free will.

He dreamed of fire. He was tied to his bed, a gag in his mouth. Daisy Fuller laughed as she poured gasoline over his body and lit a match. Flames licked up his legs.

Lynnette Braswell watched. She clapped her hands in glee and danced a little jig. In unison the girls taunted— *Don't scream, Benjamin. Don't ever scream.*

The fire savored his flesh, starting at the tips of his toes and slithering up to his elbows. He choked on the odor of burning hair. The flames singed his eyebrows, and stole inside his nostrils. His brain melted, and he felt all the little cells of gray matter leaking out his ears.

Water. Water. He needed water to cool the burning inside his scalded body.

Inching his eyes open, he found the smoke had cleared. There was no fire. He was on the floor in his little crackerbox cottage.

He lifted his hand and looked at it. *Not my hand*, his mind whispered. He felt his hair, patted it, and pulled a lock forward to examine.

Not my hair.

What was going on? He pushed to his hands and knees and crawled to the bathroom. His strength had left him. He used the toilet to pull himself upright, and looked into the mirror.

A hollow-eyed reflection stared at him. *Hello, Bennie. That was a terrible dream we had.*

Benjamin gripped the edges of the sink. His breaths came in heaves. "Go away. I'm…Benjamin."

And then there was screaming, uncontrollable screaming.

Shh..shh. Don't scream…We don't like screamin'.

His mouth was dry, his stomach churned, and his head pounded so hard he was certain it would burst. He turned on the tap and splashed cold water over his face. He bent closer, cupped his hands, and drank. Lifting his throbbing head was too much effort. He opened the medicine cabinet. His prescription bottle was empty. The refill date had expired. He counted out four aspirin and allowed them to melt in his mouth.

Only a few feet to the bedroom, and a few more feet to the bed. He turned toward the door, careful not to shuffle his feet. Each step vibrated like a tuning fork inside his brain. He sank to the mattress.

He lay facing the ceiling, his head on the pillow, an arm flung across his eyes. And though he whispered, the words seemed to echo off the walls. "I want to die and end this suffering."

Chapter Twenty-Nine

Phyllis tapped the newspaper with a loud thump. "This is absolutely frightful, Laura. Do these missing animals have anything to do with the ones found buried in the park?" She picked up her coffee cup. "The possibility of having a psycho running around loose in Cole Harbor gives me the willies."

Laura finished packing the picnic cooler. She understood her aunt's concern. "We live in a wacky world. Promise to keep the back doors locked. Until Mitch solves this case, it pays to take extra precaution."

She grabbed her tote bag and the small ice chest. "I can't believe how many art and food vendors are setting up for the weekend. Both bed-and-breakfasts are completely booked. Harmon Taylor said all of his charters for sightseeing cruises are filled. At least this type of news takes the edge off the murder."

Phyllis snorted her disgust. "Ayuh. Of course, Martha Shipley and the mayor are taking credit for your hard work."

"Don't sweat the small stuff, Aunt Philly. C'mon, walk with me."

Phyllis carried the cooler down the stairs. Laura followed her aunt through the storage area and into the bookstore's tea room. She spoke to Maudie, who commented on the news article about the missing pets. Laura made her way through the bookstore. Several patrons sat in the various reading sections. She scanned the faces of those she didn't know. Strangers. Every one a possible suspect.

At the entrance door, she took the small ice chest from her aunt. "I feel guilty. It's Monday. A work day."

"Good Godfrey, Laura. You're the boss. In fact, you're the only employee. The newspaper isn't going to fold around your ears if you take a day to enjoy yourself."

She kissed her aunt on the cheek, and Phyllis whispered, "Give Bryan a chance."

Outside, Laura drew a deep nasal breath. She resisted the urge to walk the short distance to her office. The town seemed far from perfect right now. There was something evil lurking here.

Last night she'd had that feeling, the creepy ice-slithering-down-her-spine feeling. It was the same sensation she'd experienced the night Lynnette Braswell's spirit had visited her. She closed her eyes. *Maybe Aunt Philly is right. I need a day to forget about murder and dead bodies.*

It was warm out, with the morning sun already beating down. Damn. She didn't want to go sailing. She really didn't. There was no sense arguing about it. She had agreed, and even packed a lunch. Deep down inside, she'd rather be with Mitch, helping with his investigation.

She was picking her way through the vendors' tents, mentally writing an article for the *Gazette*'s next edition. One minute she was up, the next minute she was sprawled on the ground. She hadn't given much thought to the treachery of tent ropes and the possibility of tripping over them.

Laura met his eyes, and he just stood there, mute, staring at her. She wondered briefly what he was seeing as he stared at her. Finally, she said, "Hi, Benjamin, would you mind helping me up?"

He shrugged, as if not overly concerned about her plight. His lack of enthusiasm annoyed her.

She struggled to her good knee, green from the grass staining her white pants, and then she felt a strong pair of hands lifting her. Benjamin held her at arms' length, frowning, studying her face. He studied her for a long moment and slowly his expression changed. His face, harsh before, softened just a little, and he let go of her.

Then, to her utter surprise, he reached out and ran his fingertips from the crown of her head and down her cheek to her shoulder. The touch made her nerves jump, and not in a good way. She placed a hand on his chest. "Um, you can let go, now."

He nodded, sighed heavily. "Pays to watch where you're walking."

"Laura…Laura." She turned to see Bryan sprinting toward her. "I saw you fall. Are you hurt?"

Benjamin had lowered both arms to his side. Laura thought she saw a flash of anger, but he masked it quickly.

She met Benjamin's eyes. "Thank you for your assistance."

He watched her face for a moment, as if waiting for her to say more. When she didn't, he nodded and walked away.

Bryan gathered the cooler and Laura's tote bag in one hand. He used the other to cup her elbow. She leaned into his strength.

"Can you make it to the marina, or would you rather cancel the trip?"

Although her leg ached, she kept it to herself. "I'm not hurt, just embarrassed."

He gave her arm a gentle squeeze. "According to this morning's forecast, the wind is perfect for sailing. No rain."

Guiding her down the dock, he stopped at slip five and stepped into a sleek, candy-apple-red sloop with a tall spar. The sun bounced off the all-white interior, and Laura pulled the sunglasses atop her head down to settle on the bridge of her nose.

Bryan held out both hands. "I've got you. Step on the gunwale, then onto the seat."

"Fair warning—I don't know jibbing from tacking or starboard from leeward. In fact, I'm not much of a sailor."

Bryan untied the ropes. "That's okay. I'll teach you." He pressed the starter, and the inboard motor purred to life. An expert sailor, he eased the boat out of the slip and into the channel. "Hold the tiller while I run up the sail."

She switched seats with him and held steady as he'd instructed. Lifting her face to catch the breeze, she experienced a sense of anxiety.

"Relax, Laura." Bryan took the wheel. "We'll use the auxiliary until you get used to being on the water. It won't take long for me to make a sailor out of you. Tell me, what do you like to do for fun?"

She thought for a moment. "I've never given the subject much thought. My entire life has been based around my work...the next assignment. That was my fun."

"What about now?"

Give Bryan a chance. Advice from both her aunt and Mitch. "Travel. In fact, Aunt Philly and I plan to do just that—a Mediterranean cruise in September, and though she doesn't know it yet, I think Hawaii sounds more inviting than spending a frigid winter in Maine."

"That sounds more like a destination than fun. After that, then what?"

She stifled a frown at the irritation his words evoked. "Then, one day at a time."

"What about settling down, having a family some day?"

A long silence followed. She shifted her gaze to the sparkling waters as she considered the best way to answer him. "Why, may I ask, are you so interested in my future?"

He blinked as if he hadn't expected her straightforwardness.

She decided to lay some basic ground rules. "Bryan, the reason I'm with you today is because Aunt Philly and Mitch think you're a nice guy. Plus, I was rude the last time you attempted to take me to lunch. Maybe the questions you ask are your way of making conversation, but to me it's more like interrogation. If we are to become friends, stop trying so hard. Here's what I'm not interested in: becoming a sailor, jibbing and tacking, deep-sea diving, cohabitation, settling down, or marriage."

She crossed her arms, ignoring the voice inside her head chastising her for being so blunt. Hadn't Mitch said to set the ground rules—to let Bryan know to go slow? Yeah, but Mitch didn't say to scare the hunky senior park ranger away, either.

****

Just sitting so close to Laura swung Bryan's world sideways. Behind those sunglasses her eyes were a pale blue that darkened to deep sapphire when she was annoyed, he knew. Intelligent eyes that judged him at every blink. And she should. Irritation mixed with admiration rolled off him in waves.

She pulled a sports visor out of her tote bag and tugged it on. She cocked her head and gave him an exaggerated sigh of impatience. He wasn't used to being countermanded by anyone. Mitch had warned him about Laura's leg and the possibility of a future surgery. He hadn't wanted to treat her like an invalid nor had he intended to imply she was to become a sailor. She had apparently done her homework and knew the agility required to man a sailboat. He'd grown up on the water. She hadn't. What came second nature to him might be a struggle for her.

Mitch had also warned him to go slow. Laura was a fiercely independent woman who had been forced to prove herself in a man's world. What was it Mitch had said—*she's like a wild filly who doesn't trust man. She needs gentling, and to do that you have to go slow. You'll have to earn her friendship, Bryan, or be willing to walk away.* And then he had added, *Some fillies are never tamed. They're gentled, but only tolerate man's presence.*

He hadn't completely understood Mitch's analogy comparing Laura to a wild horse until this very moment.

He saw the debate in her face. This woman took her word seriously. She had set the ground rules—go slow—allow the friendship to build—or get lost. His respect for her climbed several notches for that alone. The question remained—what did he want from her: tolerance, or friendship, or something more?

Tension compressed the air between them, forcing Bryan's attention away from her steady gaze to fix on the churning surf ahead of them.

He cleared his throat, uncomfortable as he'd been on his first date, and pointed. "A school of dolphins, straight ahead."

She reached in the tote bag and withdrew her camera. It was the first real smile he'd seen on her face all morning.

****

Benjamin watched Bryan escort Laura toward the marina. He pushed away the murky darkness pooling inside his head. He didn't want to hear the disembodied voice. *We like the way she smelled, didn't we, Bennie? Like fresh flowers. She belongs to us...not that ranger.*

He pulled the leather work gloves from his back pocket and slid his hands inside them.

He stood there, his knees feeling weak and shaky, his body slowly joining the rebellion of his emotions. Adoration. Disappointment. Anger.

She's never going to love Beenie-weenie. She likes the ranger.

Benjamin placed his hands against his ears. His voice was low and raspy. "I'm not listening to you. She touched me. She smiled at me. Do you hear—she smiled at *me*. Benjamin. Not Bennie."

Later, Benjamin's eyes sharpened and then relaxed while he eavesdropped on Bryan and Laura's conversation as they returned.

Bryan had commented, "The fireworks are

spectacular."

"So I hear from Aunt Philly. We plan to watch from the sun porch. Perhaps you'd like to join us."

Benjamin clenched his teeth until they hurt when Bryan lifted Laura's hand.

Anger punched him hard as he watched Bryan's fingers interlace with Laura's. In spite of himself, Benjamin continued to listen. "Nothing would please me more, but unfortunately, all the rangers are on duty. The Fourth is a big weekend at the park. Seems everyone wants to watch the fireworks from atop Cadillac Mountain. Can't say I blame them." And then Bryan snapped his fingers. "Why don't you and your aunt drive up? I'll arrange for you to have reserved seats from the top of Thunder Hole, and provide the chairs. I might even manage to sneak in a few minutes to watch with you."

Laura had tapped a finger against her cheek as if thinking. Then smiled. "It's a date. What time should we arrive?"

And then they had kissed. Not an intimate, passionate kiss. A mere touch of the lips. Benjamin watched as they said goodbye and Laura disappeared inside the bookstore.

He'd never physically ached for a woman. But he did now. Not just to make love to her, though that was central to his mind. He wanted to taste her, to inhale her scent, to make her his.

Everything about her drew him. Like now. She didn't belong to the ranger.

We are identical twins, Bennie. I was born with the brains, while you are destined to always do the dirty work. Do something worthwhile for once. Make her love you.

He squeezed his eyes shut and pressed his hands against each side of his head to relieve the ache. Who was he—Bennie or Benjamin? Neither was a great choice.

"How do I make her love me, Bennie? You and I are both losers."

Chapter Thirty

The following week flew by at an incredible pace. Fourth of July weekend meant the countdown of days until Sheriff Gilman returned from her honeymoon and Mitch left for Texas.

As many times as he had scoured the park areas and reviewed the autopsy report, Mitch had to admit his frustration over being no closer to finding Daisy Fuller's murderer or to connecting a ten-year-old murder to this one.

The missing pets were still missing. None of the rangers had discovered any clues that the remains had been dumped or buried in the park, and no remains had washed ashore.

To fill her days, Laura spent more time working with the tourism council and the historical society. Aunt Philly seemed inordinately pleased that Laura had accepted Bryan's invitation to watch the fireworks from atop Cadillac Mountain inside the park, and when the local celebration was not the subject, she chattered continuously about the European cruise and spending the winter in a warmer climate.

At night, Laura researched the history of the town and its buildings. Her goal was to help establish grants to preserve historical sites from outside commercial contractors whose sole purpose was to demolish the structures for capital gains and replace them with parking lots or ultra-modern architectural designs.

And, all the while, she wrestled with the question of who was sending her the white roses. After receiving another rose, she decided someone other than Mayor Shipley was the perpetrator. Whoever he was had changed his pattern. This time, she found a fully-bloomed flower on the steps at the back door of her office. She hadn't noticed the second difference until she picked up the stem and a thorn pricked her finger. Always before, the sender had stripped away the sharp barbs. She wondered if she had inadvertently offended her secret admirer and this was his way of sending her a warning.

Shaking off the doldrums, she scanned the news clipping into her computer, then zoomed in on the grainy black-and-white images of Brenda Alligood and Bennie Wiener. Twenty-plus years had passed since Dan Fuller had taken the photo and written the article about the girl's unfortunate death. Laura held a current picture of Benjamin Noone next to the screen. The resemblance she had earlier thought existed simply didn't.

The office phone rang. "*Cole Harbor Gazette*, Laura speaking."

Heavy breathing.

"Hello, is someone there?"

An unfamiliar male voice with a deep rasp whispered, "No one loves you."

"Who is this?"

The line disconnected.

Laura pushed out of her chair and walked to the back door to double check that the deadbolt was in place. Her heart thudded until the beat throbbed inside her ears.

She punched in the numbers of Mitch's cell phone. "Deputy Carter."

She struggled to keep the quaver from her voice. "Are you near the newspaper?"

"Sure. What's up?"

"I didn't tell you about receiving another rose because I still believed it was someone's idea of a sick joke. Mitch, a moment ago, I received a strange phone call. I think it was a threat."

"Lock the doors, draw the blinds, and don't let anyone in. Give me ten minutes. I'll sing out your name when I get there."

To stay occupied, she made a fresh pot of coffee. And she paced, sat down, paced some more, until she heard a tap on the glass. "Friday, it's Mitch."

She turned the lock and wanted to rush into his arms—to feel safe. Instead, she walked to the coffeepot and poured two cups. "Mitch, are you sure Elio Casper is dead? I mean…did anyone actually see him in the morgue, or in a casket?"

"What's happened to spook you?"

She set the cup on her desk and opened the large manila envelope, then carefully removed the slightly mashed but fully bloomed rose. "This arrived two days ago. Unlike the others, it has thorns. My finger is still sore from the prick."

She related about the telephone call, and repeated the caller's words.

"You didn't recognize the voice?"

She shrugged. "It was a man who sounded as if he had a bad case of laryngitis."

Mitch gave her an assessing glance. "Although my

sources are reliable, I'll contact them to double-check on Elio Casper's death."

She looked down at the cup in her hands. "I can't help but think the roses and now this phone call are connected, and that someone else is in Elio Casper's grave. I'm scared, Mitch. Not just for me. I don't want Aunt Philly harmed because I live with her."

"Friday, with the way the town is filling up for the fireworks show this weekend, I'd like you to stay at home with the doors locked. I have to work. There's no way I can keep an eye on you."

"Don't worry about us. Aunt Philly and I accepted Bryan's invitation to watch the fireworks from the park."

Mitch gave her a knowing look.

She hitched one shoulder. "Don't go reading anything into it. I took your advice and set the ground rules. Slow and easy."

In silence, they exchanged awkward smiles.

She had to remember that his time for returning to Texas was drawing nearer, and that she was staying in Cole Harbor.

Mitch checked his watch. "I'll let you know what I find out about Elio Casper. In the meantime, you know the drill…doors locked…no venturing out at night alone."

****

She hadn't slept.

At six-thirty, she carried a cup of coffee to the porch. The sun was trying to break through a blue-gray mist that hovered over the cove. Laura sat on the porch swing, dressed in a pair of flannel pajamas. The nights in Cole Harbor remained cool and damp. She sat there

238

sipping and listening to the seagulls' high-pitched mewlings.

Her cell phone vibrated against her hip. She reached into her pocket to look at the caller ID.

Bracing herself for bad news, she returned to the bedroom and shut the glass slider so her voice wouldn't disturb her aunt.

Speaking just above a whisper, she said, "Do you know what time it is?"

There was no humor in Mitch's voice. "Figured you'd be up."

Her nervousness increased. "What did you find out?"

"Hang on a second, Friday. I need to take this call."

She frowned and glanced at the clock on the bedside table.

"Friday, sorry about leaving you hanging."

A terrible feeling rose inside her. Dread. "If Elio is alive, just tell me."

"My sources sent me several pictures, which I've emailed to you. They should come through—now. Tell me if you can identify either of the two men."

Her cell phone beeped. "Give me a second, Mitch."

She viewed the gruesome images of Elio Casper and Mario Gombiana. Both on metal slabs, their naked bodies draped with white sheets. Elio's eyes wide open. Lifeless, cold, dead eyes. Bruises on his face and neck. Gombiana's picture was more graphic, with a bullet hole in the center of his forehead.

"Friday?"

"Yeah." Tears burned behind her eyes, and her throat was tight. "That's them. You're right. They are really dead. So who is after me?"

She heard him sigh through the phone. His tone was hard, intense. "The sorry bastard, whoever he is, will regret the day he harassed you when I catch him."

When she didn't answer, he added, "I'll nail this guy. You believe me?"

"Yeah, I believe you."

"Good. There's one important thing I need for you to do as soon as we hang up, Friday."

Laura could almost feel his smile through the phone. She frowned, considering his request. "What's that?"

"Go back to bed. You need the rest."

"Okay."

Sleeping would be the smart thing to do. She needed to rest and recharge her batteries. Instead, Laura opened her cell phone for a last look at the pictures of Elio Casper and Mario Gombiana. She tried to force her shoulders to relax. "I hope you both rot in hell for killing my friend."

Laura massaged the ache in her hip as she flipped the phone shut. A new worry beset her. Who was sending the white roses?

Chapter Thirty-One

The lengthening shadows of dusk surrounded the house and the woods around it. A soft breeze filtered through an open window.

Benjamin's fingers groped along the rear of the darkest corner of the shelf inside the closet until he touched the metal box. Lifting it down, he carried it to the bedroom. He sat on the bed with his back against the wall, opened the lid, and blinked at the contents.

First it was the deputy. Now, Bryan Cole. Bastard. He's gettin' in the way, and if it continues, he'll be next.

"Shut up. We're not killing anyone, anymore. Besides, killin' a man ain't as easy as you think."

As always, the voice inside him disagreed. *Aw, Bennie, you have to admit, it's kinda fun. Don't you think? If we don't do the deputy or the ranger, we can find another girl. I like that Amy girl.*

"No. She's a kid." The sudden image of a lithe, tomboy beauty with brown hair flared up in his mind's eye.

Brenda Alligood was sixteen, just like Amy.

Benjamin's eyes shifted to the grainy black-and-white newspaper photo of Brenda Alligood. He swallowed hard and looked away.

"I hate you, Bennie."

Yeah, who are you trying to convince...me or you? Thing is, you can't hate me without hating yourself.

Benjamin heaved a deep sigh. The comment sent shock waves through him.

When you were in the loony bin, didn't I tell you it wasn't going to be a one-time thing? Huh...didn't I?

"I didn't have a choice. Those girls made me do it. I only wanted to love them. They shouldn't have screamed."

His inner-twin laughed. The laughter filled the bedroom. Benjamin covered his ears to shut out the sound. It didn't work.

One more, Bennie. One more. Her.

Benjamin looked down. A finger—not his finger, pointed to another face, in a different news photograph. "No. I won't. Not her."

Oh, Bennie...Bennie. Of course, it's her. She's the best one of all. She won't scream. Now get your ass in gear.

"I won't do it. You can't make me."

High-pitched giggling rose into a loud crescendo. The walls seemed to pulsate in an erratic rhythm. Benjamin wasn't sure if the sound was real or imaginary.

He sat hunched over the edge of the bed, his hands kneaded together into fists that dangled between his legs. Maybe his brain wasn't even his brain anymore. He swayed from side to side and felt the darkness roll in. Felt himself teetering on the edge of a murky chasm. Red spots danced like chaotic sparklers before his eyes.

It's all planned. No one will know it's you.

Benjamin laughed through his tears. He drew a deep breath and looked down at the smiling face in the news article. "How will no one know it's me?"

No one...get it, Bennie? N-o-o-n-e spells—No one.

Benjamin walked into the bathroom. He turned on the cold water tap and splashed water over his face. "Not tonight. My head hurts, and I'm tired. Can't you see the blood leaking from my eyes? I'm sick."

Faker…slacker…Boo-hoo…cry baby.

He balled his hand into a fist and slammed it into the medicine cabinet mirror, and the pain brought him back to reality. The red spots in front of his eyes disappeared. Bewildered, he didn't recognize the shattered image staring back at him.

Without breaking stride, Benjamin left the bathroom. At the front door, he twisted the knob and swung it wide and walked out. The air cooled his fevered face. Bennie had picked a perfect night. Mist was rolling in over the bay. Soon dense white fog would blanket Cole Harbor. All the attention would be focused on the fireworks, and the noise. Yeah, his inner-twin had picked the perfect night.

****

"Laura?" Phyllis stood on the sun porch, staring at the growing crowd on both sides of the sidewalk. "I believe Mitch has already closed off the street to ready for the parade."

Laura glanced at her watch as she joined her aunt. "It's not five, yet. C'mon, if we hurry, we can still get out of town and drive to the park."

As she and her aunt walked down the stairs, the house phone rang. "Let it go to voice mail, Aunt Philly."

The answering machine beeped, and Bryan's voice came on. *Laura, it's Bryan. I hope you get this message. Don't try to drive to the park. Traffic is backed up from the entrance gate for approximately two miles down Cove Highway. Call me, so I won't worry about you.*

They listened, and then Phyllis waggled her neatly arched eyebrows at her niece. "Well, I guess that's that, and honestly, I'm relieved. Fog is setting in. Never did like driving in the fog."

Laura couldn't argue the last point. "I left my camera in the office. I'll call Bryan while I'm there. Might as well use this opportunity to mingle among the crowd and get a few candid shots for the paper. Maybe interview a couple of tourists."

"You know what Mitch said. Stay in the crowds—no wandering off in dark corners. I don't want to have to worry about you, either."

Laura smiled as she blew out an exaggerated sigh. Deep inside, she appreciated her aunt's concern. "Don't let me interrupt your fun. By the way, how do you normally celebrate the Fourth…I mean, if I weren't here?"

A faint tinge pinked Phyllis's cheeks. "After the parade, the girls and I indulge in a lot of junk food, several glasses of wine, and then we meander down to the dance area, hoping one of the ole codgers will ask to waltz us around the floor a time or two. Silly, at our age, huh?"

Laura arched a brow and offered an empathetic smile. "Aunt Philly, you are a beautiful, vivacious woman. There is nothing silly about enjoying life. Besides, age doesn't define you. It's only a number."

She turned and looked over her shoulder. "Don't wait up. I plan to enjoy all of the festivities, too. Maybe I'll see you at the dance."

At the bottom of the stairs and before going out the

door, Phyllis snapped her fingers. "Tell Bryan he owes us a special guided tour of the park. We'll bring the picnic lunch."

Laura nodded as she walked around the corner to the alley and the few steps to the newspaper's rear entrance. She inserted the key and turned the knob. The door didn't open. Odd, she thought, and tried again. The door creaked when she pushed it wide. A small smile tugged at the corner of her lips as she stood for a moment and listened to raucous notes from the band members tuning up their instruments. She really loved this town. It was becoming more like home every day.

As she walked through the store room, late afternoon sun filled the office area. She froze. Her eyes widened, and she felt the bottom fall out of her stomach.

"Omigod! No!"

Everywhere she looked, white rose buds, mingled with fully bloomed white roses, littered the office floor and the top of her desk, and a large sheet of paper with *No one loves you!* scrawled almost illegibly in red letters was taped to the back of her office chair.

Had she forgotten to relock the door?

Footsteps from behind caused her to turn. "You! How did you get in?"

And then she realized the door must have been unlocked, and when she inserted the key and turned, she had relocked the door. Had he picked the lock, or did he have a key?

Time blurred into milliseconds. Out of the rose-strewn area, large hands reached forward and grabbed her. She wrenched backwards. The sudden movement caused her hip to lock, and she lost her balance when she tripped over her own feet.

On her way to the floor she thought she heard him say, "It's emerging now, baby," right before her head hit the hard edge of the desk. Sharp pain riveted through her scalp.

Stars swam in a black sea behind her eyelids.

****

Benjamin grimaced when Laura hit the floor with a thud. A soft groan of pain slipped from her lips. He squatted and lifted her to a sitting position so he could feel the back of her head. A large lump had formed. Maybe she'd suffered a concussion. A moment of panic rippled through him. He placed his face close to hers to see if she was breathing.

"What should I do, Bennie?"

Benjamin listened. No answer. Disgruntled, he surmised his inner-twin had decided to remain silent, just when he needed him the most.

Her head lolled against his chest. She mumbled. The words were incoherent, something about—jolly?

Much the way one would a child, he shushed her. "I-I'm not going to hurt you." His voice was quiet.

He hadn't been touched affectionately by a female for a long time. Her hands reached out and gripped the front of his shirt as if she were seeking comfort.

Instinctively, he drew Laura to his chest, wanting to protect her. From whom—Bennie or himself? He inhaled her fragrance. Brushed his lips over the lemony scent of her hair. She had a mouth that reminded him of a pink rosebud. He wondered if her lips were as supple as they looked. Maybe he would steal a kiss, and she couldn't resist.

Her breath tickled the side of his neck. He blinked

in surprise, then grinned.

She stirred against him. Her body invited responses he hadn't felt since he was sixteen. That part of him had died with the chemical shock treatments at the asylum. He wanted to shout—*Yes!*

Outside, the band played "When the Saints Come Marching In."

His attention snapped into gear. He grabbed the tarpaulin he had stitched into an oversized sailor's duffel bag. Laying Laura flat, he lifted her feet and slid the canvas sack over her body until she looked like a large container of potting soil. He pulled the drawstrings together, and then scooped her into his arms.

He felt an odd urge to protect her. To take her out of the sack and return to his cabin, alone.

Loser.

Silence.

You hear me, loser? Big...cowardly...loser.

"Screw you, Bennie. You're making me mad, so keep your trap shut."

Benjamin shoved his black mood aside. With the stealth of a cat, he slipped out the back door, down the steps, and toward the woods.

Chapter Thirty-Two

The boom, followed by another burst of explosions, jerked Laura awake. She had been dreaming about Jolly. It took a moment to remember that it was the Fourth of July.

She opened her eyes and realized she wasn't in her office. It was dark, and she was lying in a small bed. Not her bed, and the room around her was completely different. She smelled the stale odor of sweat, which made her wrinkle her nose. Her head, when she tried to move it to take in the room, pounded so hard it made her nauseated.

She closed her eyes, and when she opened them again, the little crackerbox room came into view a bit more clearly.

Where was Aunt Philly? Where was Bryan?

Laura lifted her hand to wipe away the mist clouding her eyes. She saw the dark form standing at the foot of the bed. He was a tall, solid man.

He studied her with a gaze that swirled darker by the second, until those eyes reminded her of an ominous storm waiting to explode. His chest rose and fell with one deep breath after another.

She squirmed until his face came into full focus, then wished she had remained unconscious. Above her was the rigid jaw, sharp cheeks, and dark eyes of a dangerous predator, anticipating his plan of attack. He stared at the window, but she could tell he listened for any change in sound.

Her heart raced. She opened her mouth to scream.

He moved, cutting off the sound before it was more than a breath. It was as if he had read her mind—knew her thoughts. He put his finger to his lips. "Shh! Don't scream. Bennie and me don't like screamin'."

A chill slithered down Laura's spine. It took all she possessed to remain calm. "Why did you bring me here? What do you want?"

Benjamin massaged his temples. "Too many questions makes my head hurt."

Laura glanced around the room. "Is there another person here? Who is Bennie?"

Benjamin slammed the wall with the palm of his hand. "Bennie is my twin. He's not nice. He makes me do bad things."

"W-what kind of bad things?"

He tipped his head back and laughed and laughed, and between gusts of laughter his voice changed, his facial expression changed, and he coughed out the words, "And now…and now…I'd like you to…*ah-ha-ha-ha*…meet, *me*."

Benjamin kept on laughing, a maniacal resonance from deep within his chest. A sound utterly devoid of joy. "*Hello, darlin', I'm Bennie. You look frightened, and you should be.*"

Laura pushed to an upright position. She closed her eyes against the sudden flash of light.

Benjamin—Bennie—stood next to the lamp. "*The better to see you, my darlin'.*"

Still trying to get a handle on what was going on, Laura glanced around the room. On the wall were the newspaper pictures of Brenda Alligood, Lynnette Braswell, and Daisy Fuller. There were pictures of women she had never seen before. How many had he murdered? There was one more picture that caused her to gasp and cringe against the bed—hers.

"I found them for Benjamin, but he's such a bumblin' idiot that he made them scream."

Laura followed his gaze to a dark corner of the room. Benjamin—or was it Bennie who spoke?—said, "We don't don't like screamin' do we, Bennie?"

She decided her best defense was to humor the sick bastard. "W-what did he do to make them scream?"

Benjamin closed his eyes. It seemed he was experiencing some kind of ecstasy, or pain. Laura wasn't sure which.

He kept his eyes shut. Stood still, head tipped back. A slow smile played across his lips. He unbuttoned his pants and pulled down the zipper and spread back the fly. It took a few minutes of fumbling. It was Bennie's voice that spoke. "This is why the girls call him 'Beenie with the little weenie.' He was born deformed. Our mother screamed, too. She hated the sight of him."

Laura turned away. Rough hands grasped her chin and forced her to look. She struggled to keep her voice calm. "Where is your mother, Benjamin?"

He merely grinned. Bennie's voice, matter of fact, said, *"She's dead. Grandfather fed her to the sharks. He didn't like screamin' either."*

She swiped a trembling hand through her short cropped hair. "If you let me go, I promise not to scream."

A series of rolling booms vibrated the cabin, followed by the rat-a-tat-tat cadence of exploding firecrackers. Visible from the window, sparkling light flashed like ghostly fingers through the fog-shrouded mist.

Benjamin swayed on his feet. He beat at his head and shrieked, "Bennie...crabs...get them off...they're eating my brain!"

The voice changed. "Face it like a man. I brought the bitch here. Now are you going to do her, or is it up to me to love her?"

Laura had used her newspaper connections to gain partial access to Benjamin's medical records. Apparently something had retriggered his paranoia schizophrenia. He was clearly delusional. She waded through a mash of emotions trying to formulate a plan. With her bad leg, she wasn't much for running.

She prayed the muscles wouldn't seize up, and moved as quickly as her hip allowed. She sprang from the bed and, with a one-two punch, pushed all the force she could muster into her arm and then smashed the heel of her hand against Benjamin's nose.

He yowled and staggered backward, slamming against the wall.

Footsteps pounding behind her registered in her brain. Hands gripped her hair, jerking her head back. A hard smack of flesh against wood cracked the air.

Laura cried out in pain as her body was flung to the floor. Benjamin straddled her with his knees. The window shade hung askew from where she had torn it from the sill, allowing a view of the fireworks lighting the darkened sky.

She wasn't sure who spoke to her—Bennie or Benjamin. "Get up, bitch. I'm not through with you."

She placed both hands against his chest. "You said

you wouldn't hurt me if I didn't scream, and I didn't. Good people don't break their word, Benjamin."

He snarled and swung his meaty right paw in a powerful slam across Laura's cheek. "Scream, damn you. I can't love you until you scream."

A cut along her brow dribbled blood. Ears ringing, she struggled to push from beneath his weight. "No, I won't."

He leaned close and pressed his slobbering lips against hers. She turned her head aside, as he pinned her arms over her head, and with the other hand he fumbled with the waistline of her slacks. She twisted and reared against him, kicking.

And then the unexpected happened.

Benjamin grabbed his head and rolled to one side, knees drawn into a protective ball. He moaned and whimpered. Blood leaked from his nose to drip on the floor. "It hurts…my head…unbearable pain."

"You're sick, Benjamin. Let me help you." She patted her pants pocket. The cell phone wasn't there. Anxiety filtered through her. She challenged herself to remain calm. As an investigative reporter, this wasn't her first dangerous gig. "If you have a phone, let me call Deputy Carter to get you to a doctor. I won't press charges, Benjamin. I'll even tell Deputy Carter this was all a mistake."

With slow, precise movements, she stood, biting against the pain as her hip refused to rotate into place.

Benjamin's face twisted into an ugly sneer. He used the back of his hand to wipe the blood from his nose. For a moment, he stared at the bright red smear.

When he spoke, Laura recognized Bennie's voice and watched a feverish, rabid glow light his eyes as he unfurled and stood. "No phone, or doctor, or lawman. There's a bomb inside my head. It's going to explode soon. I can feel it, and when it does, you're going to die with me, because that's what lovers do...don't they? Die together?"

Everything slowed down. In desperation, Laura lunged, using her fingernails to gouge deep lines down his face. The assault threw him off balance. She used the momentum to escape through the front door and down the steps.

Which way...which way? Fog blanketed the area. Except for the ghostly outline of the cabin, visibility was near zero. She turned in a circle, trying to get her bearings.

A series of high-pitched, whirling whistles disturbed the silence, and a barrage of Roman candles lit the sky lending temporary light—enough for Laura to see the narrow lane leading away from the house. At this elevation the gleeful shouts of Fourth of July spectators sounded close by. Help was so near, but so far away. She suppressed the scream building in her throat.

A door slammed. His demented laughter sent a cascade of shivers over her. "Don't you understand, Laura? The only way Bennie can love you is to hear the snap of your neck...and you won't get far with your bad leg."

She knew her best chance of survival was making it to the paved road, yet she knew she couldn't outrun him on even ground. The park was closer than town. Praying she'd made the decision that might save her life, she veered right, into the woods and up the hill toward the voices.

Footsteps, and panting, and crackling underbrush.

Time slowed and blurred in her mind, but everything happened in flashes as she struggled to climb the slope. Brambles snagged her clothes; thorns tore the palms of her hands. No matter. If she could just reach the park… Hard fingers closed around her ankle and yanked her back.

She stumbled, losing her balance when her foot caught on a rut or a clump of roots. On her way to the ground, she saw Benjamin's dark silhouette through the dense white sea fog.

****

Phyllis sat on the edge of her bed, kicked off her shoes, and wriggled the toes on her tired feet. She glanced at the bedside clock. Ten o'clock. A mild concern wafted over her that she hadn't met up with Laura during the festivities. Dismissing the thought, she reached for her pajamas, then decided to read awhile before going to bed.

She hadn't realized she'd drifted off until the phone rang. Blinking away the grogginess, she said, "Hello, Laura?"

"No, it's Bryan."

"Oh, thanks for the message not to come to the park. Did Laura contact you?"

"That's why I'm calling. I was concerned that you hadn't received my message."

"She went to her office to get her camera and was going to call from there. I guess she got sidetracked, thinking about doing some man-on-the-street type of interviews. It'll probably be late when she gets in. How about coming for breakfast in the morning—around nine?"

"Sure."

Phyllis frowned as she disconnected. Laura wasn't forgetful, unless she had deliberately avoided Bryan. No, she didn't buy that reasoning, either. Slipping on a robe and slippers, she went to the hall closet and grabbed a flashlight.

Noises filled the night—car doors slamming, people laughing or shouting out their goodbyes to each other, a few firecrackers popping in the distance, the slap-flap of her slippers as she walked the few steps down the alley to the newspaper's back door. Nothing to create caution or cause concern until she reached for the doorknob and realized she stared into darkness.

It wasn't like Laura to forget to close the door. Butterflies winged their way through Phyllis's stomach. "Yoo-hoo, Laura, are you in there?"

She shone the flashlight inside the darkened storage area, then reached in to flip the light switch. Phyllis was certain an icy fist squeezed her heart when she entered the office. Her hand flew to her mouth. Even in the dimmed light the sight sent chills through her. "Oh, dear Godfrey!"

She set the flashlight on the desk. Her hand trembled as she picked up the phone and dialed.

"Deputy Carter."

"Mitch, is Laura with you?"

"Haven't seen her all evening."

"Something bad has happened. I-I think she's been abducted."

"What? Where are you?"

"In her office, and Mitch, there's white roses scattered all over the place, and it looks like she might have put up a struggle."

"Don't touch anything. I'm on foot. Too many people to use the car. Be there in ten minutes."

"Go to the back door. I'm afraid to unlock the front."

Phyllis stood in the silence and stared around the room. Tension filled her as she stared in horror.

It seemed forever before Mitch called out, "Phyllis, it's Mitch. I'm coming in."

She rushed to him. "It's that crazy Benjamin Noone. He's got Laura. Oh, wait until I tell Maudie. I've told her repeatedly not to be nice to that man."

Mitch gripped the near-hysterical woman by the shoulders. "How do you know Noone has Laura?"

By this time, Phyllis had flipped on the interior office lights. "He was so stupid he left a message." She pointed to the paper taped to the office chair.

Mitch stared at it. He took note of the scattered buds and the area's disarray. "No one loves you."

"No, Mitch. *Noone* looks like *no one* because of the gap between the two o's. The demented idiot can't even spell his own name."

He frowned, then nodded. "Oh, hell. I missed it. Stupid me."

"You're not stupid. Apparently, Laura missed it, too." She blinked at him through tears.

"Don't let him harm my niece. She's been hurt enough."

"Count on it, Phyllis. Come, let me walk you to Maudie's. I don't want you alone in the apartment. Do you need anything before we go?"

She wiped her eyes and pressed her hands to her cheeks. "Saving my niece is first and foremost. Right now, Maudine Perry is the last person I want to see."

"Maudie is your friend. She takes everyone under her wing. There's no way she or any of us foresaw Benjamin as anything more than he appeared."

"In my head, I know you're right. It's my heart that feels differently. I'd rather be alone."

He escorted her to the side entrance of the bookstore. "Do I need to remind you to lock the door?"

She cut him a smirk. "Do what you have to do, Mitch—even if it means killing the lunatic before he harms Laura. I just pray he hasn't."

She disappeared inside and clicked the deadbolt into place.

Chapter Thirty-Three

Mitch's first call was to Bryan. He explained the situation. "Laura is smart enough to know that Noone's property butts up to the park and is closer to it than to town. If escape is possible, she'll make for your direction. Alert your rangers, and Bryan, you're the official law enforcement inside the park. If necessary, don't hesitate to use deadly force."

Bryan's voice sounded as if he were speaking through clenched teeth. "The son of bitch will pay if he harms one hair on her head. Mitch, the road is jam-packed with traffic. The fastest way to get here is by boat."

"Roger that. My gut tells me the jack-off will head to Thunder Hole. That's where I'll beach."

Mitch disconnected and punched a new set of numbers.

"'Lo?"

"Where are you, Harmon?"

"At the boat yahd. Just gettin' ready to rest my tired feet."

Mitch filled in the details to the old auxiliary deputy, and finished with, "Don't remove your badge and uniform yet."

"I knew all along that pissah wasn't right in the head. I'll fire up the engines and get ready for cast off."

Mitch sprinted toward the marina. His stride built

momentum on the downward stretch to the pier. As soon as he spotted the boat, he shouted, "Cast off." In one leap he boarded the vessel.

Harmon tossed the lines to the dock. He stepped inside the cabin and spoke over his shoulder. "Fog's thicker'n pea soup. Don't mattah. I've adjusted the radar, and once we get to the first buoy, I'll breathe a little easier."

"How long until we get there?"

"Normally, ten or fifteen minutes. Mabbe thirty, in this fog, unless we get a break and the mist lifts, which is doubtful."

"Not what I want to hear."

"Can't control the weathah. It is what it is."

Mitch peered through the thick veil of gray haze. "Yeah."

There was only the sound of the boat slicing through the choppy waters, the distant clanging of the buoy, and the blip...blip...blip of the radar marking the way. The clanging grew louder.

Mitch peered through the murk, cursing the injustice of the weather. He glanced at his watch again, in aggravated disbelief.

"Lookin' at that waterberry ain't gonna make time go by any fastah."

It seemed forever before Harmon lifted his left arm and pointed. "Buoy's starboard, which means the beach is just ahead on the port side."

"What about the fog light?"

Harmon shot him a fleeting look. "All it'll do is light up the fog. Won't help with visibility until we're on top of what we're lookin' for."

Mitch's frustration continued to grow. His heart

rate jacked up a notch in anger as he glanced at his watch.

Harmon switched on the spotlight and turned it starboard. "Thar she be…the buoy."

In the veil of mist, the marker bobbed up and down like a dancing ghost.

Mitch felt the boat shift to the left. He placed his hand against the service revolver strapped to his hip.

****

I'm going to die, Laura thought. Her hip collapsed, and she fell to her knees. Her nose and lip bled. Rough hands yanked her up. They were on the path now—familiar territory. She was confident her aunt had missed her by now and notified Mitch. She needed to stall for time. Mitch and Bryan would come for her. They would figure out her strategy. She *needed* to stall for time. "Benjamin, why did you kill those girls?"

He turned her so that she faced him. It seemed as if he was experiencing some kind of pain. "I didn't want to. Bennie made me."

"You don't have to kill me. You don't have to hurt anyone ever again."

She thought she saw tears in his eyes when he said, "I do. I have to because Bennie said so."

A small smile lit his face. It grew into a grin, but there was something different about the expression in his eyes. His voice changed. *"Aw, Bennie...Bennie, don't you see what she's tryin' to do? Playin' on your sympathy."*

He grabbed a handful of hair and jerked Laura forward. *"I told you, she's the last one. I've saved the very best for last."*

"N-no, I like this one. She didn't scream."

Laura fought against the raw terror and swallowed back the sobs. "Listen to me, Benjamin. Don't you see, there is no Bennie. There is just you and me. We're in the park. Take me to Ranger Cole. We'll get you to a doctor."

Unable to catch herself, she landed hard when he shoved her backward. "No doctors. Doctors hurt me."

He leaned to pick her up. She fought with every ounce of strength left in her body. His hands went around her neck, thumbs pressed against her larynx. Dizziness washed through her until the world turned black and colored sparklers flashed behind her eyes. The voice that spoke sounded far away. *"Not yet, Bennie. It isn't time."*

The pressure eased. Wide-mouthed, she gulped in air. He lifted her into his arms. She let out a tired breath and beseeched herself not to scream. She squirmed until she could see his face. Above her were the rigid jaw and dark eyes of a madman. He studied her with a gaze that swirled more maniacal by the second. His chest rose and fell with each bounding stride.

He jogged faster. Her head lolled back and forth against his chest. She thought he scrambled over rocks. Waves seemed to lap the beach. A spray of water brought her to full consciousness. Maybe she was hallucinating from lack of oxygen to the brain.

Water gushed and surged in and out like a living creature—beckoning. Her nightmare was a reality as she remembered Daisy Fuller's nude body. Laura's eyes fluttered open. She and Benjamin stood at the edge of Thunder Hole's abyss.

He bent close and yelled above the thundering roar. "Shh. It's okay. You don't want to wake up just yet."

Her heart raced. And then she did the unthinkable. She screamed with enough force to make the dead tremble.

Benjamin laughed as he set Laura on her feet. His hands went around her neck. "I knew you would scream. I've been waiting so long. Look, Mama…Do you see?…I have an erection. I'm not a freak. Beenie with the little weenie is dead."

His entire body tensed. He moaned deep in his chest as his hands slid from Laura's neck to wrap her tight in his arms as he rubbed his body against hers. His breath came in short gasps as if experiencing an orgasm. He stared into her eyes, his own probing, searching, but for what, she didn't know.

His voice was gentle, though loud enough to hear above the waves. "I'll remember this forever. No matter what happens."

The tender moment vanished as the inner-twin emerged. In gusts of laughter, he coughed out, *"And now…and now…we…have to…we must…ah-ha-ha-ha…kill you."*

He kept on laughing.

****

Fear for Laura pulsed through Bryan in hammering waves and warred for space with his mounting anger. With slow, cautious steps, he approached Thunder Hole. He spotted the searchlight's halo beam from the boat and knew Mitch and Harmon were near.

"Step away, Noone, and let Laura walk to me."

Clouds shifted and parted. A sliver of moon peeked through the fog.

Benjamin barely turned his head, just enough for Bryan to see the expression that reminded him of a feral animal. Impatience thickened his voice. "I won't tell you again—step away—let Laura walk to me."

Bryan slowly reached one hand down to grip the Glock's butt. He eased the weapon from its holster.

The laughter died, and Benjamin issued a growl. "Take a step forward, and the girl goes with me into the bowels of hell."

Laura tried to throw herself to one side. It was Bennie's voice that snarled, "*You bitch*."

Benjamin took a step closer to the edge.

Bryan knew from the rumbling sounds of the billowing sea below that it was only a matter of minutes before the hole erupted, spewing a geyser of water some forty feet in the air. He watched Laura frantically trying to kick and twist free of her captor. She stood between his aim and Benjamin Noone.

He held his aim steady, waiting, hoping for Laura to break free long enough for him to get a free shot at the maniac. But her struggles were no match for Noone as he dragged her with him.

And then all hell broke loose.

A voice from nowhere shouted, "Laura! Go limp—now!"

She obeyed and slid out of Benjamin's grasp.

He extended his arms as if rushing toward Mitch. A deep throaty growl emitted from his throat. "She's mine...mine...Do you hear?...Mine!"

Without hesitation, Mitch fired in that same second—a pop like a firecracker, followed by a sizzle, charged the air. Benjamin Noone screamed. His body jerked upward. A crimson pattern slowly stained the front of his shirt along with the searing odor of burnt flesh. "Lauuuraaa!"

Mitch shoved the flare gun inside the waistband of his pants. He lifted Laura into his arms as Bryan yelled, "The hole…it's gonna blow. Get the hell out of here."

A loud clap of thunder vibrated the air. Water spouted with a deafening roar. Bryan grabbed hold of Mitch and helped him sprint to higher ground as a massive wave threatened to swallow them in its insidious gullet.

Chapter Thirty-Four

Laura's nerves were frayed, the adrenaline rush gone, leaving her limp and empty. She clung to Mitch. "Is it over? Benjamin's dead?"

Mitch heaved a deep breath as he set her on her feet and handed her to Bryan. "There's no way to know for sure until we find his body."

A boat horn sounded, followed by a spotlight and Harmon shouting, "Mitch…Mitch."

With Bryan assisting Laura, they walked with Mitch to the end of Thunder Hole's precipice. The fog had lifted enough to make the white tri-hull craft visible. "We're okay, Harmon. Any sign of Noone's body?"

Harmon yelled back, "Damnedest thing you ever saw. In all my years on the sea I ain't never experienced such a thing."

He shifted the boat's large spotlight to the forward deck. "I saw the flash from the flare gun, then Thunder Hole exploded, and then there was a loud whomp, and the bow of the boat dipped. I thought maybe in that gush of water a whale or a large shark had tried to swim ovah the bow. I'm tellin' you, near scared the peewaddy out of me when I saw what it was. You ain't gonna believe your eyes."

Mitch, Laura, and Bryan looked to where the spotlight outlined the inert body of Benjamin Noone, lying face down, spread-eagled on the boat's bow.

Mitch yelled, "Is he alive?"

"Well, he ain't movin', but lemme check." The boat rocked back and forth as the old sailor approached the body. Mitch and the others watched as Harmon used a toe to nudge Noone. He knelt and rolled the body over, then looked up and shouted. "Deader'n an iced mackerel."

Mitch nodded his understanding. "Can you move the boat over to the beach area and get close enough for me to wade out?"

Harmon waved. "Sure thing."

Mitch finally smiled. He squeezed Laura's hand. "Your aunt's worried sick about you. I know she'd appreciate a call." He shook a finger as if saying not to challenge his next statement. "Have her meet you at the hospital. Bryan will drive you." He'd noticed how Laura favored her right hip.

She offered a weary smile. "What happens next?"

"Harmon and I will get the body to Ken Musuyo for a routine autopsy." He shrugged. "I'll come by in a couple of days and take your statement. Right now, Bryan's going to wrap you in a blanket and get you to the hospital."

****

Days later, Laura sat on the sun porch, her hip and leg bound in a brace. She lifted the glass of iced tea and drew a sip. Mitch paused, a glass midway to his lips. He took no joy in the birds' morning songs, or the sight of tourists along the sidewalks. He hadn't changed his mind about returning to El Paso and running for sheriff. The weight of his decision settled hard on his soul. Laura was thinking of him. He could feel it.

A look of haunting anxiety sprang to her gaze. "Benjamin Noone suffered from more than paranoia schizophrenia. He was physically sick, wasn't he?"

Mitch set the glass on a coaster, and picked up the brown envelope to extract the report. "It's a wonder he was able to function as long as he did. Ken's report states Noone suffered from a massive tumor on the limbic system. This kind of tumor turns a normally gentle individual into a violent, aggressive person. Pair that type of violence with the paranoid episodes of hearing voices and it made Noone a dangerous time bomb. I guess the ironic part is, according to the report, he had maybe less than twenty-four hours of life left before the cancer would have killed him."

Laura waited a moment. "He said Bennie was his twin. Was it the schizophrenia that caused him to think he had a brother?"

Mitch relaxed against the chair. "Ken phoned the asylum where Benjamin spent ten years of his life. Since he's dead, the judge didn't have a problem issuing an order for the asylum to release his records. It seems there was a twin named Bennett. Benjamin was the older by seven minutes. At the age of three, Bennett fell from Thunder Hole and broke his neck. The mother, Rose Noone, went bonkers and blamed Benjamin for not looking after his brother. Also, according to the medical records, Benjamin was the victim of a circumcision gone bad. His mother apparently called him names—little girl, sissy boy, homo—always telling him his twin was smarter, cuter. By the time he was five, she had disappeared. The record states they resided with Rose's father in the cabin where Benjamin lived. He stated his mother was suffering one of her screaming attacks when the grandfather tried to quiet her, but he broke her neck. Instead of reporting it, he chopped her up, rowed out into the bay, and fed the remains to the sharks. Benjamin held the lantern and was witness to this. For a while he got to live a normal life, until he entered school. Apparently he was bullied by the other kids, who gave him the nickname 'Beenie with the little Weenie,' until he killed his first victim, Brenda Alligood."

Laura placed her hand to her mouth to hold back the disgust. "Poor Benjamin. How horrible." She closed her eyes and sighed. "I'm sorry for what he suffered, but I'm also relieved that he can't hurt anyone anymore."

Damn. Why did she have to be so pretty…so tempting? He would like nothing better than to stick around a while longer. His time to leave Cole Harbor was drawing close. He stood and shoved his cap on his head.

"Mitch, you could stay."

"Can't. I still have a stack of paperwork to finish before putting the case of Benjamin Noone to bed. I want everything shipshape when Sheriff Gilman returns next week."

She stared up at him, her hands folded in her lap. "I meant stay in Cole Harbor. You could run against Sheriff Gilman or whatever her married name is now."

A warm glow passed through him. "Roberta is homegrown. Her father was sheriff. I've been here less than a year, and folks take care of their own, Friday. I'm the outsider. Even if I stayed, I'd always be the deputy, and the interloper. Playing second fiddle isn't my style."

He wished he could find something clever to say. He stared down into her expectant blue eyes and drew a deep breath. "We've talked about this. There are bad guys in Texas I need to catch. I won't—can't—rest easy until they're either behind bars or dead. That's my first priority."

His feet stayed rooted to the spot while he watched the sunlight caress her skin in a golden hue.

A sudden frown firmed Laura's mouth. She crossed her arms and stared away from him.

"Laura, where are you?" A rasp of enthusiasm rang out in Bryan's raised voice.

She looked at Mitch, squared her shoulders, gave him an "oh, damn" look, and called, "I'm on the sun porch."

"Take care of yourself, Friday." Mitch turned and walked away while he still had the good sense and willpower to do so.

He met Bryan at the top of the stairs. The ranger's dark eyebrows rose into a smile. "How's our girl today?"

"Improving."

Mitch hesitated. Bryan stood there, tall, shoulders squared, his voice dropped to a whisper. "I have to ask—are you my competition? It'd take a blind man not to see how she looked at you that night at the hospital."

"No," Mitch ground out. "We're just friends."

Bryan sighed as he glanced toward the sun porch. "Thanks, Mitch."

Halfway down the stairs, Mitch turned. "I'm heading to El Paso next week. I won't be returning to Cole Harbor."

"Should I tell Laura?"

"She knows."

Bryan clenched his jaw and nodded.

Mitch didn't have that much paperwork left to close the Benjamin Noone case. In fact, he considered he was leaving the office in better shape than when he'd first arrived. Part of him thought about hitting the road earlier than planned. Just ride off into the sunset and never look back.

Outside, he squinted against the sun's bright glare and pulled the sunglasses over his eyes as he walked the short distance to his office, located inside the courthouse.

"Hiyah, Mitch."

"Mayor Shipley." His eyes went to the man's lapel. "I see you're not wearing a white rosebud."

The pudgy man's face screwed into a nervous smile. "Ayuh. Pink or red from now on." He tsked. "Terrible…just terrible about Benjamin. Who would have ever suspected we had a homicidal maniac living amongst us all these years? Why, my Martha—"

"Sorry to cut you off, Mayor, but I have a ton of paperwork to finish before leaving next week."

"Ayuh. Wish we could entice you to stay. But, you understand, small community like ours can't afford to offer you a bigger salary."

Mitch reined in his thoughts. "Have a nice day, Mayor."

"Oh, Mitch, I guess you don't know. Roberta and her new husband pulled in about twenty minutes ago. She's already at the office."

Surprise blanched him. He kept his voice calm. "Thanks for the information."

In minutes, he bounded up the courthouse steps. He slid the dark glasses over the bill of his cap and allowed long strides to take him toward the sheriff's office.

Louise gave him a cocky grin when he entered the office. "By the scowl on your face, I guess you heard. *She's ba-ack!*"

Chapter Thirty-Five

The bookstore door squeaked as he opened it. He was sorry he hadn't taken the time to oil the creak. Phyllis looked up from the computer. "Good morning, Mitch. We heard Roberta had returned early."

He reached around and removed a white envelope from his back pocket and laid it on the counter. "Would you give this to Laura after I leave?"

Phyllis frowned up at him, then stared at the envelope. "She's upstairs."

"It's easier this way."

She opened her mouth as if to form a polite denial, then nodded. "Ayuh, 'spose so."

Warm relief spread through him. He went around the counter and gathered the older woman in his arms, then released her with a peck on the cheek. "You've been a good friend, Phyllis. If you're ever in El Paso, look me up. I'll treat you to a Texas-sized steak."

She swiped a tear from her cheek. "I might just take you up on that, you handsome galoot."

He gave her an appreciative smile. "You understand why I can't stay?"

She darted her gaze toward the back room, where the stairs led to the apartment, and back again. "Ayuh. I read in a western novel where the good guy always tells the sheriff to keep the sun to his back. I hope you catch the men who destroyed your family. Take care of yourself, Mitch."

Mitch released a heavy sigh. "I'll do that."

He turned and walked out into the sunshine, closing the door softly behind him. Relief washed over him, quick and easy. He was on his way home.

****

Phyllis quickly whispered a prayer as she climbed the stairs. She knew she'd find Laura working. The sun porch had become her temporary office. Her heart swelled with love and a tinge of sadness when she spotted her niece's blonde head bent over the laptop.

A gull's shadow crossed in front of the screened area as it soared high above and then disappeared in the glare of the morning sunlight. A companionable silence filled the porch. Phyllis held out the envelope.

Laura looked up. "He's gone, isn't he?"

"Ayuh."

Laura offered a sad smile. "I don't know whether to be angry or relieved that he chose to write a note instead of saying goodbye in person."

Phyllis noted the dejected set of her niece's shoulders and the tears swimming in her eyes. "Would you like privacy while you read it?"

Laura gazed off where the sparkling aqua waters of the cove met the pale blue horizon. She sighed. "No."

She ran her finger along the sealed flap and removed the folded note. She scanned the page, and then looked at her aunt. "His handwriting is exceptionally neat for a man. I think I'll read it aloud."

Phyllis settled in a rocker and waited. The sadness in Laura's voice tugged at her heartstrings. She looked so fragile sitting there with her face flushed and somber.

"Dearest Laura…" She held the note against her chest. "Aunt Philly, he called me *Laura*—not Friday." She blinked several times, then continued, "Saying goodbye isn't easy. Maybe this note is the coward's way out. I'd like to think it's easier for both of us. We knew a storm was building between us. I'm not sure whether it was love or the kind of psychological emotion victims seek when they've experienced extreme trauma. Maybe we simply needed each other to heal our recent hurts. Either way, a future together isn't in our cards. I have bad guys to catch, and you have a lifetime of adventures to share with your aunt, and a newspaper to run. I will always adore you in a very special way.

"Bryan is a good guy, Laura. I've already told him that I'm not his competition. It doesn't take a fool to see he's head over heels in love with you. Give him a chance to prove it. Be happy!"

She racked her teeth across her bottom lip as she folded the letter and gently placed it back inside the envelope. "He's right, Aunt Philly. I'm not sure what I feel for Mitch is true love, but I sure would have liked the opportunity to find out. I'm going to miss him, more than he'll ever know."

Phyllis rose from the rocker. She patted her niece on the shoulder. "It's too hot for amaretto hot chocolate. How about a cold beer to drown our sorrows?"

Laura's cell phone rang. She looked at the ID and frowned. "It's Bryan."

"Well, answer it."

She rubbed a hand over her face and through her hair. "Hi, Bryan."

"I'm downstairs. Okay if I come up? I have lobstah rolls."

She sighed. What was it Mitch had said? *Set the rules, Friday. Let Bryan know you want to go slow and easy.* "A guy after my own heart. I never turn down my favorite food."

Her aunt smiled. "I guess that's my cue to go back to the bookstore."

"Never, Aunt Philly. Please stay. He has lobster rolls."

Phyllis laughed. "My lovely niece, you have a lot to learn about courtship. Put mine in the fridge for later."

With that Phyllis walked down the stairs, meeting Bryan halfway. "She's in a slump. Go easy."

"What's happened?"

"Let's put it this way—if you were ever worried about Mitch being your competition, you can stop. He left this morning."

Bryan pressed his lips together. "Somehow, I don't feel as glad as I thought I would. I really liked Mitch."

****

Uncertain of her feelings for Mitch, Laura felt the pain jabbing her chest and stealing her breath. If she didn't love him, then what was wrong with her? She glanced at the novel sitting in her aunt's rocker and thought about how Phyllis had complained about the ending. A small smile quirked Laura's lips as she surmised that life was like the last chapter in a book. If you don't like the ending—write a new one.

"Laura?"

"Out here, Bryan."

She sighed and slid the envelope under the laptop.

"There's cold beer in the refrigerator. I'd get it, but…"

Bryan sat down, then stood again. "Can we talk before we eat?"

She looked up at him. "Sit down, Bryan. You're making me nervous."

Today was his day off. Instead of his usual ranger uniform, he wore khaki shorts, a green T-shirt, and tan boating shoes without socks, a typical summer outfit that highlighted the blond hairs on his tanned legs and arms. Her emotions careened like a billowing storm, her thoughts equally scattered.

He leaned forward and placed his forehead gently against hers. "I know you don't like sailing or deep sea diving, and marriage isn't on your mind, but can I convince you to change your thinking about cohabitation?"

The memories of Jolly's death and of her recent violent encounter with Benjamin Noone floated through her mind. All too new and fresh to shove aside. Mitch had saved her. Bryan had held her. Mitch had said goodbye. Bryan was a safe harbor.

Like a shaft of sunlight slicing through thick fog, a warm glow spread through Laura. She leaned forward and, with a wry smile, brushed her lips against his. "Cohabitation…hmm. I'll give it serious thought."

Bryan trailed a finger down her smooth cheek. Then both his hands settled on hers. "If your leg weren't in a brace, I'd be willing to give you a lesson right this minute."

She suddenly wanted to cling to him, love him, sink into his strength, drown in the solid, muscular feel of his body and the musk fragrance of his aftershave. "Doctor's orders. Can't remove this contraption for another ten days."

"I'm not trying to rush you."

"Bryan…shut up and kiss me."

"You're beautiful, Laura."

Not quite ready for that particular sentiment, she was glad he hadn't declared his love. She laughed and plumbed his gaze. "If you're not going to kiss me, then I'm hungry. How about a lobster roll and a beer?"

He stood and, like a gallant knight, bowed at the waist. "Your wish is my command. By the way, you can cook, can't you?"

She knew what a kind heart he had as she lifted one corner of her mouth into a tiny smile. "Not really, but why should I, when there are so many fine restaurants in Cole Harbor?"

Cocking his head to one side, he studied her with mock concentration. Then as if tired of the wordplay, he leaned forward and kissed her. "Touché."

She filled her mind with pleasant thoughts, and planned to enjoy setting the rules while she and Bryan forged their lives together—slow and easy.

Loretta C. Rogers

If you enjoyed *MURDER IN THE MIST*, you'll want to read the sequel, *SHADOWED REUNION*, coming soon from The Wild Rose Press, Inc. Here's a sample:

Laura Friday peered through her sunglasses at the smiling waiter as she accepted the frosty piña colada. After savoring a long sip, she looked at her aunt. "Isn't Hawaii glorious? I can't believe we're wearing shorts in December."

Phyllis Friday wriggled her bare toes. "I don't envy our friends in Maine. Cole Harbor is a ghost town this time of year. Poor Maudine, having to shovel snow at her age. I wish she had agreed to come with us."

"Thank you, Aunt Philly."

Phyllis lowered her sunglasses to peek over the rim. "Whatever for? I'm the one who should be thanking you. You've made my long-awaited dream vacations come true. Paris in September, and now basking in the sun with my favorite niece."

Laura laughed. "I'm your only niece."

"Ayuh, and you're a keepah."

Silence stretched between the two women as if each were lost in her own thoughts. It was Phyllis who broke the interlude. "Have you given thought to Bryan's proposal?"

"I swear, sometimes I think you're psychic." Laura kept her voice casual. "He's handsome, caring, and kind, a senior park ranger. His future is secure, but we've only know each other a few months. It hasn't been a year since Jolly's death, and I'm still traumatized over being kidnapped and nearly killed by Benjamin

Noone. I need time, Aunt Philly. That's why being here with you is so special."

"Ayuh, you've had your share of grief, that's for certain. Nonetheless, Bryan loves you."

Laura harrumphed. "Love? I don't even know what that means. I loved Jolly like a brother. I love you, I love my job as a reporter, and I love the lobster rolls from the Silly Lobster. I have feelings for Bryan, but I don't think what I feel is *love*. Aren't you supposed to experience euphoria, and giddiness, and want to dance on air?"

Phyllis laughed and waved. "Yoo-hoo, waiter. Two more piña coladas, and with an extra splash of rum. Bill it to our room. Suite 2312." She turned back to Laura. "You make a good argument. All I can say is sometimes friendship grows into an even stronger affection. Remember what Mitch kept telling you— give it time. If you're not ready, don't allow Bryan to pressure you."

Mitch Carter. Laura didn't want to think about him, and decided to change the subject. "C'mon, let's go freshen up. I'm looking forward to the luau and watching the hunky male hula dancers swiveling their sexy hips."

After an evening of over-indulging in food and fun, Laura and Phyllis returned to the hotel. "Laura, I can't remember the last time I felt this alive, totally exhausted, and a wee bit tipsy."

Laura kissed her aunt on the cheek, quietly slipped into her bedroom, and shut the door. Uttering a sigh of relief, she kicked off her silver orthopedic slippers, letting her feet sink down into the soft lush carpeting. She changed into an oversized T-shirt and climbed beneath the silken duvet.

The past several weeks had a dreamlike quality about them. Could it already have been four months since Deputy Sheriff Mitchell Carter rescued her from a demented psychopath? She closed her eyes. Too much had happened since the beginning of the year. She found it all slightly overwhelming.

It was still incomprehensible that she'd let Mitch walk out of her life. Yet hadn't they both agreed the timing wasn't right for them? He was returning to El Paso to run for sheriff and to bring down the men who had murdered his wife and wounded his mother. As for herself, having given up her job as a New York investigative reporter she had just purchased the *Harbor Gazette* and was trying to recover from post traumatic stress disorder, plus coming to terms with being a cripple for the rest of her life. She had made it clear she wasn't ready for a relationship, and she certainly wasn't leaving Cole Harbor. And then there was Bryan.

It was true, Mitch had often told her to set the rules, to go slow and easy. Maybe that's what bothered her about Bryan. As much as she resisted his proposals, he pushed, always declaring his love for her. There was, as yet, no formal announcement of an engagement, but everyone in Cole Harbor expected a spring wedding.

A solitary tear dislodged itself from the corner of her eye and slowly slid down her cheek to finally fall unheeded on the pillowcase. So here she was on a beautiful breezy night in Hawaii, her hip and leg aching, and feeling a little sorry for herself.

An even bigger sigh escaped her lips as she stared up at the ceiling.

****

Just for an instant, unable to separate dream from reality, Laura believed herself back in her own bed in Cole Harbor.

"Laura!" The voice cut through the silence in the room like a knife. "Wake up!" The voice was resonant and forceful.

She wanted to shrug off this intruder. Brilliance from the bedside lamp and the persistent hand shaking her shoulder caused her to force open her eyes. She yawned. "Aunt Philly, what's wrong?"

Her aunt's voice quavered with emotion. "I don't know how to tell you!"

Laura looked at the clock. She scooted to a sitting position. "It's one in the morning." The pinched, drawn look on her aunt's face caused every muscle in Laura's body to tense. "What's happened? Are you ill?"

Phyllis stood at the edge of the bed. Hands knotted together, her voice a pitch higher, she quavered, "There's been a terrible accident... We've lost everything... Oh, by Godfrey, Laura, what are we going to do?"

Laura swung from the bed and gripped her aunt by the shoulders. "You're not making sense. Take a deep breath and start from the beginning."

"I-I actually think I might faint. I feel all swimmy-headed."

Laura steered Phyllis toward a chair and helped her sit down. "I'll get you a cold cloth." She limped to the bathroom and returned with a dampened washcloth. "Did you have a bad dream about an accident? Can I get you a bottle of water from the refrigerator?"

Phyllis shook her head as she placed the cool cloth

to her face. She drew a shuddering breath. "If only it were a bad dream. It's seven p.m. in Maine. Maudie didn't realize the time difference. There was a gas leak in the underground lines. Something happened. I don't know what or how. Maudie was near hysteria and yelling into the phone. I could hardly make sense of what she was saying. Oh, by Godfrey! This is terrible…terrible!"

"Aunt Philly, inhale, then exhale, and try to calm down. Tell me about the gas leak."

Tears stained her aunt's cheeks, and her shoulders shook as she sobbed. She did as Laura suggested. Inhaled, exhaled. "Apparently, and unbeknownst to anyone in the town, gas has been leaking and accumulating underground for quite a while. There was an explosion." She placed her hands over her face and shook her head before refocusing on Laura. "The bookstore, the newspaper office, the entire block went up in flames. The Silly Lobstah is gone, and the gazebo, too. Maudie said it looked like a bombed-out war zone. Buildings blown apart and houses burned to the ground."

Laura's heart pounded against her chest. She had difficulty getting the words out. "Was anyone hurt?"

"Maudie said ten people were killed, and about twenty-six injured. She wasn't sure exactly who or how many. Thank goodness most everyone leaves for warmer climates, and they don't return until after Easter."

A word about the author...

Loretta C. Rogers is an award-winning author who writes romance with a twist. When not writing, she enjoys reading and traveling, especially going with her husband on their motorcycle. She enjoys hearing from readers and invites them to visit her website:
www.lorettacrogersbooks.com